Gourmet Ghosts
-Los Angeles

Gourmet Ghosts - Los Angeles

James T. Bartlett

City Ghost Guides

ISBN 978-0-9849730-0-2

Special Thanks To...

Colman Andrews, Marc Wanamaker, Brett Arena, Josh Spencer, Steve Siers, Nina Monet, the History & Genealogy Department at the Los Angeles Central Library, the staff at the John C. Fremont Library (Branch #12) and Jay D. Smith at the Hearst Corporation.

Dedicated To...

My wife Wendall Thomas, who has always loved and supported me.

Introduction

Like many people, I love a good story – especially a good ghost story – and one night I was drinking at one of my favorite bars when I was told about their resident ghost and something strange that had happened to one of their employees.

As a journalist I was intrigued and as a lover of strange tales I wanted to know more, but when I went home and looked it up online I found nothing. I went to the bookstore and thumbed through some of the books published about California/Los Angeles/Hollywood ghosts and mysteries – still nothing.

There were lots of other stories in these books, but I found that many of them tended to rely on hearsay and "the legend states that…" instead of actually showing whether there was any truth in them. Of course you can't ever prove that there's a ghost, but I certainly wanted more information: maybe there was some real archive evidence that related to the story, or an eyewitness account that gave you reason to think that maybe, just maybe, there could be more to it than meets the eye.

I also found that you couldn't even visit many of the places in these books (who wants to just *look* at a house that's supposed to be haunted? Don't you want to go in? Or at least be able to?) Once I started making calls, talking to eyewitnesses, scouring the newspaper archives and being told stranger and stranger stories, I decided that Los Angeles and her visitors needed a new kind of guide that mixed history and mystery into a great night out!

Gourmet Ghosts was its name. It's a guide to some of the oldest and best restaurants, bars and hotels in town, and not only are they places you can go tonight for dinner or tomorrow for breakfast, they're places with some great – real – stories, be they of ghosts, murders, mysteries, spies or simply the unexplained.

From Downtown to Hollywood and from Santa Monica to Malibu I interviewed people and uncovered stories like the "The Night Watchman" at the Spring Arts Tower, "Glover's Ghost" at Yamashiro, "*La mujer sin cabeza* (the Headless Woman)" at Musso & Frank, "Millie" at the Paradise Cove in Malibu and Alexander Oviatt, still haunting the building that killed him.

I also unearthed some new, never-before-published stories and photographs as well, including several that really made a shiver run down my spine. They're all here for you to read so enjoy the best food, the best drinks and the best ghost stories – and if you experience your very own "Gourmet Ghost" in the City of Angels, email me at jbartlett2000@gmail.com

You can submit stories, suggest places to visit and read about some amazing and weird events I came across during my research – but just couldn't include in the book – in the "Extra! Extra! Read All About it!" section on www.gourmetghosts.com and keep right up-to-date on Facebook and Twitter (search for Gourmet Ghosts).

Note:

Apologies in advance if you go to one of the locations and find they have changed their prices, their décor, or have finished their Happy Hour. I did try to keep *Gourmet Ghosts* as current as possible.

Contents

Chapter 1

Hollywood

The Magic Castle
7001 Franklin Avenue
Hollywood, CA 90028
Tel: 323 851 3313

courtesy Magic Castle

Invisible Irma and a Ghostly Bartender

"WARNING! Visitors to the Magic Castle must be careful at all times. Many guests have reported walls that keep an eye on them. Others have seen portraits that follow them as they pass through the rooms; that tables have mysteriously moved and bar stools imperceptibly shrunk in size while someone was seated in them. Nothing is impossible at the Magic Castle! But you HAVE been warned!"

Until a few years ago, there was something rare on Hollywood Boulevard: an old fashioned store called Hollywood Magic. For years it had been the place where real practitioners came for props and advice, and where lucky tourists could get impromptu displays of close-up magic and illusions. When I visited I had been baffled by what were doubtless the simplest of sleight of hand tricks, but then the guy handed over his business card and said we should call the Magic Castle, mention his name, and make a reservation.

A rather mysterious building known around the world as the "Mecca of Magic," the Magic Castle is the private clubhouse of an organization dedicated to the advancement and preservation of this ancient art. They began with a charter membership of 150 and now have a worldwide fraternity of over 4,000, all of whom can access a unique library of the magical arts.

The Magic Castle actually began its life as a private home built in 1909 by banker and real estate magnate Rollin B. Lane, who owned much of what is now Hollywood. Lane's dream to turn the land into orange groves and farms was ended by a severe drought, and after the family moved away in the 1940s the fate of the mansion was hanging in the balance until the day Milt Larsen met the owner.

Milt's father had been a renowned magician and often spoke of building an elegant private club for his fellow artists, so in September 1961 Milt and a crew of friends and volunteers began the huge task of restoring the dilapidated building to its former Victorian elegance. Barely more than a year later on January 2, 1963 the Magic Castle opened her doors.

Unless you want to splash out $100 on a 30-day Open Sesame Membership for you and a guest, access is strictly members-only – but getting to visit is not as hard as it seems. This is Hollywood after all, and someone always knows someone who can get you in.

From the outside it looks like it was created by Walt Disney, and stepping inside the front door is like going back in time and traveling far, far away from the bustling Boulevard below. There's that reassuring musty smell, and the stained glass windows and chandeliers give the sense of somewhere very different – and a little illicit.

It's no surprise that this has been a regular hangout for celebrities since the early days, and members past and present have included "Karnac The Magnificent" (aka Johnny Carson), Liberace, Orson Welles, Mae West, Drew Barrymore, Nicholas Cage, Merv Griffin, Teri Hatcher, Tippi Hedren, Lucy Liu, Steve Martin and Neil Patrick Harris, to name but a few. Cary Grant was even on the Board of Directors at one time.

After paying an entrance charge you echo the words of Aladdin by saying "Open Sesame" to the wooden owl with glowing red eyes and a moment later – if the ancient feathered guardian is happy – the bookcase slides apart like a "Mystery Theatre" prop and you see a red carpet waiting to lead you inside.

Split into three floors and a basement, the Magic Castle almost seems like a fairground haunted house – corridors and stairs that you could swear weren't there before lead to other rooms and every wall is plastered in posters, playbills and props for the "golden age" of magic when tricks were "the like of which you've never seen" and posters used images of devils and spoke of "the other side."

"Handcuff King" Harry Houdini has his own room on the second floor, with pairs that he actually used in his feats of escapology mounted on the walls – including the only pair he couldn't escape from – and you can even hear his voice on a wax cylinder recording. Converted from one of the mansion bedrooms in 1969 and remodeled in 1997, this room also contains a green baize table used for séances, and is available to hire for your own spiritual adventures. Appropriately enough, Houdini died on October 31, 1926 and his wife Beatrice held séances every Halloween for the next ten years in an attempt to contact him.

Her last attempted séance took place with much publicity on the roof of the Knickerbocker Hotel in Hollywood, but sadly, the afterlife was one thing that Houdini couldn't escape from. She snuffed out the candle she had kept burning for him saying:

"Ten years is long enough to wait for any man."

Houdini enthusiasts and magicians have kept up the tradition in various locations though, and guests taking part in one of these "Demon" séance nights have reported the table rising into the air, floating candles and even the spirit of Houdini appearing. On Halloween night 2010 there was a small fire at the Magic Castle, but I wonder if you can guess whose room escaped damage by either flames or water?

Unsurprisingly, Milt says that the Magic Castle has more than its fair share of spooky stories:

"If any ghosts were in town, where else would they come? This building has been here for 100 years, so there are bound to be a few ghosts hanging around, and with about

4000 members and many of them writers, performers and entertainers, it's no surprise that stories tend to get embellished a little."

The most famous ghost here is Invisible Irma, an "old family friend." According to Milt, Irma was born in Chicago in 1857, the eldest of seven sisters and one brother. Entranced by music she began playing the piano whenever she could, and when the family moved to Franklin Avenue she befriended the Lanes, who were building a spectacular mansion nearby – the building that we now know as the Magic Castle.

courtesy Magic Castle

Recognizing Irma's musical talents, the Lanes asked her to give regular piano recitals and she fell so in love with the house that she vowed to return after her death so she could keep playing. When the Lane Mansion was transformed into the Magic Castle and her piano was discovered, dusted off and tuned up, she was as good as her word.

Her ghostly presence soon returned to "Irma's Room" on the second floor, and she still plays for visitors to this day.

Alongside Irma is her special friend, Katy the canary, who will sometimes twitter to guests – especially if you slip a dollar bill into her cage! You can buy Irma a drink too, though she's only allowed one per night.

Milt also said that Irma did have a couple of friends – her tap-dancing brother Invisible Irving and Invisible Isabella, a topless dancer – though Isabella returned to San Francisco and Irving's tapping has long since disappeared into the night. As for Irma, she performs every night, at Friday lunch and at Sunday brunch.

On a wall near her piano you can see a cherubic painting of a very young – and very naked – Irma. Milt didn't know it was her until she began playing "Yes Sir, That's My Baby" when he was looking at it, though her playing did once give him a real scare:

"We're more about Casper the Friendly Ghost here – pure fun and entertainment – but there was one time, soon after we had opened in the late 1960s, when something strange happened. I was here one night, alone, and believe it or not, it was a dark and stormy night – really! I decided not to risk the drive home but stay in the office and sleep on the sofa. I got woken by a clap of thunder, and the power was out. I looked out of the office window – the city was dark everywhere around too – and then I heard the piano playing downstairs. I knew that this just couldn't be if there was no electricity, so I went downstairs with a flashlight, and then just as got to the bottom of the grand staircase, the music stopped! For all I know, Irma has always played the piano in the small hours, and this was the only time anyone ever heard her."

You can find spirits of a very different kind at the five bars here. There's the Grand Salon, decorated with colorized slides from the old Los Angeles Hippodrome Vaudeville; the Palace of Mystery bar, which was originally a 17th Century London pub; the WC Fields with his trick pool table, and the traditional English Hat & Hare bar – home of some exclusive beers and the "Ghost Bartender":

"One of the bartenders was called Loren Tate, and after he died people often came up to me during the week and said that they had just been talking to a really friendly bartender there. But I knew that The Hat & Hare only has a bartender on Friday and Saturday nights – always has done."

Finally there is the tiny Owl Bar, where the walls and shelves are covered with owls of every kind – stuffed, jewelry and novelty – to commemorate the Academy logo, though you also can't help but think of Hedwig from the *Harry Potter* books and movies.

Try the favorite drink of the late magician Billy McComb, "Ireland's largest leprechaun." He would ask the barman for his "medication" – a Captain Morgan's rum and Coke – or after dinner, sample the drink named in his honor, "Billy's Nutty Irishman," which is coffee with Bailey's and Frangelico. You could also get a Corpse Reviver #2 (Lillet Blanc, gin, Cointreau, lemon juice and a dash of Galliano) – apparently four of these do the trick with the undead – and for a snack, take on the award-winning Magic Castle chili or their three-cheese garlic bread.

After spirit hunting, you make your way to the Victorian dining room. Very olde worlde, it sits right under a huge Tiffany chandelier, and the windows are the ancient etched stained glass from the Imperial Restaurant in Scotland. Except for Sunday Brunch it's strictly over 21 here, and dress codes are imposed too: business attire for men and evening wear for women.

The menu is simple but elegant "banquet" fare (shrimp, steak, lamb, salmon – my choice is the beef Wellington with potato gratin and baby vegetables), but people are really here for the spectacle and the shows. These take place in sittings in the bars, the Close-Up Gallery – a tiny theater that seats around 25 people – the Parlour of Prestidigitation, which has seats originally from the original Santa Monica Opera House and a red-curtained stage, and the large Palace Of Mystery, host for the highlight of the evening: grand illusions.

In fact, if you see or hear anything strange or unusual at The Palace of Mystery, there's a real story behind it:

"In 1986 a very good magician and a wonderful person named Chris Michaels passed away backstage. He was just sitting there in a chair, and when someone came up to him to say 'Time to go on!' they discovered that he was dead. Now, when anything goes wrong – or right – there, especially backstage, everyone blames Chris!"

In 2006 the Larsens were given the ultimate Tinsel Town honor – their own star on the Hollywood Walk of Fame – so make friends with a local, get a reservation and go see why the Magic Castle fully deserves its place in Hollywood history. One insider tip though: make reservations at least a week in advance, because everyone wants to go to this club!

Dinner: 6pm, 8pm, 9.45pm
Brunch: Saturday/Sunday 11am, 12.30pm, 1.30pm
Times of shows vary
21+ only
www.magiccastle.com
www.facebook.com/MagicCastle
http://twitter.com/MagicCastle

Roosevelt Hotel
7000 Hollywood Boulevard
Hollywood, CA 90028
Tel: 323 466 7000

Suicide, Montgomery and Marilyn's Mirror?

Right in the center of Tinsel Town, the Roosevelt Hotel is proud of its history as one of the city's most famous landmarks – the very first Oscar ceremony was here after all – and many people consider that a trip to Hollywood isn't complete without going to "the Roosevelt" for a cocktail.

It's located right across the street from Grauman's Chinese Theatre, and along the sidewalks on both sides of the street – including outside the Roosevelt – are just some of the 2,400 or so stars that make up the Hollywood Walk of Fame.

Many years ago and with great fanfare, the Roosevelt opened its doors to the world. The year was 1927 and guests such as Gloria Swanson, Greta Garbo and Clara Bow attended the opening of the newest and most glamorous hotel on Hollywood Boulevard. Nearly 60 years later the hotel underwent a $20m facelift, but as well as unearthing some of the original splendor they reawakened something more.

Just two weeks before the grand reopening in 1985, many people felt a cold spot – some 10 degrees cooler than the surrounding area – in the Blossom Room, the location of the very first Academy Awards in 1929. The very same day, an employee looked in a mirror in the manager's office and caught sight of a beautiful blonde behind her – yet there was no one in the room.

Later the employee found out that a frequent resident of room 229 – Marilyn Monroe – had once requested the mirror. She had posed for her first print advertisement – for toothpaste – on the swimming pool diving board here, and the mirror had been moved into the manager's office following her suicide in 1962.

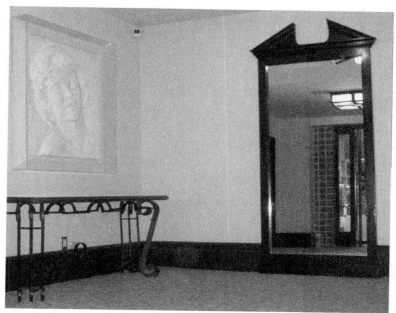

© *Tammy Melhaff*

For some time the mirror was in the mezzanine near the gift shop and many people reported seeing the blonde bombshell reflected in the glass, though on a recent visit it was gone. Nothing strange had happened – it was just in storage following more renovations – and though I was told that it was going to a sister hotel in New York or to Madame Tussauds across the street (both highly unlikely), it will hopefully it will be back on show when you pay a visit.

Also, some of the first guests after the 1985 reopening reported the sounds of children playing in seemingly empty corridors and rooms, while a ghost girl has been seen playing by the fountain in the lobby. Wearing a blue dress and known by staff as "Caroline," she and her brother were apparently staying here with their father. One night while he went out to run an errand, they decided to play at the pool – and she fell in and drowned. Some years later, the house telephone operator got a call from the lobby phone: it was a small girl "looking for her daddy," but on investigation there was no sign of the girl or her father.

Behind the scenes, most employees feel that there's something "strange" about the 9th floor – specifically room 928, the one at the end of the hall – and ever since the reopening many guests in that room (and on that floor) have reported hearing a bugle playing and the sound of footsteps. In November 1992 a guest felt an invisible hand pat her shoulder while she was in bed, and there was also a report of a female guest finding the coffee pot, television and lights in her room switching on and off.

After complaining she was given another room, but when the same things happened again she checked out in the early hours of the morning. It turned out that she had been using an Ouija board and was trying to contact the spirit of actor Montgomery Clift; he had stayed here while filming the movie *From Here to Eternity* in 1953 and was often heard practicing the bugle (his character was the company bugler) and pacing up and down the corridor practicing his lines.

There was no however no evidence in newspaper archives about any of these stories, and all the Roosevelt would confirm is that Clift did once stay at the hotel. However, on a more tragic – and real – note, the *Los Angeles Times* archive of June 20, 1929 reveals the attempted suicide of 60-year-old Frank W. Libby. He left a note for his wife at their home in North Stanley Avenue, and then checked in. Sometime later he wrapped a towel around his head, faced the bathroom mirror and shot himself. His condition was listed as "serious" and whether he recovered or not is unknown, but he was one of five people in the city who tried to end their lives that day.

SUICIDES YESTERDAY EPIDEMIC

Three Men Dead, Fourth Dying and Woman Slashed in Self-Murder Tries

Just a few years later on December 8, 1932 an actor named Harry Lee jumped to his death from the fire escape, landing on the roof of the third floor wing. He left a note saying that his wife would "know the cause of his death."

PICTURE ACTOR LEAPS TO DEATH

Roosevelt Hotel Suicide Laid to Unemployment

Harry Lee, Character Man, Leaves Vague Note

Known for Parts in Several Screen Productions

Desperate, apparently, because he could find no work in the local studios, Harry Lee, 55 years of age, motion-picture character actor of New York City, leaped to his death from a fire escape of the Roosevelt Hotel at 7006 Hollywood Boulevard yesterday. His body landed on the roof of the third-floor wing of the hotel.

A more desperate story was that of former child actor Tom Conlon. On February 4, 1940 it was reported that Conlon, 24, had tried not once but twice to take his life the previous day. In the morning his mother had found him in the garage with the car engine running, and then later he checked into the Roosevelt, slashing his wrists and leaving several incoherent notes – but was again found just in time. It emerged that several years before he'd been stabbed in a bar fight and had been suffering health problems ever since. His final movie appearance was two years later as an uncredited "Man in Ballroom" in Cecil B. DeMille's movie *Reap The Wild Wind* (1942).

If you come to the Roosevelt, you'll find that there are several bars to choose from. You can have a drink in the lobby area itself and check out who is checking in, then behind the heavy bronze doors nearby is Teddy's, a super-hip, exclusive lounge/club that is a favorite for party hounds and celebs alike – make sure you're dressed to impress if you want to go in!

Also off the lobby is the tiny Library Bar, which has plenty of books and serves cocktails in the "Omakase" style (the Japanese phrase that means "it's up to you"), but with a food twist. You can try pomegranate seeds and shitake mushrooms infused with Grand Marnier and bourbon, or even the Humpty Dumpty, a cocktail made from infused bourbon, cherry liquor, cream eggs, whites and frozen lecithin – served in an ostrich egg. You can also just ask the mixologist behind the bar to choose for you – you'll be in good hands.

Then there's the famous Tropicana Bar, which is right next to the swimming pool that's decorated with an (underwater) David Hockney mural. It's a shimmering sight when you arrive and reflects the hideaway nature of this bar – a place that turns into a busy dance lounge at night and still attracts models, starlets and young actors looking to see (and be seen). Palm trees sway as you sip your expensive drink, and this really is a chance to experience the Hollywood you see on television – though again, dress up and come early if you want to hang out.

There's also the Spare Room, a cocktail bar and gaming lounge on the Mezzanine level that features two vintage bowling lanes as part of its luxurious, clubby 1920s decor. They cost $100 an hour to rent, and for a souvenir you can try to find the secret photo booth (clue: it's near the bowling shoes). If you're in a group, order a punch bowl drink – it comes with cups and ladles – or "Evelyn Waugh's Noonday Reviver" (Guinness, gin and ginger beer) which does exactly as it promises. The best day to go is "Spare Room Wednesdays," when between 6-9pm the bowling is half-price and there are select drink and food specials.

As for restaurants, there is the Public Kitchen & Bar and 25 Degrees. Opened in late February 2011, the Public Kitchen & Bar is an American 1920s-style brasserie that's festooned with maps, flags and old photos and features huge gold chandeliers and a massive marble-topped bar that stretches into the Roosevelt's central lounge area.

The slightly pricey dishes include chicken liver Terrine with apricot mostrada, the Public Burger with four year cheddar – and an egg? ("everything tastes better with an egg on it" says the menu), though there are steaks, oysters, chicken and pot roast too, and the best nearly-always-sold-out dessert is the Pumpkin pecan pie with caramel.

I've eaten more often at 25 Degrees, which serves delicious gourmet burgers in an upscale atmosphere and is open 24/7. Big, dark burger-colored leather seats are the order of the day and your burger will be cooked to perfection with three standard choices of meat and long list of extras: dressings, garnish, cheese and other delights. Don't arrive starving though, as gourmet burgers take longer than usual to be done to perfection, which makes the daily Happy Hour ($4-6 selected drinks and $2 bar snacks) perhaps the best time to visit.

Finally, there's an unusual attraction here too – Beacher's Madhouse. Backed by actor David Arquette and accessible only though a secret bookcase, it's also a small 1920s-style club/theater that mixes Las Vegas variety, vaudeville and comedy acts and opens late. Expect burlesque, dancing pandas and flying Oompah Loompas – what some people might call a typical Hollywood night out!

Hours vary for restaurants and bars
www.hollywoodroosevelt.com
www.facebook.com/hollywoodroosevelt
http://twitter.com/hwood_roosevelt

Boardner's by LaBelle
1652 North Cherokee Avenue
Hollywood, CA 90028
Tel: 323 462 9621

The Alley and the Ghosts of Kurt and Al

Located in the Cherokee Building, Boardner's can trace its roots back to 1944, though the building itself was originally built in 1927. It first began life as a "beauty parlor" (probably a front for an illegal card club and speakeasy), and in the early 1930s crooner Gene Austin opened a club here named after his massive 1927 hit "My Blue Heaven."

It went on to be the Padres Restaurant, Cherokee House and Club 52 until January 1944 when Steve, a guy from Akron, Ohio who'd worked his way through the Hollywood bars (and got a reputation as a charming, helpful guy) cheekily put his last name over Club 52's neon sign. It's been "Boardner's" ever since.

Back then it was very much a local place, the kind of place where glamour came with dirty fingernails and there was probably a baseball bat under the bar. Everyone was treated equally, and since the local Chief of Police came in every now and then, the local cops were happy to turn a blind eye to what happened here.

Stars like Errol Flynn, W.C. Fields, Lawrence Tierney, Donald Sutherland, Vince Vaughn, Russell Crowe, Nicole Kidman, Ben Affleck, John Lennon, Slash, Axl Rose, Tommy Lee, director Ed Wood and poet Charles Bukowski have all been here at one time or another, and the "Black Dahlia" murder victim, Elizabeth Short, was a regular; she was said to be very popular with the sailors.

By 1980 things had changed in Hollywood and Boardner – who was losing his eyesight – got stung on a loan he arranged for a friend and decided to retire to Palm Spring. Some years later, current owner Tricia LaBelle found a box of pictures "under about two inches of bird shit in the loft." They were signed by a long list of vintage Hollywood celebrities and were all dedicated to Steve and to Boardner's – you can see them on the walls today.

Ed Wood (1994), *Leaving Las Vegas* (1995), *Wag The Dog* and *L.A. Confidential* (both 1997) and television shows "Angel," "Beverly Hills 90210" and "Cold Case" have filmed here, plus:

> *"If you watch old "I Love Lucy" shows, Lucy often talks about going for a drink at Boardner's!"*

LaBelle said that strange stories were easy to find at Boardner's, and that she feels there are two distinct ghosts here:

> *"When a bar has been around for nearly 70 years there's a lot of stuff to be told!"*

It's certainly true that Kurt Richter, a co-owner at the time, died here on the evening before Christmas in 1997:

> *"Yes. He was sitting at the bar drinking, and Gigi was the bartender. He was a world war two veteran, and like many then he was a hardcore drinker and a hardcore smoker, and I think he had emphysema."*

Years ago, the office was also an apartment/living area, and many times it played host to people sleeping off a hangover or who needed somewhere to stay. Richter lived here too, and LaBelle feels that he is still keeping an eye on the place:

> *"It was his home. He loved the customers and he loved the people who worked here."*

The sound of footsteps has often been heard in the office, though she feels that is the spirit of a second ghost, "a little guy named Al" who used to live there:

"He used to live (elsewhere) with his son, who treated him badly, and one day Steve Boardner and some friends went to get him and brought him back here. He became a bartender here and passed away just a few years ago. I turned up just after the ambulance had come to get him."

LaBelle also mentioned a number of other unusual experiences:

"Employees have seen, heard and felt many different things – music and televisions going on when all power is off, doors opening and closing, faces in the women's bathroom mirror, apparitions seen in the alley entrance and in the loft."

There is a photo of these apparent apparitions in the alley; it was taken by a customer who sent it in after being amazed at what he saw:

"It was him and his fiancée, and behind them through the window you could clearly see two apparitions – a man and a woman – looking in. They seem to be an old man with a top hat and woman with a shawl."

Courtesy Boardner's by LaBelle

Who is that looking through the window?

Today Boardner's is still a popular dive bar, but it's also well-known for its various music and dance nights at their B52 club, which has 22 foot high ceilings, arched windows, a large dance floor, a VIP loft area and an Art Deco antique bar. "Bar Sinister," a sinful, whip crackin' fetish/goth night is held here weekly, among many others.

Boardner's itself looks and feels like a *noir*-ish, Art Deco carriage on the Orient Express, and there's also a New Orleans-style patio if you want to move out of the darkness. Unpretentious is still the order of the day, and random specials make this a great place for a big night out.

The dinner and late night "noshing" menu comes courtesy of celebrity chef William Annesley (known as "Bloody Bill") and includes shrimp ceviche, BBQ ribs, Australian lamb chops and the exotically-named Morcilla (black sausage with fried quail eggs). You can also get a great New York sirloin or a Boardner's Big B52 Burger, a ½ lb Top Sirloin served with arugula, sliced tomato, Bermuda onion and homemade French Fries. If you're really looking to impress, then attack the 10 Layer Tortilla Tower – if you can!

As for any ghostly guest appearances by Kurt or Al while you're visiting, LaBelle is sure of one thing:

"They still love to party!"

Monday – Thursday and Sunday 5pm-2am
Friday 4pm-2am
Saturday 3.30pm-2am
Happy Hour: Monday – Thursday and Sunday 3.30pm-2am
www.boardners.com
www.facebook.com/boardners
http://twitter.com/boardners

Cat & Fiddle
6530 Sunset Boulevard
Hollywood, CA 90028
Tel: 323 468 3800

The Dead Gangster and "The Smoking Man"

A little bit of England right in the middle of Hollywood – you can't miss the jolly sign hanging outside – the Cat & Fiddle is a long time favorite for ex-pats (especially musicians) and has played host to Rod Stewart, Ronnie Wood, Morrissey, Christopher Lloyd, Woody Harrelson and countless homesick tourists.

The Cat & Fiddle is located in the Thompson Building, one of the first to be designed in the Spanish/ Mediterranean style that's become as symbolic of California as movie stars and swimming pools.

Since 1927 this complex has been a warehouse for studio make-up and costumes and home to two restaurants: Mary Helen's Tea Room and the Gourmet Hollywood, an eatery that was much loved by Humphrey Bogart, Ava Gardner and Katherine Hepburn.

Cat & Fiddle proprietors Paula and Kim Gardner first met in New Orleans in 1973, when he was recording an album with Jackie Lomax and George Harrison.

He had come over as part of the 1960s "British Invasion" and played with Creation, The Birds (with Wood, his neighbor from childhood days), Ashton, Gardner & Dyke and Quiet Melon (with

Rod Stewart and Ronnie Lane), and was always looking out for a decent pub.

In the end he and Paula opened one, initially in Laurel Canyon in 1982 and then coming to Sunset Boulevard in 1984, and though Kim died of cancer in 2001, daughters Eva, Ashlee and Camille are all involved in the family business. Kim also had quite a reputation as an artist, and you can see some of his work around the bar as well as plenty of band pictures and gig souvenirs.

Inside, the walls are covered with English paraphernalia and souvenirs; pub trays, signs and bar towels, train timetable drapes, maps, a Union Jack flag and even some antique *Vanity Fair* sketches of "Notable Statesmen" and "Men of the Day" from the 1860s.

It's a huge place – there are lots of booth and tables inside – and you can even buy your own darts if you become addicted to a game of "arrows." As you might expect, they often show UK soccer matches here and this is the home territory of soccer team Hollywood United, which was founded in the late 1980s by regulars including Steve Jones of the Sex Pistols, Billy Duffy and Ian Astbury of The Cult and Vivian Campbell of Def Leppard.

Word quickly spread among other soccer fans in town, and soon names such as Jason Statham, Anthony LaPaglia, Donal Logue, singers Robbie Williams and Ziggy Marley and even former international players Vinnie Jones, John Harkes, Alexi Lalas, Richard Gough and Frank Leboeuf began playing for the team. Over the years they've transitioned into several teams playing in different leagues, while the original members – now known as "Dad's Army" – compete in the over-40s city Metro Soccer League (Senior Division).

As for the historical side of the Cat & Fiddle, Ashlee Gardner told me that this was an area she unofficially "looks after":

"My father named it after one of his favorite pubs in Hillingdon in the west of London, where he was brought up, but it's said that the name was first inspired by Catherine of Aragon, the first wife of King Henry VIII, who was affectionately nicknamed "Catherine La Fidèle" (The Faithful)."

There were stories of a more mysterious nature though:

"I have heard the story that someone was shot here in the 1940s, in the back room."

Known as the Casablanca Room, it's available for private bookings and is on your left when you go in the front door. The story goes that a group of local mobsters were having a dinner party there when one of the guests shot and killed one of their fellow diners. Not wanting to spoil the mood, the unfortunate victim's body was dragged into another room and the party carried on as if nothing had happened – though the spirit of a well-dressed man has often been seen here since.

Gardner also spoke about the Victoria Room, a smaller room available for hire, where there have been a number of unexplained breakages and an incident of a falling lamp:

"And then one afternoon our jukebox – one of the old ones that had CDs in it – started flipping from disc to disc. It had never done that before."

Gardner suggested that Michael Savage, the Cat & Fiddle's "legendary" security guard, might know more. Savage said he worked here "for about 20 years" from 1987, and he did indeed have some very ghostly stories to tell:

"There was a shooting here in the 1930s. A member of one of the Tong gangs was shot by one of Lansky's men for an overdue debt. They just walked in, shot him in the head, and walked out – it was an execution."

The Tongs were a kind of secret organization formed for support and protection by early Chinese immigrants to the United States. Their activities were often criminal, and what is known as the "Tong Wars" between various factions raged in L.A. and especially San Francisco from around the 1860s to the 1920s.

No matter how tough the Tongs were though, getting tangled with mobster Meyer Lansky was a bad idea.

Known as the "Mob's Accountant," Lansky and his associate Charles "Lucky" Luciano were the prime movers behind the development of "The Crime Syndicate," a largely Jewish and Italian crime outfit whose enforcement men were known as Murder, Inc. They were largely based on the East Coast, but Lansky was heavily involved in gambling in Cuba, Florida, New Orleans and Las Vegas, and was allegedly the man who wanted to spare his friend Bugsy Siegel – the man behind the Flamingo Casino – from murder.

Savage didn't think this was the murder Ashlee mentioned (and there was no evidence of either in newspaper archives), but he did recount a number of strange events related to the Casablanca Room:

> *"One night I was with Brian, one of the managers. It was about 3.30 am, the front door was locked, and we were having a final pint before leaving – though we had only had a couple each. Suddenly a pint glass came flying through the air from the Casablanca Room, as if it had been aimed at us, and at the same time a load of glasses flew off the shelf nearby. I thought there was someone in here who shouldn't be, so I ran round the back to catch them – but there was no one there, or anywhere else in the bar."*

Savage also mentioned that the lights go up and down at odd times in the Casablanca Room ("Paula's had it checked out several times, and they couldn't find any explanation") and that late at night he has heard many strange and unusual noises in here "and I've heard every noise that place makes at night." He also said he's seen a "quick flash of a dark shadow walking towards the very back door, (and) late at night you can sometimes hear the saloon doors swinging in the back of the room. There are a couple of "cold spots" in here too. It's like a cold breeze – even when the air conditioning's not on."

Savage thought there was an "unhappy presence" in there, and recounted the time an elderly couple came out after having dinner in the Casablanca Room. They both claimed to be spiritual and clairvoyant, and had sensed an active, agitated spirit:

"Brian was an Irish guy and was very superstitious, and he named it a púca (Old Irish for a shape-shifting beast or ghost). He doesn't like being here alone at night, or going in there."

There could however be another explanation for that "unhappy presence." According to Savage, in 2005 a young man attempted to climb up on to the roof of the building and fell to his death:

"It was late at night, and we noticed that there was someone climbing the building. He had clambered across the door arch, climbed up to the balcony, and was standing on the balcony rail, trying to reach up to the roof, when the Spanish tile he was holding onto came loose, the stanchion too, and he fell straight down – broke his neck."

The studio watchman next door, Leonard, was also a witness, and Savage recalled a terrifying aspect of the man's sudden climb:

"Something had terrified him. He was screaming, saying 'He's coming after me!' and 'I'm not going you let you have me!' before he fell. I ran to where he was and the ambulance was there real quick, but it was too late. He looked in my eyes and died."

Savage then mentioned "The Smoking Man," a presence that he saw a number of times in 2006:

"At the front gate I saw a man leaning against a wall. He was smoking a cigarette – I saw the orange glow – and had his arms folded. Then he was gone. I wondered if it was just a shadow, but then I saw him again later that night."

Other employees saw this "Smoking Man" too:

"Ray, Bill, Johnny – he saw him twice. I was walking up the stairs to the office when he shouted out that there was a big guy right behind me. But when I turned round there was no one there. Johnny said he had had a cigarette in his hand."

I asked whether Kim Gardner was a smoker:

"He smoked like a fiend, and I got the same throat cancer that he did. Unfortunately it killed him. Perhaps he was warning me."

Whether Kim is still here or not, a glance at the menu will be enough to bring on an attack of nostalgia from even the most sun-loving transatlantic transplant. There's a ploughman's lunch, apple crumble, bread and butter pudding, bangers and mash, shepherd's pie and a $5 daily special menu (4-7pm Monday to Friday).

On weekends you can try a Breakfast From Around The World – England, America, Mexico, France or Europe – and have it with a $5 mimosa or Bloody Mary. There are of course plenty of non-English dishes to choose from too.

I had my first Scotch egg in a long while here (it's a boiled egg cooked in bread crumbs) and saw on the menu that you could order a "half" (a half pint of beer, which is a common order in England when you have started drinking a little earlier than usual!). If beer's not your thing you can keep the English theme with a Mary Poppins, a Paddington Bear or a Covent Garden cocktail – they're all good ways to take a trip to Blighty!

Try and get a table outside on the open, shady courtyard/patio. There's a great, laid-back vibe and it's the perfect place for an afternoon pint when the sun gets too much. There's live jazz on Sunday evenings from 7pm so come early, play darts and hang out under the twinkling lights.

Monday – Friday 11.30am-2am, Saturday/Sunday 10am-2am
Happy Hour: Monday – Friday 4-7pm (draft, well and wine $3.50, $5 menu)
www.thecatandfiddle.com
www.facebook.com/catandfiddlerestaurant
http://twitter.com/thecatandfiddle

Musso & Frank Grill
6667 Hollywood Boulevard
Hollywood, CA 90028
Tel: 323 467 7788

Charlie Chaplin and a Headless Woman

It's perhaps the very definition of a classic Hollywood experience – a cocktail and dinner at Musso and Frank. A much loved fixture for 90 years, they've played host to almost every movie star you can imagine, and some of the staff are as much a part of Tinsel Town history as the restaurant itself.

Named after original owners Joseph Musso and Frank Toulet (who had called it Frank's Francois Cafe), it was renamed and eventually bought by John Mosso and Joseph Carissimi in 1927. Inside, it feels and looks exactly like the most elegant of *film noir* clubs, and you can easily imagine giants of literature like Fitzgerald, Bukowski, Faulkner, Hemingway and Chandler scribbling away in a booth in their famous "Back Room," which was once nicknamed "Algonquin West."

When the owners took this space back, Musso & Frank just moved everything lock, stock and barrel into the bar (which also used to be a literary hangout – the Stanley Rose bookstore) and called it the "New Room." Chandler mentions the restaurant in *The Big Sleep*, Bukowski in *Hollywood*, and many of the veteran red-coated waiters have their own personal stories about them – it's that kind of place.

Bukowski fans meet up here every year, and on the big screen it appears in the Tim Burton movie *Ed Wood* (1994) in a scene where Wood (played by Johnny Depp) meets his hero Orson Welles (Vincent D'Onofrio), who often held court here back in those days. It's also briefly seen in the 2001 remake of *Ocean's 11* when George Clooney and Brad Pitt discuss their Vegas heist, and most recently it featured in the 1947 era Los Angeles video game "L.A. Noire."

With a reputation for being a private place where pesky paparazzi have long been banned, movie, music and television celebrities have spent countless hours here (and still do), though

Jordan Jones, great grandson of the original founder and current co-owner, noted they have fiercely loyal locals too:

> *"One of the most fun things for me is when people introduce themselves and say that they've been coming in for decades – two or three generations of a family. A woman in her 90s recently came in and she had first been here as a little girl when she was eleven years old!"*

The menu may not have changed much since the 1920s, but that never stopped Douglas Fairbanks once racing Charlie Chaplin here on horseback – allegedly. "The Little Tramp" had a favorite booth – number 1 – in the Old Room (it's the only one with a window view), and Jones suggested I look up a picture taken by a paranormal enthusiast and some friends on their visit to what's now known at the Chaplin Booth.

What seems to be a tiny, circular flash of light or glare – what's suggested as an "orb" – was captured on film, and a face is supposedly visible in the orb. Enhancement initially shows what seems to be a kind of "man in the moon" smiley face, but further magnification digitally (plus the help of a magnifying class) reveals something a little above the "orb": a man's staring left eye and a long, straight nose.

It doesn't look like Charlie Chaplin, but you can decide for yourself at www.hauntedplayground.com/photos.htm (it's under "Musso & Frank's").

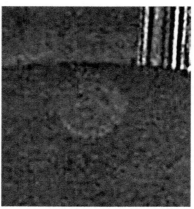

© *Tammy Melhaff 2006*

Jones also related another very frightening apparition that appeared to Ignacio Soriano (known as "Nacho"), one of his grill counter men:

> *"He works late, and speaks little English. One time he came to me and said he had seen 'La mujer sin cabeza' (an apparition or ghost) of a woman without a head. Lots of friends of mine and lots of regular customers say that there's something paranormal here, and I've experienced a few strange things myself."*

As for a possible historical explanation of any paranormal happenings in Musso & Frank, Jones mentioned the Vogue Theatre (now the Supperclub) with whom they share a wall on one side at the back (and whose owners took back the "Back Room" in 1955):

> *"It's supposed to be the most paranormal place in Los Angeles. I have heard stories that it used to be a schoolhouse and that when it burnt down in a fire, lots of kids died."*

Whether this is true or not, Jordan knows how you can find out about any spooky stories at Musso & Frank:

> *"Just come in and sit at the bar. Talk to the barman or some of the regulars."*

Barman Ruben Rueda has been working here since 1967 and over the years he has served everyone from Steve McQueen to Sam Peckinpah and Keith Richards (the Rolling Stone even gave him a guitar once). Johnny Depp still comes in to say hello, apparently.

Although "Musso's" is known for staying exactly the same, Jones has made a few little changes. Aside from keeping the bar open later on Friday and Saturday nights he introduced some background music – Billie Holiday, Ella Fitzgerald, Duke Ellington and other classics from that era – and made sure that the speakers were designed to fit right in (they look just like the old 1940s intercom system).

As for the food, there's one dish that everyone knows and is practically obligatory: chicken pot pie. It is (and will probably always be) the Thursday Special, so order any cocktail with that (a dirty martini is my recommendation) and you're set – simple but elegant. Jones, whose parents were served by current waiter Juan Ramos when they were dating, notes that Gore Vidal used to drink with Faulkner in the Back Room and still comes in today:

> *"He's says that coming to Musso's is like stepping into a warm bath."*

Some say – with justification – that the menu is very expensive, but for a slice of Hollywood nostalgia that's good enough for Gore Vidal et al, everyone who comes here is bound to agree with Jones:

> *"I want Musso & Frank to go on for another ninety years – and beyond that!"*

In late 2011 the "Back Room" between Musso's and Supperclub reopened as a tiny, separately-owned exclusive bar called The Writers Room. It features a 1920s elevator cage complete with a day bed and curtains for those looking to sip cocktails in private. Entrance is round back, and though it's nothing to do with Musso & Frank's, its design is certainly inspired by it.

Tuesday – Saturday 11am-11pm, bar until 2am Friday/Saturday
www.mussoandfrank.com
◼️Musso & Frank Grill

Pig 'N Whistle
6714 Hollywood Boulevard
Hollywood, CA 90028
Tel: 323 463 0000

The Lost Little Girl

Back in the days when Los Angeles was fast becoming the center of the movie industry, a street called Hollywood Boulevard became home to the biggest movie theaters of the day. Back then the Grauman's Chinese and El Capitan didn't have the kind of huge concession stands we're used to today, so on July 22, 1927 the Pig 'N Whistle opened its doors.

Though it was part of a chain started by John H Gage in 1908 (the first one was downtown), he had cannily seen the opportunity to provide food and drinks for moviegoers and took a prime spot next to the Egyptian Theater (there's still a side entrance from the Theater's forecourt).

Surviving both the Depression and WWII made it a landmark in a town of fleeting fame, and thanks to its connection to the Egyptian it soon became a favorite watering hole for stars to meet up and celebrate, commiserate, gossip and perhaps be inspired

(Porky Pig anyone?). More often than not they were dressed in their best following a premiere, and Cary Grant, Spencer Tracy, Clark Gable, Judy Garland and Barbara Stanwyck all came in here at one time or another.

Child actress Shirley Temple often visited too, but that's not as odd as it sounds – in those days the Pig 'N Whistle had an ice cream parlor and a candy counter in front, and was known as a "candy and luncheon" place. Another Pig 'N Whistle opened down the street by the El Capitan Theater in 1929 but closed less than ten years later, then the early 1950s saw the closure of this Pig 'N Whistle too.

Nearby restaurant Miceli's grabbed some of the "Pig's" furniture and decorations following a later fire, and though it went through various incarnations over the next few decades it still popped up in the classic movie *Chinatown* (1974) starring Jack Nicholson and Faye Dunaway.

The ongoing renaissance of Hollywood Boulevard inspired the new owners to invest over $1m for a full restoration in 1999, and in March 2001 the glory days were back when the Pig 'N Whistle opened its doors once again.

Sako Spruill, who has been with the company that owns the Pig 'N Whistle for over eight years, said that there was apparently a speakeasy in the backroom at one time, and then mentioned the name of actress Elizabeth Short. She was seen here several weeks before her murder in 1947 – a gruesome event that gave her the nickname "The Black Dahlia" – though that isn't the spookiest story from the Pig 'N Whistle:

> *"About five years ago, one of the chefs was clearing out an old storage room and he found a 1930s doll house, girl's clothes, toys and stuff."*

Spruill further explained that several staff members have apparently felt the presence of "a little girl" a number of times, and one female bartender once reported that she felt a strong tugging at her pants leg, as if a child was trying to get her attention:

> *"No one has ever seen anything, but this bartender was certain it was a small girl – it was just the feeling she got."*

Later online research noted that the ladies room is supposedly haunted by a woman who lost her young daughter in a fire back in the 1950s, and it's possible that these two stories – a girl wanting someone to play with and the child lost to fire – could have been born out of the story of the actual 1950s fire, the find of the doll's house and past visits from Shirley Temple.

The *Los Angeles Times* archives did reveal that there had been a tragic accident at the Pig 'N Whistle. In November 1932 new kitchen worker Dominic Stratton was "working for his breakfast" and had been "severely scalded" after falling into a large pot of boiling water. This however was at the Pig 'N Whistle by the El Capitan, and though the archives didn't have any stories about deadly fires, Spruill was certain of one thing:

"The manager, bartender, chef – they've all mentioned many times that they don't like being here late at night. There's definitely an eerie feeling."

If you sit inside, make sure you look up at the ornate, gothic carved wood ceiling and try to count the number of vintage pig and whistle tiles – they're everywhere. Joint owner Chris Breed noted that "people love the historical feeling they get when they walk in. They stare up at the ceiling before they've even ordered a beer – it really has that "wow" factor."

Some of their signature cocktails like the Margarita Hayworth, the Halle Razz Berry and The Dude celebrate their starry connection, and the latest, A Clockwork Orange, celebrates actor Malcolm McDowell, whose Walk of Fame star is right outside. Though the short menu of standard American food is a rather pricey tourist favorite, my server told me that the Philly cheese steak would "put a smile on your face" – and he was right.

Being at such a prime location "The Pig" is always busy, but if you do manage to snag one of the few tables outside it's a perfect place to watch some of the wild locals walking by.

Sunday – Tuesday 12pm-11pm
Wednesday – Saturday 12pm-2am
www.pignwhistlehollywood.com
www.facebook.com/pignwhistlehollywood
http://twitter.com/PigNWhistleHW

Yamashiro
1999 North Sycamore Avenue
Hollywood, CA 90068
Tel: 323 466 5125

Glover's Ghost and The Woman at Table 9

At the top of a hill some 250 feet above Hollywood Boulevard, Yamashiro arguably has the best view in Los Angeles – and has stood guard over Tinsel Town for nearly 100 years.

As the old black and white photographs on display show, it was here when everything around it was fields, and it was here when the fledgling movie business came west to take advantage of the endless sun (and to avoid paying fees to camera inventor Thomas Edison).

But there were difficult times for Yamashiro too.

During the years of World War II it suffered graffiti attacks and was even closed for a while, but the everlasting appeal of the Far Eastern culture and architecture has continued to this day. Just stroll around the tranquil gardens and you're transported to a different place and time; it's easy to see why this is a popular place for weddings and special occasions.

Described as "what will possibly be the finest, and certainly the most unique bungalow in the United States," an April 7, 1912 *Los Angeles Times* article included an artist's impression and was in awe of $100,000 plans for the "luxurious" private estate planned by new owners Adolph and Eugene Bernheimer.

Two merchant brothers from Germany, they wanted to build a mansion for their many imported Asian treasures at what was then known as Whitley Hill No. 2, and "Live Like Real Mandarins" in a home of teak, ebony and colored tiles.

Inspired by a palace located in mountains near Kyoto, Japan, construction began later that year on a replica inspired by both the design and the name "Yamashiro," which translates as "mountain palace" (though most people simply referred to it as Bernheimer's Japanese/Oriental Palace or Gardens).

BORROWED FROM THE FAR EAST.

Noted Importers Completing Unique House.

Hollywood Hill Mansion a Striking Object.

Asiatic Even to the Teak in Its Walls.

Hundreds of skilled craftsmen were brought from the Orient, and by 1914 Yamashiro was completed. 300 steps led up the hillside through the landscaped Japanese gardens to the 10 room teak and cedar mansion, where the rafters were lacquered in gold and tipped with bronze dragons. Inside, a sacred inner court garden took pride of place and was decorated with plants, trees and stone pools, while the surrounding rooms were draped with luxurious silks and ancient tapestries.

Luxurious Oriental Bungalow to Crown Beautiful Foothill Back of Hollywood.

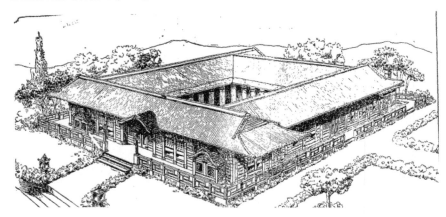

Los Angeles Times

The garden landscaping cost a rumored $2-$4m (a huge sum of money even then), and the hillside terraces were decorated with 30,000 varieties of trees and shrubs, waterfalls, hundreds of goldfish and even a private zoo with exotic birds and a monkey house. Miniature bronze houseboats floated along a maze of tiny canals through a miniature Japanese village, and though some of those features have passed into history (or storage), the famous 600-year-old pagoda is still here.

Brought over from Japan at great expense, it was placed next to a lake that was once home to rare black Australian swans. The birth of six swan signets here even made the *Los Angeles Times* (February 27, 1938) when it was reported that the protective "father swan" once shattered the walnut barrel of a shotgun and "dotes on wrecking cameras." Today the pagoda watches over guests at the small Pagoda Bar/Lounge, a hidden-away location that has that great view and gets my vote as the most romantic spot at Yamashiro.

In the late 1920s Yamashiro changed hands again and became the headquarters for the ultra-exclusive "400 Club," the first celebrity hangout in town. In the *Los Angeles Times* of November 1, 1925 celebrity reporter "Stella" (real name Grace Kingsley) noted "A brilliant gathering of film folk" at the opening, and members of the Hollywood movie elite such as Lillian Gish, Ramon Navarro, Rudolph Valentino and many others made it their home-from-home. "Maybe there will be a ghost!" said "Stella," showing that there may have been some strange stories even then.

During the Depression, tours of the gardens and a chance to gaze at Los Angeles and the Pacific Ocean beyond were available for just 25 cents, and there were rumors of a vast basement and a tunnel that ran all the way down to the Grauman's Chinese Theater (and was a secret route for alcohol smuggling and beautiful wannabe actresses and models who were available here – for a price).

Anti-Japanese sentiment spread rapidly at the start of World War II though, and with memories of the German Bernheimers, Yamashiro was mistakenly thought to be a signaling tower for ships and submarines out at sea. Vandals attacked the building and even the gardens, so Yamashiro was boarded up and painted over, the estate showing its patriotic colors by becoming a boys' military school.

Following Adolph Bernheimer's death in 1944 the gardens were closed for several years, but in 1948 the estate – now almost unrecognizable from its halcyon days – was bought for $50,000 by Thomas O. Glover. He initially planned to tear down the palace and develop a hotel and apartments, but then he uncovered the ornate woodwork and silk wallpaper hidden under layers of paint, and decided to restore the property to its full glory.

That planned 20 year project is still going on, with Glover's son (also named Thomas) the driving force behind the restaurant's Sunset Room, the main dining room terraces, the bar lounge and Skyview banquet room. He also renovated the inner courtyard and garden and added rare koi fish to the pools, though most of the Asian collection – the Buddhist and Satsuma art, the rare jades, tapestries and chandeliers – had sadly been auctioned off in 1922 when Eugene Bernheimer had died.

David Comfort has been General Manager here for the last seven years, and replying to my emails about any supernatural stories he said that there were "too many stories" and that "I can't tell you how many security guards (Yamashiro) has gone through."

When I visited he explained how many guests insist that there really is a secret tunnel (even that they'd been in it themselves), and then he took me on a rare tour into the basement. After passing a small but creepy display put up for a Halloween event a couple of years ago (it included two rickshaws, one of which was used in the 1957 Marlon Brando movie *Sayonara* and still has a California license plate), we browsed through some forgotten antiquities – bells, pictures, wooden fixtures – in an area that used to be an underground bowling alley.

After passing head bartender Steve's office we were standing among shelves of wine and spirits, and I noticed that if you tapped a couple of the red floor panels it sounded hollow, as if there was nothing underneath. Was this the entrance to the rumored tunnel? Comfort said that he had even drilled a hole in the floor to try and see what was down there (you can see the hole in the photograph), but that he didn't really want to know – just in case.

As for being here at night, Comfort said that "multiple" Security Guards had "quit on the first night," and that one even left mid-shift and never came back. As for what they saw, he mentioned Tony, a 25-year-old Security Guard who said that he once saw "guys walking through walls." Jason Ram wrote a piece for the restaurant's website called "A Heavenly Haunt" about his experiences as a Security Guard here and he mentions "sudden chills" and "heat sensations." One night he was alone in the locked building, and most of the lights were turned off:

> *"I had just finished with the main floor and was on my way up to the second via the East-wing stairway. Striding up the stairs, flashlight in hand, a tune in my head and Starbucks on my mind, I heard the faint, yet distinct sound of two voices briefly conversing in the (inner court) garden; lasting only a few moments until fading into silence. I could have sworn the voices were those of a man and woman walking by the garden."*

Regardless of what anyone has seen or heard here, it does seem that Thomas Glover Sr. still seems to be looking over his mountain palace. Tommy Zoobharasee, a previous General Manager, told the story that one night after closing up he saw a man sitting in the inner court area; Glover ashes were laid to rest in the north east corner under a tree in the inner court garden, as were his wife Jane's.

Comfort has had several experiences here too, the most recent of which was just a few days before we visited:

> *"The other night I kept hearing the sound of someone walking up and down the stairs to my office."*

Four years ago, Comfort – who considers himself a "very realistic person" – was upstairs when he saw a light downstairs switched off. He went down to see if there was anyone there and clearly saw the silhouette of a person passing right in front of him:

> *"I ran! Steve at the bar took one look at me and said 'You saw something, didn't you?' Just a few weeks later, one of the other managers, Jack, a super guy, saw the silhouette too."*

Soon after that Jack found that there was a light on in the groom's room (which is only used for weddings), and once inside he heard the distinct sound of a child crying:

> *"He switched off the light and came downstairs, pale as hell. He and the security guard went up again. They could both hear the crying, but there was no one there – and the light was back on."*

Other staff members have had strange experiences here, but they all seem to see it as just part of a working day at Yamashiro:

> *"Tabitha, our receptionist, just accepts the ghosts here. A few years back there was talk of selling Yamashiro and the Glover Family was split on a decision. Thomas Sr. seemed to decide though, as out of nowhere dishes started flying off a shelf – and Tabitha heard all the crashing and*

smashing. This was no earthquake, and the Glover Family decided not to sell. Now she even says hello to the ghosts."

As he walked past, another employee named Omar stopped and added that he "sees and hears weird things here – I always turn on the lights at night!" and there's also the intriguing story of table number 9 (the last one in the far corner) in the Sunset Room:

"As soon as Steve's mother-in-law, who said that she was psychic, walked in, she said that there was a 'woman waiting for her husband' at the empty table. A year or so later, some paranormal investigators came into Yamashiro and said the same thing."

Comfort has no idea who the lonely woman could be, and that table remains the most popular in the Sunset Room – it has the best view.

Table 9 – with guests

Lastly, one of the upstairs bedrooms here used to be the old carriage house, and a maintenance person said that he once woke up feeling a huge, crushing weight on his chest – as if someone was sitting on top of him. "He quit right away," said Comfort.

Even the Japanese gardens have their own strange stories. One night at around 2am, former general manager Zoobharasee heard a woman walking round the gardens in high heels. As she got closer and closer he noticed that some of the lights were going on and off. He moved aside to let her pass and even felt a wisp of wind as she passed by – but there was no one there.

Also, as noted by Ram in his article, there are spooky stories outside the walls of Yamashiro too. The most infamous one is that of a man who hung himself from a tree in the grounds of the Hollywood Hills Hotel, which is perched on the same hill. He was found with divorce papers in his pocket – possibly the reason for his desperate act:

"His body was only discovered (a few months after his death) when one of his shoes fell upon a gardener. His ghost has been known to stalk the road leading up to his tree and he chased away one security guard who fled his post in the middle of the night."

Ram told me that the current Hollywood Hills Hotel owners (who saw the body) asked that the victim's identity remain anonymous, though further archive research uncovered another event that happened just yards away from Yamashiro.

Back in 1955, the *Los Angeles Times* of May 22 reported the suicide of movie producer and writer Fayette Moore. Dead from a gunshot wound to the head – a .38 revolver was on the seat next to him – he was found in his car, which was parked at the curb right by Yamashiro. Apparently in poor health, Moore left behind a simple note that read: "In case of emergency, please contact my son."

Fayette Moore, Film Producer, Ends His Life

Inside, Yamashiro is a glamorous maze of endless rooms and wings – all of them with a great view over Los Angeles – though I like to sit at the lounge bar and watch as the lights (and sometimes spotlights) come on across the city. If you're there on a clear day you can see all the way to the ocean, and my drink of choice to gaze over the city is "Norman's Mai Tai". He was a bartender here for over 30 years (even living here at one time), and he bought the recipe – and its "secret ingredient" – with him from Hawaii. It has been said that his ghost is still tending bar.

As you might expect, executive chef Brock L. Kleweno has fashioned the menu for lovers of sushi and seafood (though I've yet to try the spicy tuna black rice roll, better known as the "Darth Vader"). There's an intriguing choice of sakes and beers as well, but if you can't make it for dinner then you can come here for one of Los Angeles' more unusual Farmers Markets.

One of my favorite nights out, they start in April and take place on Thursday evenings between 5-9pm. Come early to get a table and avoid the lines because the market is packed with local organic produce, crêpes, barbeque sauces, cheeses, cakes and cookies. There are also food trucks offering ice cream sandwiches and one with lasagna cupcakes (strange, but it works!). There's live music too, and the Yamashiro grill stand does a roaring trade in mini-tacos (I recommend the braised ribs). Last time I went, a guy with a telescope was offering a free look at Saturn!

Valet parking is standard, but there is free parking further down the hill and a shuttle bus to save you from the climb. However, if you're feeling brave – or want to make room for that ice cream sandwich – then walk up the (admittedly very steep) hill.

En route you'll pass what was originally the carriage house, and at the summit you can survey the city as the sun goes down.

Hours vary for restaurant and bars
www.yamashirohollywood.com
www.facebook.com/YamashiroLA
http://twitter.com/YamashiroLA

Miceli's Restaurant
1646 North Las Palmas Avenue
Hollywood, CA 90028
Tel: 323 466 3438

Toni's Still On The Clock...

The oldest Italian restaurant in town, Miceli's really is the definition of a family business – Carmen and Sylvia Miceli, their sisters Angie and Millie and brothers Tony and Sammie all joined forces to open Miceli's in 1949. Using secret family recipes bought from Sicily via old Chicago, they soon had people lining up along the block to taste a new, exotic dish they offered – something called "pizza".

Celebrities were soon coming here too and everyone from John F. Kennedy and Richard Nixon to actors Jim Carrey, Adam Sandler and Julia Roberts have popped in. It's also Hollywood legend that Lucille Ball came here to learn how to toss dough and make a pizza for a famous episode of her "I Love Lucy" show.

You might spot a few flute-playing dancing pigs on the walls here, and that's because they were originally from one of Hollywood's most famous restaurants, the Pig 'N Whistle, which is located just round the corner. When "the Pig" was gutted by fire in the 1950s, the industrious Miceli family grabbed all the hand-carved booths, wall panels and fixtures out of the dumpsters, and brought them home.

Frank Miceli laughed off their website's claim that Union leader Jimmy Hoffa is buried in the events-only basement (he's also supposedly buried in the New Jersey Turnpike and under the New York Giants Stadium), but it is possible that The Beatles came in one night for beer and pie after recording at Capitol Records (or performing at the Hollywood Bowl – they're both near each other). Marilyn Monroe was said to drink the odd martini here too, and there was even a late night rendezvous between gangster Bugsy Siegel and actor Sal Mineo over (what else?) spaghetti and meatballs.

There's no archive evidence for any of these of course, though Frank did say that family friend and regular Gene (or Jean)

Goh passed away here a couple of years ago. He was down in the basement it seems, and his body was found the next morning:

"Soon after a kid came in (to Miceli's) and, out of the blue, said to me: 'You have a spirit in here.' His parents said to me that 'he sees dead people,' just like in that movie. I've never heard any stories or seen anything myself, but when I walk down into basement in the dark, before the lights come on, the hairs on the back of my neck do stand up. People do come in and say that they feel things."

However, Frank was more than happy to confirm that there is one "ghost" here – the spirit of Antoinette "Toni" Heines, who worked here for 52 years and, understandably, is still keeping an eye on her tables:

"Whenever a light goes out or a glass breaks unexpectedly, we always say that it's Toni. She gets the blame for everything!"

There's a stained glass portrait of her in what was her section, so say hello and make sure there won't be any strange "accidents" while you enjoy your pizza (I recommend the Special with pepperoni, Italian sausage, meatballs, salami, bell peppers, mushrooms and onions, though there's a long menu of lamb, pasta, veal, chicken and seafood dishes too). If you still have room, try Uncle Frank's Tiramisu: Mascarpone mousse with lady fingers flavored with rum, espresso and Kahlua.

Monday – Thursday 11.30am-11pm
Friday – Sunday 11.30am-midnight
www.micelisrestaurant.com
Micelis Italian Restaurant
http://twitter.com/micelis1949

Couldn't Get A Table - Hollywood

Despite my best efforts to find an eyewitness or something in the archives, these places just didn't have enough to make it into the chapter – but still had a great ghost story.

TCL Chinese Theatre (formerly Grauman's)
Tel: 323 461 3331

Victor Kilian's Ghost – and a Serial Killer?

Bang in the middle of Hollywood Boulevard, the distinctive TCL Chinese Theatre is one of the most popular tourist attractions in Los Angeles. It's known for its glamorous movie premieres, and at night you have a good chance of seeing cameras flashing endlessly as movie stars walk the red carpet.

In fact, many people say that a trip to Hollywood isn't complete without seeing how you measure up against around 250 of the biggest names in Hollywood, all of whom have happily stuck their hands and feet in concrete to be preserved forever right here. It's strange to think that this unusual tourist attraction began accidentally, when Sid Grauman stepped into wet concrete during construction.

Grauman had already masterminded the Million Dollar Theater downtown and the exotic Egyptian Theatre nearby, but he wanted a dream venue. Actress Norma Talmadge dug the first spade of earth in January 1926 and $2m later the theater opened for its very own movie star premiere on May 18, 1927 and then to the public the next day.

Designed by Raymond Kennedy, the Theatre features specially-imported bells, dragon heaven dogs and other artifacts, while its red pagoda towers 90 feet high over the Boulevard. The golden dogs still guard the entrance today, and between the red columns is a 30 foot high stone dragon, just in case they need more bite than bark to chase away the press photographers.

"Grauman's" was bought by new owners TCL in 2011, and they plan to bring back some of the 1930s glamour by re-lighting the forecourt and restoring the old signs, and also preserving and repairing some of the older cement tributes. There are also plans to include athletes and musicians handprints in the adjacent Hollywood & Highland mall, which they also own.

No matter what happens, the theatre is known around the world as a symbol of Hollywood and the movies, so it's no surprise that some sources have reported that an actor's ghost often roams the theatre forecourt at night, apparently in an endless search for his murderer.

According to the *Los Angeles Times* and *Los Angeles Herald-Examiner* of March 12 and 13, 1979 respectively, on the last night of his life actor Victor Kilian (best known for his role as the "Fernwood Flasher" on the 1970s television series "Mary Hartman, Mary Hartman") apparently met a man in a bar near the theater, and invited him up to his apartment in nearby Yucca Street for some drinks.

His body was found the next day, beaten to death, and the police report said that "robbery was a possible motive," though the apartment doors were apparently locked.

The very next day the shocking news was announced that another elderly actor named Charles Waggenheim had also been beaten to death in his home in the Hollywood Hills earlier that same week. Was there a serial killer on the loose?

Police Checking Possible Link in Actor Slayings

Two elderly character actors beaten to death within a week at their Hollywood homes appeared together in a taping of the TV show All in the Family shortly before they were killed, Hollywood detectives said Mon-

After several months both the *Los Angeles Times* and the *Los Angeles Herald-Examiner* reported that police had arrested their "prime suspect" in the Waggenheim murder: her name was Stephanie Boon and she was a nurse who looked after Waggenheim's invalid wife Lillian.

Nurse Arrested in Slaying of Actor, 84

Tragically, Lillian's stroke meant she was unable to tell the police anything about that fateful day, and the LAPD eventually ruled out any connection with Kilian's death – which they never solved either. Bizarrely, it also later emerged that Kilian and Waggenheim had both just taped appearances for the television show "All in the Family".

There have also been reports about a mysterious curtain "twitcher" backstage at Grauman's. Is it the ghost of Grauman himself or Fritz, an employee who apparently hung himself there? There was no evidence in newspaper archives of the latter, and since there is supposedly also a "Fritz" who died at the former Vogue Theatre (now the Supperclub and just a few blocks away) it seems that this story at least is an apocryphal one.

On a recent visit staff members mentioned that the ghost of Marilyn Monroe is often in the ladies bathroom – they usually just wave and say hello – while one noted that Grauman himself is regularly seen on the right side of the lobby, where there's a good view of the screen:

> *"He's still here. After all, Grauman was all about entertainment, wasn't he?"*

A hot dog, popcorn and soda aren't really a meal, though there are countless restaurants nearby – especially in the glitzy Hollywood & Highland complex – and you can try to see Kilian's lonely vigil from anywhere by clicking on their webcam.

Hours vary
www.tclchinesetheatres.com
www.facebook.com/TCLChineseTheatres
http://twitter.com/chinesetheatres

Supperclub
Vogue Theatre
Tel: 323 466 1900

Miss Elizabeth and the Fire

Designed by architect S. Charles Lee, the man behind several hundred movie theaters across California and Mexico, the Vogue Theatre opened on July 16th, 1935. There was a seating capacity for nearly 1000 people inside and for many years it was one of the most notable theaters in Hollywood, enjoying a long and successful run before it closed its doors in the early 1990s.

Over the next decade this prime spot on Hollywood Boulevard became a temporary home to award ceremonies and movie and television crews on location, though it did have some notable tenants: in 1997 it was acquired by the International Society for Paranormal Research as an office, and they – perhaps unsurprisingly – identified a number of ghosts here.

The building still shares a rear back wall with the Musso & Frank Grill next door, and Musso's owner Jordon Jones mentioned that the Vogue Theatre "is supposed to be the most paranormal place in Los Angeles. I have heard stories that it used to be a schoolhouse and that when it burnt down in a fire, lots of kids died."

Online research suggested that over 100 years ago, when Hollywood Boulevard was known as Prospect Avenue, the Prospect Elementary School – or its playground – was indeed located in what would later become the Vogue Theatre's auditorium. This was apparently the schoolhouse that burned to the ground in 1901, killing 25 children and their teacher "Miss Elizabeth," and was doubtless the origin of stories about the smell of smoke, sightings of small children, a little girl skipping in the aisles, and, most chillingly, people feeling that they were being pushed aside on the stairs in the theatre.

However, extensive research in Los Angeles newspaper archives found no record of such a fire or the Prospect Elementary School, with the nearest thing being a non-fatal blaze that destroyed the nearby Hollywood Community Theater School and several buildings in August 1939.

Union High School was mentioned in reports around the turn of the century though, and on January 7, 1910 the *Los Angeles Times* reported that a student from the school, Elizabeth Taylor, ("Miss Elizabeth"?) had been thrown from her buggy when its horse was frightened. Her brother Henry escaped with lesser injuries, as did the occupants of two other buggies involved in the accident. "Death Near Young Woman" said the headline, noting that sophomore student Taylor had suffered "concussion of the brain" and "recovery was not considered probable."

Injured in Wild Ride Down Cahuenga Pass.

Horse Runs Away and Girl Is Thrown from Buggy.

Five Others Narrowly Escape Serious Injury.

HOLLYWOOD, Jan. 6 — Miss Elizabeth Taylor, daughter of D. Taylor of Lankershim and a student in the sophomore year at the Union High School, is at the point of death in a ward at the Sisters' Hospital, Los Angeles, as the result of a runaway in Cahuenga Pass this morning.

She had broken her leg in a similar accident in almost exactly the same place the year before, and maybe this second – seemingly fatal – accident stayed in the memories of her fellow students and combined with the later school fire to become the more shocking story.

Two other entities were found to be in residence by the ISPR: "Fritz," a German who worked as a projectionist here for decades, and "Danny," a maintenance engineer for the theatre company.

Both apparently died in the 1980s and though "Danny" died elsewhere, "Fritz" apparently died in the projection booth – possibly by committing suicide.

When the ISPR left in 2001, parapsychologist Dr. Larry Montz said they had "cleared" the building, but a story in the *Hollywood Independent Newspaper* in February reported that the vintage 1940s-themed All Star Café and Speakeasy was going to open here, and the owner was bringing some ghosts from its old venue – inside the Knickerbocker Hotel – with him.

Legendary director D.W. Griffith died shortly after collapsing in the Knickerbocker lobby, costume designer Irene Gibbons jumped to her death from the 11th floor and, most famously, Bess Houdini – widow of legendary showman and escape artist Harry, held séances for years on the roof in the hope that he would contact her from the afterlife – though he never did.

The ISPR held a special séance to help finance the move and restore the lobby to attract more tourists, but – ghostly help or not – the All Star Café didn't last long and the Vogue was again shuttered to the world.

Then the Supperclub – a worldwide chain of lavish, glossy theatrical restaurants where you relax on couches and enjoy performances by dominatrixes, opera singers, acrobats and midgets between courses before then clubbing the night away – announced they were coming to Hollywood. Early publicity even mentioned "Fritz," and when I spoke to managing partner Alan Hsia he confirmed some early experiences definitely got them wondering:

> *"During construction, people would come in off the street and tell us 'Watch out! Fritz will get you!' and when we were here at night we could hear banging and knocking in the ceiling. But then we realized that the rooftops of this building and next door are connected, and when we went up there we found empty water bottles and stuff. Squatters had been living up there. Once we locked off all the entrances, we never heard any sounds again. No more Fritz!"*

Hsai said that though nothing else strange happened, they did their own research anyway – but were still unable to find anything to back them up:

"We even asked the Los Angeles Fire Department, and they had no record of a fire here."

It's a dead end then, though since "Fritz" is reportedly haunting Grauman's Chinese Theatre too, he'll doubtless be thrilled that "his" old Vogue projector is going to live on:

"The projector, old marquee letters and a ticketing machine were here when we arrived. The projector is being refurbished, and we're going to donate it to the Hollywood Chamber of Commerce."

Hours/events vary
www.supperclub.la
www.facebook.com/supperclub.los.angeles
http://twitter.com/supperclub_la

Chapter 2
West Hollywood & Beverly Hills

Barney's Beanery
8447 Santa Monica Boulevard
West Hollywood, CA 90069
Tel: 323 654 2287

The Man In Black and the Sunset Strip Love Triangle!

When hapless barman Moe opened his Family Feedbag restaurant in "The Simpsons," one of the big selling points was "a whole lotta crazy crap on the walls." Barney's Beanery is a bit like that; an old bungalow shack with a small stoop/porch outside, and yes, lots of crazy crap on the walls.

The original of what is now a chain (the others are in Santa Monica, Burbank, Westwood and Pasadena), Barney's is a neon heaven of beer signs, tiffany lights, memorabilia, license plates, autographed pictures, yellowing newspaper articles and souvenirs from the famous and infamous of movies, television and music. Inside there are flat screen televisions all over so you don't miss a minute of the game, arcade games in back, pool tables, a foosball table and air hockey.

After serving chili burgers to soldiers during his Navy service in WWI, John "Barney" Anthony first founded his restaurant way back in 1920, and a few years later in 1927 he relocated roadside to the new Route 66, which ran all the way from Chicago to Los Angeles. It was a genius move, and newly-arrived pioneers looking for a fresh start in the sunshine were soon coming in for a bite and a beer. Movie stars such as Jean Harlow, Clark Gable, Errol Flynn, Judy Garland and Rita Hayworth began paying a visit too, and it's still a celebrity favorite today.

The credit-giving John was a popular guy, and "Barney's" soon became a favorite hangout for poets, artists and musicians as well. The emergence of the nearby Sunset Strip as a major music scene in the 1960s also meant that singers like Jim Morrison became regulars (even though he was once thrown out for relieving himself on the bar – there's a plaque there now).

The movie *The Doors* filmed here, and Quentin Tarantino wrote most of *Pulp Fiction* sitting in his favorite booth by the bar; on their website it even quotes him as saying that:

"Whenever someone comes to town and hasn't been to L.A. before, I like to take them to the Beanery. It's such a great experience."

Perhaps most famously, this was the place where another regular, singer Janis Joplin, had her last drink before dying of a drug overdose on October 4, 1970 (her favorite booth was #34). Charles Bukowski drank here too – as he seemed to do in most of Hollywood – and Ed Kienholz even created an anti-war tableau sculpture (complete with beer smell) inspired by and called "The Beanery." It got its grand unveiling in the parking lot in 1965, and has been on exhibition around the world ever since – most recently in the National Gallery in London.

Barney's was home to controversy too. In the 1940s a sign appeared among the paraphernalia that said "Fagots (sic) – Stay Out." Most of the regular gay clientele dismissed it as a joke, but after protests and nearly 15 years of the sign going up and down off the wall it was finally removed for good in early 1985.

Bonnie Ajemian has been a waitress and manager here for over a dozen years, and she feels that not all the customers come through the front door:

"There's definitely stuff there (at Barney's) and although I've always had strange experiences in my life, I always feel that there must be a rational explanation."

Nevertheless, some experiences at Barney's have been difficult to explain away, and the most striking of them involves a strange "Man In Black":

"One of the previous managers, Michelle, had closed up one night, but when she walked past the ladies room she saw a man in black standing in there. He was wearing a black hat and a black coat, (but) as soon as she said something he was gone."

Ajemian's husband Doc, who worked at Barney's before her, had some clues about this strange "Man In Black":

"This place has had a lot of remodeling over the years, and he told me that before it was the ladies room, that area was a back room where there was a pool table and gambling."

There could be an explanation for the story – or the root of it – in the archives. On September 15, 1973 the *Los Angeles Times* briefly reported on a murder that took place here; 25-year-old Leonard "Tony" Taylor was arrested several days after he had allegedly shot and killed Barney's bartender Robert H Rush, 34, following an argument over a game of pool.

Suspect in Pool Game Slaying Seized at Home

A 25-year-old suspect in a shooting at Barney's Beanery, 8447 Santa Monica Blvd., was arrested Friday and booked on suspicion of murder.

Maybe the "Man In Black" is Rush, still waiting for his winnings (or his revenge), and perhaps he was there the night Ajemian said she felt someone pass behind her:

"On the ceiling in the middle of the restaurant is the hood of the old kitchen, and I was standing right under it. The aisles here are narrow and the tables are close together, so whenever anyone wants to get past they usually say something or touch you on the back. I was taking the order when I felt someone touch the small of my back and squeeze past. I looked up a moment later, but there was no one there. It was early and the other tables were

empty. I asked the people on the table, and they hadn't seen anyone either."

A few years ago the "Man In Black" appeared again:

"A waitress called Denee went into the walk-in fridge. Inside is a smaller walk-in freezer, and she went in there to get ice cream. As soon as she opened the door she saw that there was somebody in there. He was dressed in black, and when she said something he just disappeared."

Understandably "freaked out," the waitress came running back upstairs and spoke about what she had seen:

"We checked all the staff that were there – who could have gone down into the walk-in – but only one of them was wearing a black t-shirt, and he was nowhere near the walk-in. Those walk-in doors are heavy, and who'd lock himself in the freezer like that?"

Ajemian also mentioned that she has felt her hair being pulled, and when she was working as a manager she and the lone Security Guard had a strange experience after closing one night:

"There are swinging doors on the kitchen, and suddenly they flew open as if someone was running through them. We thought it must be an open door or a draft from other doors nearby, so we tried to make it happen again – and couldn't do it."

Also, another employee had such a strange experience that he left Barney's:

"One of the cooks, Raul, was downstairs in the dry storage area to get one of the kegs out of the cooler. He got a keg and put it in front of the ice machine, then started to walk back up the stairs. He'd hardly taken a step when he heard a dragging sound. He turned round and watched the keg slide about 20 feet across the floor from the ice machine to the washer/dryer. The floor isn't

on a slope or anything, and those kegs are very heavy –
they wouldn't just slide on their own. He quit and started
working at the Barney's in Pasadena (nearly 10 miles
away) soon after."

Other experiences in the keg room/cooler were mentioned in the October 30, 2011 edition of the *Los Angeles Times*. Bartender Chanhsy Khamta had been in there when she felt someone walk in and then disappear – though the door was shut – and while she has "gotten used to it," waitress Ashley Lawyer refuses to go in alone after hearing "a whoosh sound go by." The article also mentioned the appearance of a strange figure in a white shirt passing outside the rooftop office. Manager Jonah Dumont has seen it "20-plus times," and other employees have seen it elsewhere in the building too.

Finally, jealousy was the motive been behind a murderous story that Ajemian had heard took place here in the 1960s:

"A waitress working here at the time had a boyfriend who
was very jealous. One night he came to Barney's and, angry
at how she was talking to one of her male customers, took
him outside and shot him – right out front."

The newspaper archives showed no such story at Barney's, though it did unearth an incident that took place half a mile directly west of here, and could be the original source of the story. Under the eye-catching headline

SUNSET STRIP TRIANGLE!
SWANK HOTEL MAN SLAIN

the January 29 and 30, 1963 edition of the *Los Angeles Herald-Examiner* noted the shooting of Robert I. Ingram, 41, in another restaurant – the Aware Inn – by the 40-year-old owner, James Edward Baker. It seemed that Ingram's actress wife Jean had struck up a relationship with the married Baker, and though they were separated, Ingram was jealous.

Beauty in Case
—The Fight Over Her

By permission of Hearst Communications, Inc., Hearst Newspapers Division.

A meeting was arranged, but Ingram came armed with a .38 revolver. Baker disarmed Ingram with a judo blow, but then there was a struggle and Ingram was shot in the head.

Baker was convicted of manslaughter and sentenced to 10 years in prison, though this wasn't his first dice with death; records showed that in 1955 he was cleared of the murder of a neighbor in a fight over a dog, his lethal judo then considered justifiable homicide.

However, Baker was quickly paroled in the manslaughter case and his life took a bizarre turn. Up until his death in a bizarre hang gliding accident in August 1975 he was known as "Father Yod" or "YaHoWha," the leader of a seemingly harmless sex, drugs and rock n' roll hippie cult commune known as The Source Family.

He had 13 wives and 140 "spiritual" children and they lived in eccentric harmony on the earnings from The Source, his popular vegetarian restaurant, until his fears of apocalypse led to them to move to Hawaii. Well, it was the 1970s!

Many years later in September 2008, something happened at Barney's that really was chillingly close to the story Ajemian heard. Two men – Justin Michael Acosta, 34, and Damon Gerardo Acevado, 36 – got into an argument with 40-year-old Michael McClure. The argument moved outside where McClure was stabbed, dying later in the hospital.

Finally, the *Los Angeles Times* archive tells of a "very bloody night" at Barney's Beanery. On February 20, 1969 a man named Robert Griffin, 29, rushed into the bar, grabbed the chef's cleaver and lunged at local resident Joseph Swartz.

Ketchup 'Massacre' Has the Beanery Bouncing

The chef and several of the customers jumped in to help, and one of them smashed a bottle of tomato ketchup over Griffin, who ran from the restaurant looking like he was covered in blood. An LAPD deputy later commented that it looked like a "massacre," and Griffin was charged with suspicion of assault with a deadly weapon and possession of amphetamine pills.

As for the food, it's always delicious and the prices are nice n' low (unlike the calorie count of most of the menu). There are hundreds of choices (the menu is like a newspaper and is probably the longest I've ever seen), but my favorites are their hamburgers and pizzas (pick any one) and of course their special chili (said to be Marilyn Monroe's personal favorite). Breakfast is served all day, and you can even have a champagne breakfast – a bottle of Dom Perignon with a giant cheese chili dog – for the princely sum of $250!

When I drop in, I usually take a seat at the bar. Nearly 100 beers are on offer from places as diverse as Argentina, Namibia, Alaska and Louisiana, and there are different specials during the daily Happy Hour, as well as a handful of cheap snacks to go with your drink. If you're not sure about what you want to drink, there are cocktails and a number of Red Bull-based revivers, though a good idea if you like beer is the sampler: several small glasses of Domestic and Imported specialties.

Over 90 years young, Barney's is perhaps the ultimate hip dive bar in town, and really is a must-visit. A mecca to all things American it may be, but with the comfort food to match (and plenty of it), as the menu says:

"If we don't have it, you don't need it!"

Monday – Friday 10am-2am, Saturday/Sunday 9am-2am
Happy Hour: Daily 4-7pm
www.barneysbeanery.com
www.facebook.com/theoriginalbarneysbeanery
http://twitter.com/Barneysbeanery

Chateau Marmont
8221 West Sunset Boulevard
West Hollywood, CA 90046
Tel: 323 656 0575 (Bar Marmont)

DaVinci and Boris Karloff

Few would argue that the Chateau Marmont holds center stage in the history of Hollywood; their guest list reads like a Who's Who of celebrity and has been an endless source of gossip ever since it opened. Even if your favorite star hasn't stayed here, they've probably partied here – it's even said that The Eagles' hit "Hotel California" was written about "the Marmont," (though that's actually the Beverly Hills Hotel on the album cover).

Named after the hilly street running alongside the chateau – Marmont Lane – it was originally opened as apartments, but the Depression forced a change of plans and it became a hotel whose design was inspired by the Chateau d'Amboise in the Loire Valley, France. The hotel quickly bought the nine cottages built alongside in the 1940s, and in 1953 architect Craig Ellwood designed two bungalows here in the style of his other "Case Study Houses," experimental model homes built for the millions of returning World War II soldiers.

With so many big names passing through their doors, it's amazing that the Marmont has managed to maintain a reputation for utter discretion. The bungalows and cottages have their own (much loved) private entrances too, and this is just two reasons their famous clients come back time and time again.

It also ensures that word gets around; even if you're in town for a short time, this is the place to stay. Services here include secretarial/translation help, personalized stationery, packing and unpacking, dry cleaning and chauffeur-driven cars: why would you ever leave?

"I would rather sleep in a bathroom than at another hotel," said writer/director Billy Wilder (*Some Like It Hot, The Apartment, Double Indemnity, Sunset Boulevard*), and he did indeed sleep in an anteroom attached to the ladies toilets for a while in 1935. He'd foolishly arrived at Christmas time without making a reservation, and the hotel was booked out. "It's the only time I had a room with six toilets," he joked.

Famously heralded as completely earthquake-proof when it was built in 1927 (and it's survived shaky moments in 1933, 1953, 1971, 1987 and 1994) it's possible that suddenly-falling pictures or moving chairs could be explained by the Richter scale, though not everything can.

Novelist Elaine Dundy felt that the "resident" ghost here was not dangerous, and was more out for fun – even if things did get broken along the way. In the book *Haunted Hollywood* (edited by the current owner, Andre Balázs) she even suggests a name for this ghostly mischief maker – Leonardo da Vinci:

"His ghost would go west. Leonardo would want to go where the action was. Wouldn't he?"

Da Vinci had been a guest of King Francis I at Château Amboise, though he had actually stayed and worked in the nearby Close Luce, which was connected to the château by an underground tunnel. Like many other places in Los Angeles, the Marmont supposedly has an underground tunnel too; it was built in the 1940s to allow easy access to screwball screenwriter Preston

Sturges' nightclub "Players" on Sunset Boulevard below, though today it's said to be bricked-up.

Writer L.M. Kit Carson also confidently asserts that there are several ghosts spending their time at the Chateau Marmont. His first encounter came some 28 years ago when he was staying in Suite 23 and working on the American remake of the French movie *A Bout de Souffle* (his version, *Breathless*, starred Richard Gere). Carson reported that a ghost would make regular appearances at around 3.30am:

> *"It would wake me up and make me go work. It happened all the time."*

Like Dundy, he didn't feel in any way scared or threatened and referred to it as a "rosy presence" – so much so in fact that he specifically asked for Suite 23 every time:

> *"That's my lucky suite. I stayed in a couple of other suites, and it didn't happen."*

The closest that the Chateau Marmont has to a ghost story owes more than a little to Boris Karloff, the actor most famous for his terrifying performance as Frankenstein in the 1931 horror classic. In reality Karloff was a very shy man, but when he and his wife moved in to the Chateau Marmont in 1955 for a stay of what turned out be seven years, a few ghostly things began happening. Two guests reported a woman dressed in white hovering above their bed, and there were stories of faucets turning on after being turned off.

In March 1982, the calm of the Chateau Marmont was truly shattered when actor John Belushi (best known for his performances on "Saturday Night Live" and as Jake in *The Blues Brothers*) was found dead of a drug overdose in bungalow #3. More recently, in 2008 there was a report that actor Adrian Grenier (who played actor "Vincent Chase" in the HBO series "Entourage") had a spooky experience while he was staying here, though no specific information was ever released and his PR representative declined an interview.

Unless you're staying here the chances of seeing any supernatural guests are almost nonexistent, though on arrival you'll pass the place where German fashion photographer Helmut Newton died in January 2004 – his car crashed into a wall opposite the driveway after he had suffered a heart attack. An accident like this was recreated in the background of a scene in *Somewhere*, a 2010 movie about an actor staying at the Marmont. Writer/director Sophia Coppola had spent so much time here as a child (she's the daughter of Francis Ford Coppola and cousin of Nicolas Cage) that they allowed her full access to shoot it.

If you are lucky enough to be dining at the reservations-only restaurant you're on safe ground with the Damn Good Burger or the sheep's milk ricotta gnocchi, while the Sunday Night Special (buttermilk fried chicken with biscuits, mashed potato, gravy, kale and hot honey) is a treat. If not, you can still pay a visit and have "libations" at the Bar Marmont next door (warning: the menu has no prices, so expect to spend big cash on your cocktails).

Order a Marmont mai tai (Nicaraguan Flor de Caña rum, orange Curaçao, fresh lime juice and orgeat syrup topped with dark rum and a mint leaf) and see whether you can sneak a peek at a celebrity. No matter what time you're here the odds are very good (though they're almost zero that anything you see will be in the papers/television/on the internet the next day).

As Harry Cohn, legendary founder of Columbia Pictures famously said to young Hollywood hopefuls William Holden and Glenn Ford:

"If you must get into trouble, do it at the Chateau Marmont."

Bar Marmont: Daily 6pm-2am
www.chateaumarmont.com/barmarmont.php
www.facebook.com/barmarmont

Formosa Café
7156 Santa Monica Boulevard
West Hollywood, CA 90046
Tel: 323 850 9050

The Ghost at Booth #8...

As soon as you go through the padded red leather door, the Formosa Café hits you like a blur.

Red and black throughout, the dark atmosphere is very welcoming, romantic and perhaps just a little bit forbidden. No wonder it's been a Hollywood favorite for movie stars, musicians and mere mortals for over 70 years.

A glance up at the walls reveals some odd Toby jugs and liquor paraphernalia, but also over 250 head shots and pictures of almost every star you can imagine, including Bogart, Gable, Monroe, Dean, Sinatra, Newman and Brando.

Movie fans will immediately recognize the Formosa from *Swingers* (1996) and *The Majestic* (2001), but especially from *L.A. Confidential* (1997) and the scene when rookie detective Exley – played by Guy Pearce – embarrassingly mistakes the real Lana Turner for a hooker "cut" to look like the actress. In fact, Lana Turner and her gangster boyfriend Johnny Stompanato were regulars here, and her daughter famously stabbed him to death in self defense some years later.

As you can see, the back part of the Formosa is fashioned from an old train car. It's hard to imagine now, but from 1880 to 1950 trolley cars ran all over town, and this particular one was built in 1896 and was one of the original Pacific Railway Cars that ran down Santa Monica Boulevard. Mobster Mickey Cohen ran a bookie operation out of this train, and if you look carefully around the booths you can see his old floor safe.

The train car was set to be demolished when it was added to the Formosa in 1945, and many years later *L.A. Confidential* director Curtis Hanson helped save the Formosa itself from bulldozers when it was under threat from development. Apparently Hanson met actor Kevin Spacey here to persuade him to do the movie, and it all worked out well; Hanson was nominated for the Best Director Oscar and won as co-writer for the Adapted Screenplay, Kim Basinger won for Best Supporting Actress, and it was nominated in six other categories too.

Vince Jung is the current owner of the Formosa, and he said that over the years there have been many reports of an elderly-looking Asian man walking around – and he's in no doubt about who it is – Lem Quon:

> *"The Formosa was my grandfather's life – he was here pretty much every day until he died – and the staff experience strange things almost on a weekly basis. Pots and pans banging suddenly, doors closing, footsteps – even having their name called. It's like he's still the boss, walking around, checking on everyone and saying 'Get to work!'"*

Quon took over the Formosa in partnership with Jim Bernstein – Cohen's friend – and was a huge lover of all things Hollywood:

> *"He loved celebrities, loved hanging out with them, and he'd even bring them home to party – and they all came in here over the years. He was also a huge Elvis fan. Elvis's manager Colonel Tom Parker hung out here and the owner of the record studio where Elvis recorded – just up the street – hung out here too. He loved Evel Knievel as well. He came in all the time, and my grandfather collected Evel's paintings."*

The ghost of Quon tends to appear more in the kitchen and the main bar area, but his favorite booth was #8 – right in front of the bar – and sometimes he seems to be in his seat again:

"Some staff have said that if you stand too long in front of table number eight you get pinched! He hated people standing around – it's a family trait!"

On a more recent visit we asked about booth #8, and server Deanna confirmed that the Formosa was definitely haunted:

"One time I was here at night, standing at the till, when someone called my name. I clearly heard someone say 'Deanna' and I turned round – but there was no one there."

Strangely, neither Jung nor his father – who ran the Formosa with Quon before he took over – has actually seen the family ghost:

"We're kind of pragmatic about it. It's just never happened to us, but he's been seen by others many times since he passed away in 1993. The cleaning crew is often here at all hours, and one night they saw this figure. One of them described the figure and what he was wearing – a cardigan – and I described a very specific kind one that my grandfather used to wear, and that he wouldn't ever have seen. He looked at me and said: 'How did you know?'"

The Formosa stands out like a red beacon on Santa Monica Boulevard, and inside the first section has a lengthy green-lit bar with black stools and red booths. There are a couple of big booths for groups and the table-lined train car in back, but it's lucky that there's a candle on your table, as the Chinese tasseled lanterns aren't strong enough for reading the menu!

Formosa has perhaps my favorite Happy Hour, and the main attraction is the tempting selection of $4 appetizers from their Nuevo Asian cuisine menu. Though they're smaller dishes than the regular menu, it means you order several at once –

perfect for sharing a romantic dinner or catching up with friends. All of the dishes are great, though the huge plate of sesame fries, the chili ribs and the chicken shu mai (dumplings) are definite favorites.

On the regular menu, the Kobe burger is the most popular choice (choose the classic onion bun over the brioche) and it comes with jalapeno jack cheese topping and those sesame fries. The cocktails all hit the spot too (the mai tai especially doesn't skimp on the rum), but do make sure you keep your eye on the time – once Happy Hour is over, the prices go up quite steeply. It's an easy mistake to make!

Whether Grandfather Quon's ghost welcomes you or not, keep an eye out for celebrities – they still pop in occasionally for a slice of true Old School Hollywood.

Monday – Friday 4pm-2am, Saturday/Sunday 6pm-2am
Happy Hour: Weekdays 4-7pm (beers $3, well drinks and wine $5, spirits $6, $4 appetizers)
www.formosacafe.com

Jones
7205 Santa Monica Boulevard
West Hollywood, CA 90046
Tel: 323 850 1726

Table 34, a Secret Tunnel and the Ghost of Jock?

Gourmet Ghosts began when I heard a story here one night; that there was a ghost in the building and that it may have something to do with a tunnel connected to the old Warner Hollywood studios opposite – a secret tunnel that actors used to get to their favorite bar stool.

Bar Manager Eric Tecosky noted that "Jones often gets used in movie shoots, and older members of the crew always come up and ask: 'So, where's the tunnel?'" but said that the story pre-dated Jones's opening in 1994 and went back to the time when the site was another bar/restaurant called Ports.

To learn more about Ports I tracked down *Gourmet* magazine restaurant columnist and founder of *Saveur* magazine, Colman Andrews. He sent me his article titled "In Any Storm" and explained that although Ports was in a rather seedy area, it was the place to be seen in the 1970s and 1980s:

> *"One evening I walked into Ports and saw sitting, at three of the five tables in the restaurant's small front room,*

Claes Oldenburg, Michelangelo Antonioni, and Milton Glaser. Ports was that kind of place."

He wrote that Ports was a place of "diverse cuisine," books, card games, showboating and the odd fistfight – a haven for classic Hollywood stars including Warren Beatty, Julie Christie, Robert Redford, Francis Ford Coppola and even a young Oliver Stone, who was "always insulting the waiters." Andrews also remembered that before it became Ports, it was called the Sports Inn:

"It became "Ports" in 1972 when the new proprietor climbed up on a ladder and painted over the "S" and the 'Inn'."

New Yorkers Jock and Micaela Livingston were the painters, and after helping to open the nearby Studio Grill a couple of years before, they ran things here for nearly two decades. It was suggested that the ghost might even be Jock, a colorful but complicated character who was mentioned in Andrews' article:

"Jock was an imposing man, big, bearded, deep voiced, an Orson Welles-like presence. For years, he greeted guests wearing a long white lab coat, which made him seem at once avuncular and vaguely sinister. He was widely traveled and well read; he spoke fluent, often impolite Spanish and used to bid me good-night in Serbo-Croatian. At his best, he was great company, charming, erudite, obscure. But he had demons, which he tried constantly and unsuccessfully to drink away. He would end many evenings at Ports sitting almost comatose at a back booth, rising occasionally to lurch across the floor in search of another drink – sometimes, with no warning, erupting into an outraged bellow directed at nobody and everybody."

Jock died in 1980, and after his death an actor named Philip Compton helped Micaela run the restaurant for the next decade or so – her Greek Pie was a favorite with the locals – until hotelier/restaurateur Sean MacPherson bought the bar in the early 1990s.

Research across the road at the Warner Hollywood studios (now called The Lot) revealed that the story of the secret tunnel was well-known here too, and that there were other exotic tales at the studio; that Howard Hughes had an underground running track built so that he could run naked, or that there was an underground swimming pool. Marc Wanamaker, co-author of *Haunted Hollywood*, had visited The Lot, and replying to my email he noted that it has underground springs, which may explain why he had been unable to find any tunnels:

"There are utility tunnels all over the city leading under the streets and interconnecting with other buildings. There is nothing unusual about them. Usually the stories say that the tunnels were built to hide contraband during prohibition or to sneak prostitutes into a studio, but none of these stories are true other than there are tunnels here and there."

Andrews hadn't heard any spooky stories related to Ports either:

"I have to say that I spent most evenings at Ports for most of the seventies, and I never heard of either. The only ghosts I ever encountered there were old girlfriends."

MacPherson said that he loved the story of a ghost, but in the first days of refurbishing what was to become Jones he never saw any blueprints that indicated a tunnel, nor did he see a pentagram on the floor, as several people had suggested:

"On the other hand, just because I never saw them doesn't mean they don't exist."

However, when I later visited Jones several staff members immediately confirmed stories of strange things happening – often late at night. Table #34 (where I recently saw one of the "Desperate Housewives") was known as "the haunted table," and pizzas falling off their stand and glasses suddenly spilling were so common that they were listed as "Promo – Ghost" on server slips. There were also stories of table candles suddenly catching aflame.

Unsurprisingly, the story of Jones' ghost was often told to new staff (especially those working the night shift or closing up in the wee hours), but one night a very unusual incident was caught on one of the security cameras when server Storey Cunningham entered the back room and was almost hit by a box of ketchup bottles that fell from a high shelf:

"I wasn't touching the shelf or even near it. I felt the box brush the back of my head as it fell. If I'd been a second slower, it would have landed on top of me."

Other staff members "took turns" to watch the security tape, and it certainly seemed that the box was pushed off the shelf with some force; it didn't slide or slowly tip over. There was no sign of what made it fall though, and it wasn't on the edge of the shelf:

"It certainly freaked me out, and we were going to send it to (television show) "Ghosthunters" – it seemed that creepy."

Sadly the installation of a new security system meant that this footage was lost, and though the running track and the swimming pool were definitely just rumors, it does seem that the story of the "ghost" of Ports and now Jones has persisted over the years. Perhaps, as the city of West Hollywood's urban planner John Chase told me:

"It's a case of "wishtory" – a history that we wish were true."

Supernatural stories aside, Jones is a popular bar/restaurant that attracts a hip, hot, rock n' roll crowd like moths to a flame. The blasting jukebox, dark corners, risqué pictures and lines of Jack Daniels bottles above the bar tell you all you need to know; this is a place where the beautiful people – and some big stars – come to eat, drink and be merry. You can add "flirting" to the list too; the angled walls mirrors allow you to check out people at faraway tables.

You can order cocktails named in honor of Joplin, Hendrix, Joan Jett, Keith Moon and John Bonham, or you can take a liquid ride on the Magic Bus, The Stone Pony or even the One Night

Stand. Jones is certainly more than just a bar though, and they really have an extensive and impressive (if rather pricey) menu.

Their big, thin crust pizzas are enormously popular, and maybe the secret is in their wood burning oven, because I have to admit that I rarely stray from ordering the BBQ chicken. Their Quattro formaggi pizza, Meatball Hero sandwich and carbonara pasta have all been excellent when I've tried them too, and try and save some room for their Yummy Brownie desert, which comes with vanilla ice cream and chocolate sauce.

Visiting the bathrooms – male and female – is a trip, and sometimes you can spend too long looking at the walls. There are snaps of celebrity guests dotted around, and many revealing photos of some wild nights out – it's appropriate that Jones's motto is "Don't Play With Fire."

Monday – Friday 12pm-2am, Saturday 6pm-2am, Sunday 7pm-2am
Food served until 1.30am
www.joneshollywood.com
www.facebook.com/jones.hollywood.1

The Comedy Store (formerly Ciro's)
8433 Sunset Boulevard
West Hollywood, CA 90069
Tel: 323 650 6268

Comedy Suicide and a Beast in the Cellar

Over nearly 30 years, The Comedy Store has seen all manner of laugh merchants grace its stages. Some have gone on to great fame on television and the big screen, while others have gone back out onto Sunset Boulevard, never to be seen again.

Many years before it launched the careers of comedians, this was the location of Ciro's, a fashionable nightclub opened by Billy Wilkerson in early 1940. Just like in his other joint the Cafe Trocadero, the biggest names in show business came to Ciro's: Sinatra, Monroe, Dietrich, Bogart, Bacall, Judy Garland, Joan Crawford, Cary Grant, Mickey Rooney and Lucille Ball and Desi Arnaz.

On stage the lights burned just as brightly for the acts: a zany comedian and his crooner sidekick – Jerry Lewis and Dean Martin – started out here in 1950, as did Sammy Davis Jr. Other entertainers like Andy Williams, Xavier Cugat and Nat King Cole made Ciro's the hottest nightspot in town, and for a while at least it was on a par with Las Vegas, where Wilkerson had been involved in the first strip casino (until gambling debts and Bugsy Siegel left him with just a share in The Flamingo).

Ironically, it was the huge fees that the Vegas casinos offered to singers and entertainers that was the beginning of the end for Ciro's, and eventually Wilkerson sold out to businessman Herman Hoover. Hoover was undone by the IRS over unpaid taxes, and after years of the building standing largely idle, in the early 1970s comedians Sammy Shore, Rudy de Luca and Sammy's wife Mitzi leased part of it and started The Comedy Store. Mitzi later received the Comedy Store in her divorce settlement, bought the whole building and was the driving force behind it until recent ill health kept her from coming to the office.

Perhaps the most ghostly story associated with The Comedy Store is one that came to a sudden and tragic end on June 1, 1979 when a comedian committed suicide by jumping from the roof of the 14 story hotel next door.

The Tragic Death of a Comic
100 Grieve at Memorial Rite

Where Lubetkin's body was found: between the hotel and The Comedy Store

The *Los Angeles Times* of June 5 reported that a suicide note was found pinned to his body, and it read:

"I used to work at the Comedy Store."

Steve Lubetkin had performed at the opening night of The Comedy Store and regularly at their other location in San Diego, but he hadn't been able to "break through." That year he was heavily involved in short-lived labor union CFC (Comedians for Compensation) who protested against the policy of not paying comedians for their appearances on the famous stage. An agreement was negotiated that led to far fewer slots at the Comedy Store, and Lubetkin began to get fewer bookings. Convinced he had been targeted for his protesting and increasingly depressed at his prospects, one night he left a CFC meeting and went straight to the hotel.

The *Times* noted that comedian Mitchell Walters, possibly the last person to see Lubetkin alive, said that he had told him he was just "going for a walk" and would "be right back." Lubetkin had another plan though, and in trying to land on top of The Comedy Store, perhaps felt he was making the ultimate statement.

Blake Clark, a comedian who often appears in Adam Sandler movies, worked the door when he was first trying out his act here. One night he was checking the main room after closing time when he saw a chair slide some 20 feet across the main stage – but he didn't stay long enough to see anything else.

He also reported being watched; he once spotted a man in a brown bomber jacket, but when he turned to him the man slowly faded away. The man appeared again later that day, crouching in the corner of an office on the third floor – but again disappeared. When the female employee working there mentioned it too, they realized it was the same man.

Early one morning – around 3 am – Clark heard a low growl coming from the basement, which was reached by going through a locked metal gate. Suddenly it seemed like something huge was pushing the gate, almost ripping it off its hinges in an attempt to get out. Seconds later the door snapped back into place and Clark was staring at a dark, seven foot high being. He turned and ran, never looking back.

A team of parapsychologists from UCLA actually investigated the basement in 1982, and member Dr. Barry Taff suffered extreme pain in his knees; they concluded that there may be lingering spirits back from the days when Ciro's was a mobster hangout. In those days the basement may have been used as a secure, soundproof place where "problems" could be sorted out – broken legs and maybe worse – by mob muscle (maybe big, seven foot tall mob muscle?)

That could help explain the terrified man in the brown jacket, but either way, in 1994 a local television news crew was filming a piece called "Haunted Hollywood" when Dr. Taff saw three men in 1940s style suits watching them – but when he approached them the trio disappeared.

There have been other reports of two female ghosts. One is apparently named Ellen, and she is a woman in her 50s who used to perform backstreet abortions for the Mafia (in the basement?)

while the other is apparently a young woman who died during one of those "operations."

Eerie basement or not, nothing could be found in any of the Los Angeles newspaper archives to back up these stories. There were no reports of anything unusual either in Halloween 2010, when the Comedy Store apparently offered a rare "behind-the-scenes" tour of now-sealed passages that lead to tunnels under Sunset Boulevard (and were said to contain several dead bodies).

As for the menu, it's a very short one – you're not here for the food – though aside from pizza and chicken tenders and wings, you can have milk and cookies. Like most entertainment venues there's a two drink minimum (don't forget to tip your waitress!) though with $4 PBR you needn't break the bank for a night of laughter.

Daily, hours vary
21+ only
www.hollywood.thecomedystore.com
www.facebook.com/thecomedystore
http://twitter.com/thecomedystore

Couldn't Get A Table –
West Hollywood & Beverly Hills

Despite my best efforts to find an eyewitness or something in the archives, these places just didn't have enough to make it into the chapter – but still had a great ghost story.

Kate Mantilini
Beverly Hills
Tel: 310 278 3699

The Lady Ghost of "Hustler"

Named after a pioneering boxing promoter (and the mistress of the original owner's uncle Rob), Kate Mantilini's is a favorite for those involved in the movie business – über-talent agencies ICM and William Morris Endeavor are just a short walk (or limo drive) away.

Before "Kate's" there was Hamburger Hamlet, which came into being on the very first date between actor Harry Lewis and his future wife Marilyn. Harry said that his dream was to open a small bistro where movie industry people could meet, and she immediately got working on a menu and finding a location.

Harry invested his $3,500 in the lease, and despite the fact that Marilyn was a clothing designer and didn't even know how to cook (she took the orders and he handled the kitchen), they opened the doors of the first Hamburger Hamlet in 1950. The name was suggested by Harry, who had once been on the books at Warner Bros. (he played "Toots" alongside Humphrey Bogart, Lauren Bacall and Edward G Robinson in 1948's *Key Largo*) and it came from the idea that every actor dreams of playing Shakespeare's legendary character "Hamlet."

By 1987 there were 23 more restaurants in the HH chain, but after they sold out for $33 million they concentrated on Kate Mantilini's, the crowning glory of their original idea – though this time it was Marilyn that chose the name. Just a few years later, Robert DeNiro and Al Pacino spent three days here shooting their major scene in the movie *Heat* (1995), and over the years it has been name checked in novels by Robert Crais, Michael Connelly and John Irving.

As for any supernatural stories, the only one I found suggested that Althea Flynt, the fourth wife of Larry, first centerfold and co-publisher of *Hustler* magazine, still haunts Kate Mantalini's and the building – even though she overdosed and drowned in her bathtub at home.

Before *Hustler* was based at the former Great Western Bank nearby (the one with a bronze statue of John Wayne on horseback outside), the magazine was indeed based here, Mantilini's co-owner Adam Lewis confirmed when we spoke on the phone. Laughing happily, he admitted:

"I've been here 21 years, and I've never heard that story about Althea Flynt – though I wish it were true. It's great!"

He was unaware of any other strange stories or mysteries, but if you do come and visit check out the boxing mural on the wall and make sure you order a side of "Those Potatoes" – two layers of hash browns with sour cream and spring onions in between – as they're a legendary dish in this town.

Monday 8am-10pm, Tuesday – Thursday 8am-midnight
Friday 8am-1am, Saturday 11am-1am
www.katemantilinirestaurant.com
www.facebook.com/KateMantiliniBeverlyHills
http://twitter.com/KateMantilini

Beverly Wilshire Hotel
Beverly Hills
Tel: 310 275 5200

The Woman in White

Located right on the world famous (and rather Stepford wife-ish) shopping paradise of Rodeo Drive, the Beverly Wilshire Apartment Hotel first opened for business in 1928, even though the city of Beverly Hills barely had 20,000 residents and definitely no designer stores. Owner and real estate developer Walter G. McCarty was sure that he was on to a good thing though, importing Tuscan stone and Carrara marble to bring his plans of Italian Renaissance and French neo-classic style to life in the original Wilshire Wing (10 floors).

Later owners dropped the "Apartment" from the name and over the years a ballroom, Olympic-sized swimming pool and championship standard tennis courts were added. The Beverly Wing (14 floors and a bigger ballroom) was added in 1971 and immortalized forever in *Pretty Woman* starring Richard Gere and Julia Roberts (1990), while HBO series "Entourage" filmed here several times every season.

As for unusual stories, there have been reports of a ghostly woman in white on the eighth floor of the Wilshire tower. She has long, blond hair and has been seen on numerous occasions, peeking around corners or looking through doorways, and some employees believe that she's the spirit of a woman who lived most of her life in a suite on this floor but died a few years ago.

A search of the newspaper archives revealed a possible connection with one of the hotel's most famous residents: Barbara Hutton, a woman with long, blond hair who was nicknamed the "poor little rich girl."

Barbara Hutton, Reclusive Woolworth Heiress, Dies

On May 12, 1979 the *Los Angeles Times* reported that she had suffered an apparent heart attack in her penthouse "atop the Beverly Wilshire Hotel" where she'd been living for the last few years, and died soon after in the hospital.

Married seven times – including to suave actor Cary Grant, whom she apparently said "I loved most" – her mother committed suicide when she was aged just four, and she was shuttled among relatives until she inherited around $28m of the Woolworth stores fortune a few years later. It was worth around $40m when she turned 21 and became one of the richest women in the world, and though she was poorly advised by lawyers and exploited by husbands she still spent lavishly – until her only child, Lance, was killed in a plane crash in 1972.

In the following years she sold almost all she had, and, dogged by addictions and poor health, lived out a reclusive life at the hotel. On her death her fortune was rumored to be barely $5000, and the inevitable television movie: "Poor Little Rich Girl: The Barbara Hutton Story" starred Farrah Fawcett.

However, there are some discrepancies in linking the woman in white to Hutton. The newspaper said Hutton lived "atop the Beverly Wilshire Hotel" (presumably the Royal Suite), though the hotel's director of public relations noted in an email that this suite had in fact been occupied by philanthropist Caroline Leonetti Ahmanson from 1975 until her death in 2005. This was "a few years ago," though Ahmanson had dark black hair, not blond. It seems that perhaps these two lives have combined into one story – though the Woman in White could still be in residence.

There are several places to dine here, and the most notable restaurant is Cut. Only open for dinner, it serves a steak and seafood menu courtesy of celebrity chef Wolfgang Puck and is glamorous and very expensive. There are two rooftop terraces here as well, and though you'll have to be a guest in the Royal Suite to see the 360 degree view over the Hollywood Hills and beyond, the Rodeo Terrace offers a front row view of Rodeo Drive – perfect for you to check out which stores you'll be visiting (or at least window shopping in).

Hours vary for restaurants and bars
www.fourseasons.com/beverlywilshire
www.facebook.com/BeverlyWilshire
http://twitter.com/BeverlyWilshire

Beverly Hills Hotel
Beverly Hills
Tel: 310 276 2251

Ghost Musician and Ghost Comedian

Fabulously painted pink, the Beverly Hills Hotel has been welcoming royalty, legends and world leaders since it first opened its doors in 1912. Best known for its celebrity hangout The Polo Lounge (Raquel Welch was "discovered" by the pool here), few people know that the city of Beverly Hills was virtually built around this castle-like hotel.

After Burton Green struck water instead of oil in the area, he persuaded Margaret Anderson and her son Stanley, owners of the Hollywood Hotel, to open the grandest of hotels here – and to be the lynchpin of a new city in Southern California. Within two years the City of Beverly Hills became official, and when Mary Pickford and Douglas Fairbanks built their house in the hills here in 1920, its status as neighborhood of the stars was assured. Charlie Chaplin, Gloria Swanson and Rudolph Valentino soon moved here too, and the Beverly Hills Hotel was at the center of it all.

The Depression forced the hotel to close for a while, but Bank of America vice president Hernando Courtright organized a buyout and became manager, changing the name of the El Jardin Restaurant to The Polo Lounge in honor of actors such as Will Rogers and Spencer Tracy, who played polo nearby and celebrated here afterward. Humphrey Bogart was a regular too, and Marlene Dietrich (bungalow #11) changed the "No slacks for ladies" rule. Years later, the Rat Pack – Frank Sinatra, Dean Martin and Sammy Davis Jr. – relaxed here as well.

In 1942 Howard Hughes took up residence in four bungalows (two were decoys) and lived like a hermit for decades, while in the 1970s John Lennon and Yoko Ono hid out here for a week. Elizabeth Taylor shared bungalows with six of her eight husbands here as well, while Marilyn Monroe preferred bungalow #1.

The distinctive exterior was the result of a 1948 facelift (this is Beverly Hills!) and then Detroit real estate millionaire Ben Silberstein fell so in love with the place during his stay that he bought it for $5.5 million in 1954. It went through several owners after his death, and then a few years after celebrating its 75th Anniversary in 1992 the hotel closed for a huge $100 million restoration, opening again in June 1995.

Today it's still the place for stars to see and be seen. Actor and producer Mark Wahlberg regularly has meetings in his favorite restaurant booth here, though years ago Clark Gable and Carole Lombard met secretly in one of the bungalows before his divorce came through and they could be married.

The hotel is reportedly haunted by two musical ghosts – Russian composer Sergei Rachmaninoff and harpist and comedian Harpo Marx – but the hotel's director of public relations was less than keen to talk about any strange stories (they're very careful to protect their famous guests, dead or alive):

> *"While there may have been an occasional reference to a paranormal experience at the Beverly Hills Hotel in the past, we have never actually participated in stories relating to this and we do not have any anecdotal references that we can provide."*

Archive research may provide some answers why; actor Peter Finch (best known for his "I'm as mad as hell, and I'm not going to talk it anymore!") role in *Network* (1976) had a heart attack in the lobby here, and died soon after. Until Heath Ledger in 2009, he was the only posthumous winner of an acting Oscar.

Rachmaninoff toured the US extensively from 1918 and made his home in Beverly Hills at 610 Elm Drive, where he died on March 28, 1943. Elm Drive is just a few blocks from the Beverly Hills Hotel, and it's very likely he visited or maybe even stayed here.

As for the curly-wigged Arthur Adolph "Harpo" Marx, the "Gadabout's Notebook" of the *Los Angeles Times* on December 2, 1936 notes he was staying at the similarly-named Beverly Wilshire Hotel while waiting to move into his new house with bride Susan Fleming. Marx may have visited and stayed here too, so perhaps both stories have become entwined and the hotel's name was changed by accident – or design.

Ghost or not, there's no question that a reservation at The Polo Lounge – or even spending time at the coffee room, poolside café or the Nineteen 12 bar – definitely puts you in the center of Beverly Hills history, and it can certainly call itself the inspiration for The Eagles' song "Hotel California" – they were the hotel on the cover of the album.

Hours vary for restaurants and bars
www.beverlyhillshotel.com
www.facebook.com/Beverlyhillshotel
http://twitter.com/bevhillshotel

Chapter 3

Downtown

Biltmore Hotel

Bonaventure Hotel

Checkers Hotel

Cole's & Varnish at the P.E. Building

Figueroa Hotel

Grand Central Market & Angels Flight

La Golondrina

Oviatt Building & The Cicada Restaurant

Philippe The Original

Redwood Bar & Grill

Spring Arts Tower

The Alexandria Hotel

Traxx at Union Station

Biltmore Hotel
506 South Grand Avenue
Los Angeles, CA 90071
Tel: 213 612 1562 (Smeraldi's/Afternoon Tea/La Bistecca)
213 624 1100 (Sai Sai Noodle Bar), 213 624 1011 (Gallery Bar)

The Black Dahlia and Unexpected Guests

A downtown landmark for nearly 90 years, the Biltmore Hotel takes up half a city block and is 11 stories high. It was designed by Schultze and Weaver in the Spanish-Italian Renaissance style with a Beaux Arts influence, and if you look carefully you'll see the "Biltmore Angel" design is everywhere. Movie fans will recognize it immediately too. The entrance and lobby were in 1984's *Ghostbusters* (it was the fictional Sedgewick Hotel), and *Vertigo* (1958), *The Sting* (1973), *Chinatown* (1974), *Splash* (1984), *In The Line Of Fire* (1993), *Independence Day* (1996), *Spider-Man* (2002) and *National Treasure* (2004) have filmed here too.

Though the Roosevelt Hotel in Hollywood hosted the first ceremony, the Biltmore was actually the birthplace of the Oscars. The Academy of Motion Picture Arts & Sciences was founded over lunch in the Crystal Ballroom in May 1927, and it's said that MGM art director Cedric Gibbons sketched the design for the Oscar statue on a napkin.

Eight Oscar ceremonies were held in the Biltmore Bowl room in the 1930s and early 1940s, and in 1977 Bob Hope hosted the Academy's 50th Anniversary here. You can see some huge black-and-white pictures from those days in the Historic Corridor, which is just by Treasurer, a store that proclaims it sells Cigars & Novelties ("novelties" such as expensive watches, jewelry and lighters – it's that kind of hotel).

Known back then as the Los Angeles Biltmore Hotel, it opened its doors for the first time in 1923 and visitors still marvel at its opulent murals, frescoes and fountains – it's as if a luxury liner from the golden era of ocean travel had come ashore. In 1929 a luxury liner really did pay a visit: an LZ 127 Graf Zeppelin hovered over the Biltmore before landing at Mines Field (now Los Angeles International Airport). The crew and passengers stayed here, and the hotel re-stocked the zeppelin's kitchens before it left to continue its round-the-world journey.

As well as the glitz and glamour, the Biltmore has many spooky stories to tell. Perhaps most famously, it was here that Elizabeth Short was last seen alive on January 9, 1947.

May.Have Been Followed

Donahoe considered the theory that the "Black Dahlia" fell into the hands of her murderer immediately after she was dropped at the Biltmore Hotel by the man who drove her here from San Diego.

The *Los Angeles Times* on January 24 also reported that Captain Jack Donohoe, head of the investigation, had another suspect – "a mysterious 'Thin Man'".

Seen Loitering in Shadows Near Where Murdered Girl Was Found

However, the gruesome killing was never solved, and it quickly became Hollywood's most notorious murder, inspiring movies, books and songs ever since.

It's also true that on March 7, 1952 the well-known yogi and author Paramahansa Yogananda – the man who introduced yoga to America – died of a heart attack in the Music Room, just after finishing a speech in honor of the Indian ambassador. Today this location within the hotel is revered by many as the place of the yogi's *mahasamadhi*, or conscious leaving of the body. "Strange things really do happen here," someone on the front desk mentioned cryptically, and this was confirmed by James Russell, the front desk manager who had worked here since 1993 and was the resident expert on unusual happenings:

> *"The elevator stopping on the 8th floor for no apparent reason – that happens all the time. I myself have never seen an entity, but I have definitely felt one – many times. There's a lounge on the 10th floor – it was first opened in the 1960s – and it was reopened after a refurbishment in 2002. I spent a lot of time alone up there at the time, working on the computer, and many times I felt that someone was walking around behind me. I was sure that someone else was there. I just feel a chill, you know?"*

Right at that moment, our phone call was interrupted by a loud crash:

> *"They're filming (television show) "Numbers" here today. We've had around 300 movies and television shows shoot in here – The Italian Job, Wedding Crashers, all the Beverly Hills Cop movies. Many people come in here and recognize the lobby ceiling from the ballroom scene in 1970s movie The Poseidon Adventure."*

Russell further explained that many guests come to the Biltmore and ask for a haunted bedroom – and several of them have actually gotten their wish to see something strange:

> *"In many rooms on different floors guests have woken up at night and seen entities, but they never seem scared by it, or even ask to be moved. About nine years ago, three ladies here for one of the regular fashion shows were sharing a room. They were woken up and saw the ghostly figure of a man in the room with them."*

Beware though, as two guests who were openly skeptical then had a scary experience:

> *"A couple of women had come in, asking if the hotel was haunted. They went downstairs to the Biltmore Bowl room, and on the way back up the staircase they were saying how any talk about ghosts was just a story when the chandelier above them started shaking. They carried on walking up the stairs, and when they got under the next chandelier it started shaking too! They were convinced the place was haunted by then – and no, we didn't have an earthquake that day!"*

Russell also said that many people have reported being touched on the back, perhaps as if by a guiding hand, and more recently a handful of staff working on one of the floors that's mainly used for storage had a much closer encounter:

> *"They saw a woman, transparent, hovering about a foot off the ground. When she started moving towards them, they got out of there real fast!"*

On a return visit I found out that Russell had left the Biltmore, but another employee named Louie soon mentioned that he had a number of his own stories:

> *"I was on stairwell four, on the graveyard shift, when I heard loud whispering. Just before I got to the landing I actually shouted out "I can hear you whispering!" but*

when I came round the corner I saw that a door – a door with no handle on the outside – was open slightly. Then it suddenly closed!"

Since he was new to the job Louie reported this to his Supervisor, who explained that there was only a power panel inside, and why hadn't he gone in to check?

"I said that if there were people in there, then they were probably doing something I didn't wanna see. If not, then I was quitting the job!"

He also mentioned that a man in a stove pipe hat – "like Abraham Lincoln wore" – has been seen in the corners of the Tiffany Room, and that a boy and girl have often been observed running across the balcony in the Crystal Ballroom:

"There was a conference being held in there one time, and a woman came up and asked me why children were allowed up there."

Louie showed me a room just off the Rendezvous Court and said that it used to be a four star restaurant named "Bernard's" (the name is still by the door). After the rundown Biltmore had been sold for $5m in 1976, it was one of the first features of a major restoration – though today it's a meeting room. Two mirrors are opposite the door inside, and behind them are the bathrooms:

"One night I came in to check the place. I went into the men's bathroom, bleeped the receiver (which notifies electronically that he was there) and came out and locked the bathroom door behind me. The second I took my key out of the lock, there was a huge bang – one of the stall doors slamming shut. I knew there was no one in there, and there's no windows or ventilation system that could have caused it."

Very soon after this he met one of the maids, Lourdes, and mentioned the bathroom to her:

"She said a Mexican word for 'black ghost' or 'black spirit,' something like that, and then I told her about the banging door. She turned to her colleague and said: 'I told you!'"

Louie also mentioned that on the B4 level passageway he saw what seemed like a "black triangle shape" in the distance – "as if someone was carrying a tarp over their shoulder" – but then he got a call on his radio and had to leave, so we couldn't discuss it any further.

Visiting the Biltmore is like losing yourself in luxury, what with its marble floors, chandeliers and wood paneled elevators, and though just walking around is a treat, it's also home to several restaurants and the very decadent-looking Gallery Bar.

My favorite thing to do here though is something very old fashioned: taking afternoon tea in the Rendezvous Court. The original lobby of the Biltmore, it's decorated with Moorish carved wood ceilings, Italian chandeliers, travertine stone walls and a rose marble fountain, but do look out for the mermaids on the carpet and brickwork as well. Walk down the huge bronze Baroque staircase overlooking the lounge and you'll find figures of the Roman goddess Ceres and Spanish conquistador Balboa at the bottom. If you're lucky there will be a pianist playing so it really feels like you're making an entrance!

Wednesday through Sunday from 2-5pm you can choose a Victorian Tea ($29), which includes an assortment of tea sandwiches, freshly-baked scones with homemade Devonshire cream and jam and a selection of miniature pastries, or the more expensive option that includes a glass of Sherry, Kir or sparkling wine ($33 or $46 with champagne).

I prefer the simple Princess Tea experience ($24), which includes a pot of tea, freshly-baked scones with Devonshire cream and jam and an assortment of miniature pastries, but whatever you choose be sure to make a reservation, as it's one of the most popular afternoon events around.

If you're not a fan of cream teas or want something quick, then the nearby Café Rendezvous offers coffee, pastries, bagels, panini, cheese plates, yogurt, biscotti and sweets, plus cocktails, bottled water and juices.

In the evening you can dine at Italian steakhouse La Bistecca, which is in the Rendezvous Court area itself, while elsewhere there's a weekday seafood lunch buffet and homemade Italian and Continental food at Smeraldi's, which is named in honor of Giovanni Smeraldi, the artist who carved and painted the hotel's original ceilings.

Finally there's Sai Sai Noodle Bar, a fast-paced place that offers a variety of Vietnamese Pho and Japanese Udon/Ramen noodles in a healthy soup base; try the Bubbies Mochi (ice cream flown in from Hawaii) for dessert. They have a Happy Hour too, and if you feel inspired there's an "Artistic Corner" where you can add to a customer canvas – though be aware that it will be on display afterwards!

These restaurants all service the Gallery Bar, which has a reputation that goes beyond downtown. Dark and elegant, it serves a long list of signature martinis, bourbon, fine wines and exclusive liqueurs, all under the eyes of the carved angels that float above the shiny, granite bar. They'll mix you six unique versions of a Manhattan, and then you can get lost with your drink in one of the leather banquettes or go into the Cognac Room, a lounge with big couches and cabinets full of Biltmore memorabilia. There's also live jazz here on Friday and Saturday nights from 8.30pm.

In fact, since you are facing the Gallery Bar when you go back up the Rendezvous Court staircase, you could spend your whole day here and finish the evening with one of their most popular cocktails (vodka, Chambord black raspberry liqueur, Kahlua). It's called (what else?) a "Black Dahlia".

But before you visit, take some advice that Russell gave me:

"Some say that when you first go to a new hotel, somewhere you haven't stayed before, you should knock on the front door – just to let the people inside know that you're coming in."

Hours vary for restaurants and bars
www.thebiltmore.com
www.facebook.com/MillenniumBiltmoreHotelLosAngeles

Bonaventure Hotel
404 South Figueroa Street
Los Angeles, CA 90071
Tel: 213 624 1000

Horror on the 24th Floor

With its five distinctive circular glass towers, the Bonaventure Hotel looks like a spaceship that's just touched down among the skyscrapers, and at 367 feet (112 meters) high it's the largest hotel in Los Angeles. It has nearly 1350 rooms and 35 floors, though the six story central atrium itself is also home to dozens of businesses, restaurants, retailers, "pod" booths and a running track.

External – and ear popping! – elevators offer amazing views across the city, and every one of the odd-shaped rooms has a floor-to-ceiling window, so breathtaking views are guaranteed whether you visit, come for a meal or drink, or stay overnight.

Architect John Portman's design also includes large water displays and fountains inside the huge lobby area, and though the Bonaventure is a youngster downtown – it was completed in 1976 after a couple of year's construction that included sinking its foundations into an abandoned Pacific Electric subway tunnel – its silver exterior quickly made an impression.

It's been seen on the big screen in *Rain Man* (1988), *Lethal Weapon 2* (1989), *In The Line Of Fire* (1993), *True Lies* (1994), *Strange Days*, *Forget Paris* and *Nick of Time* (all 1995) – keep an eye out for plaques celebrating some of them – and has also been depicted in video games "Grand Theft Auto: San Andreas" and "Midnight Club: Los Angeles".

Also, since it looks like a mix of *Blade Runner* and *2001: A Space Odyssey*, the Bonaventure was an ideal filming location for the television show "Buck Rogers in the 25th Century."

1980s sitcom "It's a Living" (later known as "Making a Living") went one better – it was actually set in the restaurant on the top floor.

As for the Bonaventure's most famous feature, that's something quite unique. Take the red tower elevator (they're all color coded) up to level 35 and walk down into the BonaVista Lounge. Not only does it have one of the best views in town, but because it's a revolving restaurant it lets you see the whole 360 degrees of Los Angeles in one journey.

However, guests enjoying the night lights on October 7, 1979 had no idea that below them in room 2419 (now 2418-20), a gruesome and bloody murder was taking place. In a dispute over a cocaine deal, Eli and Esther Ruven were shot and killed and their bodies chopped up with a cleaver in the bathroom, alleged witness Eliahu Komerchero, who had bought the couple there believing they were just going to "scare" them.

Witness Gives Grisly Details of Couple's Slaying, Dismemberment

The bodies were later found in trash bins in Van Nuys and Sherman Oaks, and the *Los Angeles Times* and *Los Angeles Herald-Examiner* of January 5, 1982 reported that Yehudi Avatal had been convicted of first and second degree murder, and had received life without parole.

Man Convicted in 2 Dismemberment Murders Sentenced

Joseph Zakaria was sentenced to 21 years to life for the slaying of Esther and mutilation of Eli Ruven, while Komerchero was allowed to plead guilty to manslaughter and received four years in prison for helping to clean the room and transport the bodies away from the hotel in a suitcase.

Even though the murders occurred over 30 years ago, a scary reminder of the Ruven's horrific ordeal may still be lurking underground here. In early 2010 a concierge named Jorge told me that all the parking attendants are "terrified" of the far corner of the basement because of the "strange noises" that have been heard there – they "hate" having to park cars in that area and then walk back alone.

Once you're safely in the BonaVista Lounge and have got used to the unusual sight of a column or pot plant slowly moving towards you, you can sit back and enjoy the view. The best time to visit is at dusk, when the 60 minute revolution will change from the setting sun to streetlights and stars – and maybe even the odd helicopter, blimp or studio searchlight.

As for your choice of drink, the most amusing choice is one of their hard-to-get novelty cocktails in take-home themed glasses (and I don't mean plastic ones). The best seller is "The

Cloudbuster" (cranberry juice, vodka, Coco Lopez and Chambord black raspberry liquor) which comes in a glass shaped like the Bonaventure Hotel itself, plus there are also crystal skull shot glasses served with vodka.

Above the BonaVista on the top floor is L.A. Prime, a New York-style steakhouse that opened in 2000 and replaced the Top of Five restaurant. It has amazing à la carte steak, though it's very expensive and is somewhere most people would only go for a birthday or a big occasion.

In late 2010 a major $30m renovation began, and saw Art Deco-style dark brown wood and leather furniture, cigar-shaped lights and tube light "water towers" appearing around the Lobby Court bar, which circles around the center "white" tower. A water feature winds around all the other towers and stairs, making it an ideal place to enjoy the ambiance and hear the relaxing sound of the splashy fountains (though watch out for the bronze fishes and their arching jets near the Concierge Desk).

Since the BonaVista lounge doesn't open until 5pm, you're likely to visit the renovated Lake View Bistro for lunch. You can make your own omelet, but there's also sandwiches, pasta and chicken.

Later in the day, the Lobby Court bar gets very busy. It has the same menu as the Bistro and plenty of televisions showing every sport you can imagine (the Bonaventure is a popular hotel for visiting athletes and sports teams). There are a number of other separate restaurants within the Bonaventure building complex – everything from a Subway to Chinese to Korean BBQ – and on the 4th floor is the Bonaventure Brewing Co., a restaurant that was here long before the current Californian trend for microbrews.

It opened in 1998, and you can peek at their silver brewing vats before taking one of their four homebrews (I prefer the Bonaventure Red Ale) or a taster set of five small samplers out onto their circular Patio. Their weekday Happy Hour bar snacks are a real steal (I had some very hot wings for $3, while beers, wine and well drinks are $4) and if you want to know more about what goes into your glass, you can book a tour of the brewery.

Then there's a glitzy and very, very red bar/lounge called Suede on street level. It has a small menu of Mexican-influenced bar snacks and opens – and is always busy – from weekday Happy Hour onward (beers, wine, well drinks and small plates $4).

The renovation bought changes in the BonaVista too. The great Happy Hour ended, their menu was upgraded to tasty, high-end bar snack fare, and the drink prices went up ($8 for a bottle of domestic beer, $11 or more for a glass of wine). Still, even though you're definitely paying for the view, the BonaVista Lounge can't be missed; there's nothing like sipping your drink while the sun goes down and the city lights up – it really is one of the hidden treasures of Los Angeles.

Finally, a word of warning about downtown: parking can be extremely expensive (even if you're parking in the hotel where you're staying), so check out the buses and Metro subway system at www.metro.net and enjoy a drink while saving yourself time and money.

Hours vary for restaurants and bars
www.thebonaventure.com
www.facebook.com/TheBonaventure
http://twitter.com/thebonaventure

Checkers Hotel
535 South Grand Avenue
Los Angeles, CA 90071
Tel: 213 624 0000

"Miss X" and the Unknown Disappeared

One of the older hotels in downtown Los Angeles, the trident-shaped Checkers Hotel is away from the hustle and bustle thanks to its unique location – adjacent to the long, winding walkways that lead out of the Central Library – and while it's just yards from the more famous Biltmore Hotel, "Checkers" has a history that more than lives up to its name.

Built in 1927 at a cost of $1.2 million, it was one of the first newly-allowed 12 story buildings in the city and originally opened as the Mayflower Hotel. Designed by C.F. Whittlesey, an architect known for his work in San Francisco and San Diego, it was initially planned to be the location of stores, a barber shop, a beauty parlor, cafés and bars, but after barely five years the hotel went into bankruptcy. In early 1948 the Mayflower changed hands for $1m, and in 1952 they became part of the large Hilton Hotel group (which later became the biggest in the world).

This may have been part of the attraction for actress Mary Pickford, the girl who was known as "America's Sweetheart" and was arguably the most powerful women ever seen in Hollywood thanks to her co-founding of United Artists with Charlie Chaplin, D.W. Griffith and her husband-to-be Douglas Fairbanks. Her halcyon days were behind her by this time (the *Los Angeles Times* described her as an "erstwhile leading lady") and around 1956 she took an interest in the Mayflower – but then suddenly backed out of the deal.

She was sued by her business partners, and when the case finally came to court in 1961 she testified that she had been told the hotel seemed a bad investment. Also, the hotel had a bar and Pickford – who battled with alcohol and whose family had been badly affected by it – said that she "opposed morally to the commercial aspects of the liquor trade" and could not become a licensee.

In 1989 the hotel underwent a major redecoration, and a faded mural in reception was lost to history. Painted decades before by Danish muralist Einar Petersen, a Hollywood-based artist who had created similar works on other downtown hotels and across the country, it featured pilgrims and the famous Mayflower ship that landed at Plymouth, Massachusetts in 1620. But now of course, the hotel was reopening with a new look and a new name: Checkers.

At the same time, the huge building behind Checkers – which until a few years before had been home to the Church of the Open Door – was demolished after being damaged in an earthquake. A couple of years later a 28 story skyscraper called 550 Hope Street (and also known as the California Bank & Trust Building) took its place, and now there's a large courtyard with some modern sculptures between it and the back of Checkers.

The hotel underwent another renovation in 2008 and changed hands for $46m in June 2010, but back in August 1953 it was in that courtyard area – among lumber and debris in one of the small, inaccessible walkways then behind the hotel – that a crumpled woman's body was found.

WOMAN'S BODY FOUND IN AIRSHAFT AT HOTEL

The body of an attractive and well-dressed woman, about 35, was found yesterday morning by police in an airshaft between a hotel at 535 S Grand Ave. and a church building at 558 S Hope St.

ture could provide any clue to the location of the spot from which she tumbled.

Officers said she wore a blue and white two-piece suit, black oxford shoes and had no jewelry, hat or purse.

As reported in all the Los Angeles newspapers, detectives had no clues about the unidentified woman – nicknamed "Miss X" by the *Los Angeles Herald-Express* – or how she came to be there, though a broken ladder under her body seemed to indicate she had climbed or jumped from a great height.

Death Plunge
Identity of 'Miss X' Still Unsolved

However, the next day she was identified as Teresa Drauden, a guest who had registered at the hotel a few days before, though exactly where she jumped – or fell from – remained unclear.

One of the newspapers reported that the body was found in an air shaft, and looking at the back of the hotel today (see picture) you can see a few feet of an old, brown, stained air duct leading into a newer concrete shaft running to the ground. This shaft/duct is in the corner of the rooftop pool area – certainly a fatal drop, accidental or not.

Middle left of photo:
Was Mrs. X's body found at the bottom of this airshaft?

Back in the hotel, employees said that there have been other unexplained events here, and Ruben – who has been a valet for over seven years – told me about something he found to be "very weird." He was taking two guests – a couple – up to "maybe the 8th floor; it was certainly one of the higher floors," but when he showed them in to their room:

"There was a person asleep in the bed. We closed the door and waited a few moments, but no one came out. Of course they were upset, so I took them straight back down to reception then the Supervisor and I ran straight back up, but when we got there the room was perfectly normal, the bed made up as if it had never been slept in."

There was no missing room key and the previous occupant had checked out, so just whom the person was – and whether it was a man or woman – was never explained; they just disappeared from the hotel.

On my next visit, Ruben confirmed what front of house employee Rashad had told me: a few years ago one of the front doors opened on their own, as if someone had left the hotel – but there was no one there. They checked the CCTV several times and it clearly showed the (non-automatic) door had fully opened on its own, but they could never explain how and why.

Though it looks deceptively small from the street, Checkers is nonetheless rather elegant inside, what with the marble foyer, golden décor and mirrored elevators. Directly on your right is the Checkers Lounge, a lounge/bar with large leather chairs and a chess board ready-to-play, while further into the hotel is Checkers Restaurant, a modern eatery with minimalist artwork, and there's an outdoor patio area featuring a fountain and deck wicker furniture.

Together these areas are known as Checkers Downtown, and the restaurant menu mixes American cuisine with French and California influences and is as high-end as you'd expect from the only Hilton in downtown. Standouts include the Wet Breakfast Burrito (chorizo, potatoes, onions and cheese) and the Checker's Cheeseburger with wild arugula, cave-aged cheddar, red onion and bacon aioli.

If you're there for dinner – be aware, it's expensive – two of the best choices are the Downtown braised short rib "Potpie" with wild mushrooms, celery root purée and baby root vegetables or the grilled Black Angus 10 oz filet mignon with roasted root vegetables, crisp ricotta gnudi and pinot noir sauce.

Like most places downtown the parking fee here is pretty steep, but the stunning rooftop view (especially at night, when the skyscrapers and downtown are lit up) is worth a visit by itself.

Hours vary, Lounge/Bar menu 3pm-1am
www.hiltoncheckers.com
www.facebook.com/HiltonCheckers
http://twitter.com/hiltoncheckers

Cole's and The Varnish
Pacific Electric Building
118 East 6th Street
Los Angeles, CA 90014
Tel: 213 622 4090 / Varnish 213 622 9999

"A mass of broken bones and bruised flesh."

As you can tell from their fantastic neon sign, the logo and even the website, Cole's Pacific Electric Buffet (to use its full name) is certain that it's not only the originator of the French-dipped sandwich, but that it's the oldest restaurant/bar in Los Angeles as well. Philippe's also claims to be the home of this culinary landmark, but it's hard to know for sure because the legend goes that both venues created it at around the same time.

In Cole's case, they say that the chef came up with the idea when a customer who had recently had some dental work found their French bread too hard to chew. Henry Cole dipped the bread in *jus* to soften it up, other customers liked the look of it, and a legendary meal was born. There are other stories too, and regardless of who was really first, the debate is likely to go on forever – especially since it's just as difficult to say which restaurant is more famous in downtown.

Located on the ground floor of the Pacific Electric Building – formerly the main terminal for the mass transit Pacific Electric Railway – Cole's opened its doors in 1908. The building itself was constructed for Pacific Electric Railway magnate Henry E. Huntington in 1905, and was originally known as the Huntington Building. Designed by Claud Beelman it stood over downtown at nine stories high, and at the time it was not only the biggest building in Los Angeles, but one of the largest in this part of the country.

At its peak around 100,000 Angelenos a day passed through this downtown transit hub, and most of them probably stopped in for a French Dip sandwich and a drink before catching a train, bus or one of the distinctive red trolleys home.

After the terminal closed in the 1960s the building spent a number of years lying dormant, but then the Pacific Electric

Building (as it's now more commonly known) underwent a $20m conversion to apartments, and in 2005 – almost exactly 100 years from the day it first opened – it was open to tenants looking for a downtown address. Pictures and souvenirs of the Pacific Railway days can be found in the apartment lobby, and though you can't go inside unless you're visiting a resident, a 2008 online story by then-resident Javier Ortega noted that there were some strange stories here:

> *"Since living here, I've heard stories about the 5th floor on this building. Stories that include loud bangs, whispers and the occasional apparitions of ghosts in era clothing. Now, at first I dismissed this as just talk, or regular man-produced noises, but as I talked with the maintenance crew in the building they would tell me that most of it was true. They also told me that a very uneasy feeling was felt by the whole crew on that floor. Uneasy enough for one of the crew members to refuse to work on that floor... she proceeded to tell me that most of the times it's a very uncomfortable feeling, as if you are being followed or watched."*

He adds that the Office Manager confirmed they had heard "rumors" but could not confirm anything – though a female 5th floor tenant did ask to be moved as her apartment was "haunted."

Also, Leonard Greco, a contributor to a downtown blog/online group, responded to an email I sent: he had also "heard (that) one of the floors of the PE Building on Main is haunted," and he thought it was on the second floor.

As for Cole's, it was given an extensive $1.6m renovation in 2007/8, and patrons were happy to see that it had retained all its style. The glass lighting, penny tile floors and 40 foot mahogany "Red Car" bar were all preserved, as were the bordello-red wallpaper, the table tops made from old Red Car doors, the Tiffany glass lampshades and the ancient clock. It brings to mind the saloons that dotted the west around the early 1900s, while the dark interiors make it feel like a *noir*-ish gangster hangout – which is exactly what it was at one time.

Back in those days, gangster Mickey Cohen was dating one of the girls from the long-gone Follies Theater. It was close enough to walk to from here, and he used to come in regularly for a cocktail, a beer, or something harder. Look on the wall for the sign that's a reminder of those days: "Ladies, kindly do your soliciting discreetly."

A search of the newspaper archives about Cole's and the building uncovered two stories, the first of which made the front page of the *Los Angeles Evening Herald* and was in the *Los Angeles Times* of August 21, 1918: "Seven Stories He Leaps: Cannot Die."

Los Angeles Times

Distraught over the death of his wife the month before, Edward P. Michener jumped from the seventh floor window of the PE Building but landed on trolley guy wires, and was flung down the remaining short distance onto the pavement. He was only cut and bruised and told passersby:

"I want to die, why can't I die?"

Michener had taken elevator number 2 up to the seventh floor and then dived headlong from the window as the Operator watched in horror. Ironically, it was this dive clear of the building that saved his life and was shown in a illustration of him tumbling, almost like a circus gymnast, his hat flying off his head as he fell.

Unfortunately, another person who actually helped construct the building back in 1903 wasn't so lucky. The *Los Angeles Times* of September 10 that year reported that iron worker Russell Morehouse, 24, was laying planking on the exterior of the fourth floor when he missed his footing and fell, striking an iron girder on the second floor as he plummeted nearly 60 feet to the ground.

TWO FEARFUL FALLS, TWO MEN KILLED.

CARL HUNT AND RUSSELL MOREHOUSE THE VICTIMS.

Former Fell from Telephone Pole and Latter Crashed Down from Top of Huntington Building, Becoming Mass of Broken Bones.

When his fellow workers reached him he was said to be "a mass of broken bones and bruised flesh" (the *Los Angeles Record* described him as "a shapeless corpse") and the actual moment of Morehouse's death – when he struck that iron girder – matches Greco's observation that the second floor was haunted.

On the floor below in Cole's – whether you choose to sit at Mickey Cohen's favorite table, take a stool at the bar or find a quiet booth (I like the one right by the door) – it's going to be hard not to order the French Dip sandwich (beef, pastrami, lamb or turkey), which comes with one of their huge "Atomic" pickles. There are other sandwiches and salads on the menu, but this is what Cole's is famous for. Try and save room for their dark chocolate cream pie too.

The items on the menu are oddly priced ($6.83, $7.06, $3.19 and so on), and I'll often stay in this odd frame of mind and order a Guinness float (Guinness with an ice cream top) to drink. Their root beer floats are delicious too, but it would be a crying shame not to sample something from the main "Red Car Bar." As well as a special monthly cocktail selected from the 1930s menu, the Red Car Named Desire (rye whiskey, cynar, luxado, maurin liquor) is recommended, and the "Saloon Special" half dip with fries ($5) is an ideal bite-sized snack.

At the back of Cole's is an unmarked, small door that's easy to miss. Try not to though, as it's the entrance to "The Varnish," an elegant, wood paneled, speakeasy-type bar. Despite the "secret" location and high prices it's always busy, but then HBO Prohibition-era gangster series "Boardwalk Empire" gave a secret password to viewers for a complimentary drink here – that's how cool this place is. Ask for a "Bartender's Choice" to be in cocktail heaven, though see if you can get a Ginger Rogers (gin, ginger syrup, fresh lime juice, mint and ginger ale) – it's really refreshing and has a kick to match.

As you leave Cole's, you might notice there's a "Payroll" part on the neon sign. Henry Cole operated the first check-cashing service in Los Angeles from here, and the savvy guy realized many customers would naturally spend their just-received cash on food and drink. One of their busiest days was when the end of Prohibition was near, and California lifted the ban on beer: Cole's sold 19,000 gallons (or 58 kegs of it) that very same day.

Sunday – Wednesday 11.30am-midnight, Thursday – Saturday 11am-2am
Happy Hour: Monday – Friday 3-7pm, Tuesday all day (well cocktails $5, specialty $8, Schlitz beer $3, half dips with fries $5)
Varnish: Daily 7pm-2am
www.colesfrenchdip.com
www.facebook.com/colesfrenchdip
http://twitter.com/harrycole1908
www.thevarnishbar.com

Figueroa Hotel
939 South Figueroa Street
Los Angeles, CA 90015
Tel: 213 627 8971

"I killed her. I killed her because I loved her."

Originally built as a hotel for professional people by the YWCA, it opened its doors in 1925 with the bottom two floors set aside for men with children, while the other nine were for women. At a cost of well over a million dollars it had been a huge investment for the organization, and it quickly began to struggle financially. By 1930 the Depression probably required more of the YWCA's efforts, and the building was sold.

Today the colorfully-fronted building is still known as the Figueroa Hotel and a glance inside shows the gorgeous and decadent Moroccan/Spanish-style ambiance they created. With skyscrapers nearby and the unmissable blue Vegas-style hotel right next door, stepping inside is like stepping into an oasis in the middle of downtown. In a moment you feel like you're in Morocco, and far away from the street outside. The décor is so exotic and opulent – tin lanterns, chandeliers, palm trees, rugs, throws, drapes, goddess statues and sculptures, dark wood furniture, fountains and amazingly elaborate Moorish tiles – that you feel instantly relaxed.

When I interviewed the General Manager and asked about any "unusual" visitors or happenings here, he said he had been working there since 1976 and that there were "some of the usual hotel stories," but he wasn't prepared to speak any further. Some online research about Hotel Figueroa did mention strange sounds emanating though the hallways and rooms, televisions turning themselves on or unable to be turned off, and empty elevators running on their own and stopping at certain floors.

However, the newspaper archives did reveal three stories connected to the Figueroa Hotel, one of which is a still-unsolved murder and was – at the time – a huge sensation.

RADIO MAN HELD CABIN PRISONER

Wife of Banker Found Slain in Apartment Closet

Tallman, Her Admirer, Denies Any Part in Crime

Accused Deeply Tangled in Net of Circumstance

In June 1929, the press reveled in the murder of Virginia Patty, 26, who had been beaten with a brick and then trussed up in a closet in a "love nest" on South Union Avenue.

A "W.C. Johnson" had recently rented this apartment, and he was later identified as "dapper" radio ship operator William L. Tallman, Virginia's longtime lover.

He had been staying at the Figueroa Hotel, and after checking out had rented the room where Patty's body was found.

Love Nest Murder Suspect Arrested Aboard Steamer

He was arrested on a ship bound for San Francisco but later escaped and allegedly jumped overboard, though there was speculation that he had instead stowed away on the liner *Parthenia* bound for Liverpool, England.

Over the next three years there were sightings of Tallman in Ohio, Alaska, Texas, Wisconsin, Louisiana and even Guatemala. A body found floating in San Francisco Bay and the suicide of a Hoover Dam laborer in Las Vegas were also rumored to be him, though Los Angeles police dismissed both possibilities and, despite a $2000 reward and a murder warrant being issued (his fingerprints were found at the scene of the crime) it seems that he remained at large and was never bought to trial.

Secondly, the newspapers of April 6 and 7, 1950 reported the murder of Hallie Cecilia Oswald, whose naked body had been found in one of the rooms here.

Confesses
Weird
Slaying

Mystery as No Marks of Killing Found on Woman

The killer had apparently written on her chest and back, the most intelligible message being "And I love you. It is for THE BEST."

Cryptic Messages Scribbled Across Dead Divorcee's Body

Her ex-husband reportedly said that she had spoken of "living in constant fear" of a man named "Gordon," though it later emerged that she was a heavy drinker, and had just been on a 10 day drinking spree with a waiter named Harry Gordon.

The Los Angeles Coroner's Office was cautious about declaring the cause of death, but the next day Gordon was arrested and placed in a psychiatric ward after causing a car accident. The suicidal Gordon quickly confessed to the murder, telling detectives:

"I killed her. I killed her because I loved her... I wrapped a towel around her neck and squeezed tightly."

'She Was Happy'

"So I wrapped a towel around her neck and choked her until she was quiet. I choked her and she was happy to go that way, as she was smiling when she went. I wrote across her body a farewell message that I wanted her to take with her."

A little over a year later in September 1951, the *Los Angeles Examiner* reported that elderly Ray D. Bowen had checked into the hotel and drowned himself in the bath. He left a suicide note, and his wife later confirmed that he had indeed been in poor health:

"I don't want to be a burden to you," It read. "I have been suffering for two years."

Barely five years later, the *Los Angeles Times* was full of coverage of the Rose Parade in Pasadena, but featured a story – and picture – that was truly heartbreaking. On January 2, 1956 Harold Chester looked out of the window of his room and saw a group of people gathered around the body of a woman who had jumped from the unfinished 4th Street bridge nearby.

Curious, Chester approached the crowd – and to his horror, saw that the dead body was that of his wife Bettie. Weeping as he spoke to Officer James Staurakes, Chester explained that she had "kissed him good-by… saying she was going for a walk," and that she was suffering from cancer and had attempted suicide before. The couple had only arrived in Los Angeles from Dallas, Texas a few days previously.

The Lobby Café menu is pretty standard (steak, chicken, burgers), but you should come here for a cocktail at the Veranda Bar out back. It's a small bar/patio (check out the red and gold four poster "Sultan's" bed with pillows at both ends) and faces out onto a hexagon-shaped pool bordered with a little garden of bougainvillea and cactuses. It is a gorgeous spot, though on April 21, 1946 school principal David Ray Arnold, 57, jumped from the fire escape on the 11th floor "landing in the courtyard below" – which is right where you are now!

School Principal Killed in Plunge From 11th Floor

David Ray Arnold, 57, principal of Santa Catalina Island High School, leaped or fell to his death from an 11th floor fire escape at a hotel at 939 S. Figueroa St. yesterday.

Lobby Café: 6-10.30am and 5-10pm
Veranda Bar: Monday – Friday 4pm-midnight, Saturday/Sunday 4pm-2am
www.figueroahotel.com

Grand Central Market & Angels Flight
317 South Broadway / 351 South Hill Street
Los Angeles, CA 90013
Tel: 213 624 2378 / 213 626 1901

Mysterious Passengers

The Grand Central Market has been a downtown hub for 95 years, but one of the main reasons it's here is because the "shortest railway in the world" is right across the street. That may seem like an unusual decision, but for many years the city's wealthy elite lived on Bunker Hill, and from early morning until late at night they would ride down on the Angels Flight funicular railway and often go right into the market.

Designed by architect John Parkinson (who was also responsible for City Hall and Union Station, among many others), the market is on the ground floor of the Homer Laughlin Building, which was Los Angeles' first fireproof structure and opened its doors in 1897. Named after the building's funder, an Ohio businessman who had made a fortune in China ceramics and dishware (his company is still operating today), the ground floor was originally a department store, with the market opening later in 1917. Together with Angels Flight, they're about as close to the old Los Angeles as you can get.

MARKET OPENING.

New Broadway Establishment to
Begin Operation Next Saturday.

Inside, the market is a prime example of Beaux-Arts architecture, and though it has undergone many interior cosmetic changes to keep up with the fashions, the sawdust-sprinkled floors, neon signs and the exterior façade have remained true to its heritage. In the 1920s noted American architect Frank Lloyd Wright had an office in the building, and it's impossible to think that he didn't eat lunch – or do some shopping – here.

Many Bunker Hill residents probably came through here on their way home as well, and when you take your own journey on Angels Flight you'll be following in the footsteps of over 100,000,000 others; that's the estimated number of passengers that Angels Flight carried in just its first 50 years of operation – more passengers per mile than any other railway in the world.

Today you'll be one of the 1,000 passengers per day that takes a seat in "Olivet" or "Sinai," the two orange train cars that counterbalance each other on the 33% slope. The fare is just 50 cents each way (it went up from 25c in March 2011), and during the minute-long journey you'll hear trundling cable drums, creaking wood and a bell-like ring of cables – the same noises that millions of passengers have also heard over the last 110 years.

UP AGAIN, DOWN AGAIN.

It Will Take Two Minutes, Perhaps Three, for the Round Trip on the Angels' Flight.

The new inclined railway up the Third-street hill from Hill to Olive street, the franchise for which was granted to J. W. Eddy by the City Council last May, will be in operation, so the builder says, by December 1.

Masterminded by lawyer, politician and engineer Colonel James W. Eddy, the Angels Flight "hillevator" opened on New Year's Eve 1901 as a quick way for people to travel up and down Bunker Hill. Passengers paid a penny fare for the 315 feet journey, and from the very beginning it was popular.

They were mentioned in Raymond Chandler's novel *The High Window* and short story *The King in Yellow*, and also in the children's book *Piccolo's Prank* by Leo Politi. Even the main character in John Fante's novel *Ask the Dust* knew Angels Flight – though "Arturo Bandini" always walked the 189 step staircase alongside, since he couldn't afford the fare.

It's been a regular on the silver screen too, and was first seen as early as 1920 in one reel comedy *All Jazzed Up*, as well as in *The Unfaithful* (1947), *M* (1951), *The Glenn Miller Story* (1954), *Kiss Me Deadly* (1955), *The Exiles* (1961) and in a "Perry Mason" television episode called "The Case of the Twice Told Tale." It also featured in the recent 1947 era Los Angeles video game "L.A. Noire" and Olivet had a cameo in 2011's retro hit movie *The Muppets*.

Angels Flight was originally located by the 3rd Street Tunnel – just at the end of the block from where it is now – and in 1969, despite protests from singer Peggy Lee and others, it was closed to passengers when the area underwent major development.

It wasn't until 1996 that the rebuilt Angels Flight welcomed riders to its current location, and that was after test runs had been made with cases of beer and soft drinks weighing 9,000 pounds.

Sadly, Olivet and Sinai were again silent in 2001 following an accident in which one person died and seven were injured, so the second reopening of Angels Flight in 2010 was a very big story in Los Angeles, and the year ended with a celebration of the 109th Anniversary when passengers could travel for the 1901 price – one penny – on December 31st.

Sailor Killed as He Walks Angels Flight

An unidentified sailor attempting to walk up the tracks on Angels Flight, Third and Hill Sts., was crushed to death last night when he was hurled by one car under the wheels of the descending tram.

Firemen worked for 20 minutes before his body was extricated from the wheels of the car halfway up the steep tracks.

Few people know that September 1943 was in fact the first death associated with Angels Flight.

Both the *Los Angeles Times* and the *Los Angeles Evening Herald-Express* of September 1 reported that a sailor named John Gaddy had walked up the track and was struck by one car and then crushed by the other.

After the accident, heavy jacks were needed for the very gruesome task of removing his body.

I always take a trip on Angels Flight when I'm downtown, and on a recent visit Bill, the Angels Flight operator, told me that there had been some ghostly sightings on board:

> *"I've heard several stories that, especially in the early morning, the figure of a person has been seen sitting alone on the cars, yet when it arrives at the top (where the ticket office is) they're gone."*

I asked whether this figure has been seen on one of the cars in particular, as newspaper reports seemed to indicate the 2001 accident fatality occurred on Sinai:

> *"No, they've been seen on both Olivet and Sinai and no one seemed to know if it was a man or woman."*

There was another clue about the origin of this story when Bill mentioned the 1999 mystery novel *Angels Flight* by Michael Connelly (a copy of which is displayed in the ticket office window). In this fictional story the Olivet car was the location of a double murder that set LAPD Detective Harry Bosch on the trail of a killer.

Bill said that it was around this time that the ghost sightings started – a case of life imitating art, perhaps? You'll have to take a ride yourself to find out for sure.

Across the road, the Grand Central Market is a food lover's paradise and a real feast for the senses. As you wander down the sawdust-strewn aisles you'll note the aromas of sizzling meats and freshly-caught fish, but make sure that you smell the dried chili peppers (my favorite is *pasilla*) and sample some sweet Mexican treats – watermelon, sweet potato or a stick of *jamoncillo* (milk fudge).

For more than a snack, try one of the packed burritos at Ana Maria's, watch your Salvadorian pupusa get patty-caked together at Sarita's, enjoy a beer with your chow mein at the China Cafe (it has a great red neon Chop Suey and Chow Mein sign) or simply shop. Most people leave with armfuls of fruit and vegetables, which are cheap and abundant here.

One of my favorite spots in Los Angeles, the Grand Central Market is a busy, bustling place where people from all neighborhoods come together. Any time is a good time to visit, though it tends to be quietest after lunch.

Also, if you leave the Grand Central Market's main exit onto Broadway, you'll see the famous Bradbury Building opposite. Probably best known for its appearances in 1982's *Blade Runner* and 2011 Oscar winner *The Artist*, it was designed by rookie craftsman George Wyman. Unsure about the assignment, he contacted his dead brother Mark through a device similar to an Ouija board and supposedly received the message:

"Mark Wyman / take the / Bradbury building / and you will be / successful"

Finally, if you happen to be in L.A. around August 20th, have a look at Angels Knoll, the very steep, grassy piece of land next to Angels Flight, or see if you can hear any bleating. For the last few years the city has bought in dozens of goats to eat the grass here, so you might get a chance to see that rarest of things: an animal lawn mower.

Grand Central Market: Daily 9am-6pm
Angels Flight: Daily 6.45am-10pm (or later)
www.grandcentralmarket.com
www.facebook.com/grandcentralmarket
http://twitter.com/GrandCentralMarket
www.angelsflight.com
http://twitter.com/angelsflight

La Golondrina Restaurant
17 Olvera Street
Los Angeles, CA 90012
Tel: 213 628 4349

"La Consulela"

Olvera Street may seem like just a long alley, but it's the oldest part – and the beating heart – of downtown. It was on a site very near here that the city now known as Los Angeles was established as a *pueblo* (town) by eleven Spanish families of *pobladores* (settlers).

The City of Angels has come a long way since then, but Olvera Street is still a busy, wild, colorful place where you can hear mariachi bands, buy beautiful candles, sample a *churro* and maybe visit La Golondrina, the very first Mexican restaurant in Los Angeles.

Named after a sort of Mexican "Home, Sweet Home" song about the migrating swallow bird, the building is one of the oldest in Olvera Street too. It was originally built in the 1850s by an Italian winemaker, the grandfather of current owner Vivien Bonzo, and the main dining room (the one with the black roof beams) was once his wine cellar. Vivien's grandmother opened the doors in 1930, and Vivien – whose parents first met and fell in love here – took over in 1980.

I spoke to staff member Eduardo, who has been working at La Golondrina for 14 years and said that there are stories of "La Consuela" or "The Mistress" appearing upstairs in what used to be the living quarters. It's now the office and employee dining room, and he said that when he's closing up and finishing paperwork late at night, he always wants to leave before midnight so he doesn't see her.

As for Ms. Bonzo herself, she talked to me from her home in New Mexico and said that she feels La Golondrina is home to more than one ghost:

> *"The building has been here so long, and so many people have been here over the generations, that there's not only one ghost here – there are many. To my mind it's fairly natural. When one of the cooks comes in, he often says*

that he hears someone calling his name, and when I used to close up late on Wednesday and Thursday I always heard big thumps and bangs upstairs. I often called security, but there was nothing there."

Bonzo recounted a sighting of "The Mistress" and said that she thought it was probably the ghost of her grandmother, the "Queen of Olvera Street," Consuela Castillo de Bonzo:

"There was a guy here at night painting and putting in tiles. He clearly saw a ghostly woman coming down the stairs."

She further explained that in Mexican folklore, the appearance of a ghost often means that there is buried treasure. Strangely enough, in an article in the *Los Angeles Times* on April 25, 1962 the Consuelo de Bonzo talked "over a beef taco" about when they first moved to the current location:

"But," she added, eyes twinkling, "we had it blessed to drive away the evil spirits."

Unfortunately the age of the building – as well as city ordinance and regulations – meant that hunting for that buried treasure wouldn't have been allowed, even if there was something hidden under the floorboards. In fact, Bonzo recalled that L.A. City employees had also had some strange encounters at La Golondrina "at least 15 years ago":

"A law had been passed and they came to do some seismic work on the building, but after going away for short time they returned to find their equipment had been unplugged and moved to the other side of the room. They ran out of the building."

It seems that various repairmen and construction workers have been favorite targets for the spirits of La Golondrina:

"One worker was doing some painting overnight, and then the next day he came along with his wife and children. He said he had watched as the bathroom door – a heavy door, not on a spring or anything – had just slowly opened wide. He wouldn't come back on his own."

With all these unexplained stories, there seems to be a definite feeling about the place – at least at night:

"It can be frightening to be in here. I've often worked here through the night, and I always felt that someone was watching me. Sometimes I slept here, but I always had nightmares. Years ago, after my parents were divorced, my father often slept here. He was a big, macho man, but he always left all the doors unlocked and open so he could run – he was frightened to be there at night."

Pointing out the faded picture of Consuela Castillo de Bonzo on the wall by the bar, Eduardo added that "some of the old timers" have heard voices, doors slamming and chairs being scraped across the floor upstairs, although no one seems to feel that the spirit of La Consuela is frightening.

Though I was tempted by their Mexican meatballs (and weekend diners can try steamed goat or lamb), I enjoyed their Burrito Especial, which has shrimp instead of the more usual pork or beef. It was more expensive than most other Mexican restaurants (Olvera Street is very much a stop on the tourist trail), but they use health conscious olive and soybean oil for cooking, and for the first time in my experience, my beer glass was lined with salt and a slice of lime.

Most people like to sit on the patio here – even if that does pretty much guarantee a visit from the strolling mariachi bands – though in the newer section of the restaurant at the back you'll notice a small balcony on the second floor.

I learned that it used to face right out onto the street, so keep an eye out when you are here – maybe La Consuela will come out to see you!

The balcony at La Golondrina

Monday – Thursday 9am-8pm, Friday – Sunday 9am-9pm

Oviatt Building and the Cicada Restaurant
617 South Olive Street
Los Angeles, CA 90014
Tel: 213 488 9488

Haunting the building that killed him...

Perhaps the most suave, snazzy and snappily-dressed story in *Gourmet Ghosts* is about the Oviatt Building and its flamboyant mastermind, James Z. Oviatt. He lived in his luxurious penthouse here until the day he died and – evidence seems to show – ever since.

Back in 1907, an ambitious and talented 18-year-old Oviatt left his home town of Salt Lake City for Los Angeles, where he began working in haberdashery at Desmond's Department Store. Just five years later in 1912 he opened his own exclusive men's haberdashery with Frank Baird Alexander, and the assurance of quality, luxury and elegance soon saw movie stars like Douglas Fairbanks and John Barrymore leaving Alexander & Oviatt looking like a million bucks.

They were soon expanding, and Oviatt didn't rest on his laurels. In one of his many research trips to Paris for fine fabrics he attended the 1925 Exposition Internationale des Arts Decoratifs et Industriels Modernes – and was inspired. He immediately commissioned leading European designers and craftsmen – including the "great French genius" Rene Lalique – to bring a magnificent style emporium to life, and architects Walker & Eisen helped design a new Art Deco home for Alexander & Oviatt, which opened in May 1928.

Alexander & Oviatt
HILL AT SIXTH STREET
LOS ANGELES' FINEST MEN'S SHOP

Over 80 years later, the interior furnishings and paneling are still impressive to see. There are the Lalique glass elevator doors –

he used some 30 tons of glass, the biggest shipment ever to pass through the Panama Canal at the time – magnificent chandeliers, many tons of French "Napoleon" marble and a massive tower with a chiming neon clock, which was also imported from France.

The Penthouse was for Oviatt, and was fitted out with custom lighting and exquisite floors and cabinetry from celebrated French firm Saddier et Fils. There were also bi-level rooftop gardens with a 360 degree view of downtown, a swimming pool, tennis court, putting green, the clock tower and even a "beach" of imported

French Riviera sand.

Oviatt and his wife Mary played host to many parties over the following decades, and autographed photographs of their many friends (and clients) still line the Penthouse walls – Barrymore, Errol Flynn, Leslie Howard, Charles Boyer and Howard Hughes among them. Oviatt expanded his empire too, opening his own branch in the luxurious Beverly Wilshire Hotel from 1933 until 1958, when the lease expired.

Many years later on April 13, 1965 the *Los Angeles Times* reported that Oviatt had been a brief financial backer of racist organization the Christian Defense League. He claimed that he merely rented them office space and that this was "a damned lie," though he did say the League was "a great organization."

By 1968 the party was over and the haberdashery closed, though Oviatt continued to live in the Penthouse until his death in 1974 – when there was no expansive obituary in the *Los Angeles Times*.

> OVIATT, James, beloved husband of
> Mrs. Mary Oviatt, father of
> James Oviatt Jr.
>   Private services to be held at
> Forest Lawn-Glendale. Forest
> Lawn Mortuary. In lieu of flow-
> ers, contributions may be made
> to the Heart Fund.

A decade or so after Oviatt's death the new owners restored the Penthouse and lobby to their former glory, while the ground floor is now home to the Cicada Restaurant. Only party goers, wedding couples and movie crews can visit the penthouse today – it's been un-lived in since Oviatt died – though Marc Chevalier, producer of *The Oviatt Building*, a documentary made to celebrate the 80th Anniversary, has heard stories that say otherwise:

> *"Jen, who was one of the managers at Cicada a little while ago, also used to show prospective clients up to the Penthouse. One day she was really busy and sent a couple up in the elevator to look around on their own. After a while they came back down and said they loved it, especially the 'wonderful, pipe tobacco smell.' Jen knew that the building was a non-smoking one, and that no one ever goes up to the Penthouse. Turns out that Oviatt was a rabid pipe smoker, and I mean rabid – every picture he has a pipe in his mouth."*

Chevalier also recounted the earliest story he heard about the Oviatt – a story never before revealed to the public – from Maureen Vincenti, the wife of the late owner of Rex Restaurant, which occupied the space before the Cicada:

> *"She only told me this about six months ago, and it happened back in the 1980s. Maureen said that she was often the last person there at night, locking up, and the first there in the morning as well. Many times, she said, she would arrive to find the old clothing drawers all pulled out, though they were definitely closed when she left the night before."*

Speaking from her current restaurant Vincenti, Maureen confirmed the story about the drawers, and revealed that she wasn't the only person to have this experience:

"My husband Mauro – he passed on – experienced it too, because after the first couple of times I asked him if he'd done it. He said no, and said that he'd seen the open drawers before too, though he hadn't said anything as he didn't want to scare me. He really believed that there was someone was there – he was very susceptible to feelings like that."

Like the menswear cases, the drawers – and there are dozens of them – date back to the days of the haberdashery, and are like ones that you would find in a kitchen, only deeper. Most of them are used to store extra supplies for the restaurant, while the rest are empty. Maureen added that she never felt scared, and that both Mauro and she found the Reservations Book open in the morning "periodically" too.

Manager Richard Liberman, who has been at the Cicada for over 10 years, spoke further about his own unusual experience:

"One night about six months ago I had closed all the walk-ins (refrigerators) and went to the office to do some paperwork. When I came back downstairs one of the doors – and they're heavy doors, six foot by four foot across – was wide open. Doors open and close here a lot too – other people have seen that – and recently my waiter Rich Lopez said that on table 17 (the south wall) the chairs kept being pulled out and the silverware moved around. It's a fascinating building."

Richard says that he has never felt scared by anything that's happened, and that about seven years ago he actually had a healer come into the building:

"He was an Austrian healer and he worked in a metaphysical way, putting the negative energy he found into water, which we then threw out. He said there were the spirits of lots of little children under the stairwell, and many other things – I had no idea there could be that much in one place!"

He also mentioned that "lots of women tell us they feel something in the women's bathroom," and added further confirmation to the reports of the smell of pipe tobacco in the elevator and up in the Penthouse – the place where one of his fellow employees said he actually saw Oviatt:

"Ray has worked here longer than me – he's part time now, and works in maintenance – and he has said that he several times has clearly seen Oviatt sitting on the bed in the Penthouse."

Most recently, Richard said that Ray had a ghostly experience with someone who had more recently died:

"One of my employees, Daniel, his brother died suddenly in October last year. Ray saw a "man walking" in the restaurant, and when he described this man to Daniel, he immediately said: "That's my brother Mike."

The entrance to the Oviatt Building – and the Cicada Restaurant is open

The Cicada is kind of hidden gem in this part of downtown, and a table on the ground floor (or even better, on the upstairs mezzanine) is a perfect way to experience the 1920s design; no doubt that was the reason contemporary silent movie *The Artist* chose to shoot here. Some of the fixtures and fittings from the haberdashery are still in use – the mahogany menswear cases make a perfect wine rack – and the European influence that Oviatt loved continues with the food.

It's a Northern Italian menu, and their appetizers include stuffed tiger shrimp, blini with scallops and pan-baked asparagus with parmigiano. The beautifully-presented entrees include lamb, duck, steak, chicken and fish. The smoked apple bacon-wrapped veal chop is a standout, though I will often go for the Chef's Choice of gnocchi.

Since you'll have hit the wallet pretty hard already, indulge in one of their many specially-themed desserts including the Alexander & Oviatt tiramisu and Prohibition crème brûlée.

To set the mood the staff are dressed in their historical best, and if you can get hold of a tuxedo and cocktail gown you can opt for a high-end dinner and some exercise by coming to the Cicada Club, a swingin' good time that celebrates the Roaring Twenties with songs, dancing, cocktails and glamorous entertainment direct from the Jazz Age. Boasting a different menu, it takes place on Sundays and is run by Maxwell DeMille, the "Impossibly Impeccable Impresario" who also says that Oviatt is definitely still around the building that he made his own:

> *"One of the restaurant managers says that light switches turn themselves on and off here all the time. It really seems that things seem to work outside the building, then suddenly don't inside. I recently got a new microphone cable and when I tested it at home during the day, it worked perfectly. Then, in the club that night, it just suddenly stopped working – dead. We say "Blame Oviatt" every time things go wrong."*

Though admittedly a huge admirer of the building, Marc Chevalier noted that "some crimes definitely occurred here," and talked about the final moments of the man behind the name:

"Oviatt himself was rather a troubled character. He was charismatic and charming certainly, but he was also very paranoid and prejudiced. He was also not afraid to cut corners, shall we say, in running his business, and soon after his death, his wife attempted suicide by trying to jump off the building. His death was odd too; he was woken by an earthquake and got up to see what was happening. The lights were out, and he tripped on a step, fell and broke several bones. He never really recovered from his injuries, and died soon after. In a way, his building kind of killed him."

Visiting the Oviatt is like stepping back in time (especially if you eat in the restaurant or attend the Cicada Club), but remember that they're only open a couple of days a week, so be sure to check and make a reservation.

Dinner: Thursday/Friday 5.30-9pm
Club Cicada open most Sundays 6-11.30pm (show 8pm)
www.cicadarestaurant.com
www.clubcicada.com
www.facebook.com/cicadaclub
www.oviatt.com

Philippe The Original
1001 North Alameda Street
Los Angeles, CA 90012
Tel: 213 628 3781

Georgina and The Lady Upstairs

One of the most famous restaurants in Los Angeles – and maybe even Southern California – Philippe's was established over 100 years ago by Philippe Mathieu, the man who claimed to have invented their famous "French Dipped Sandwich." One day in 1918, a customer asked Philippe to cut a beef-filled French loaf into two, so he could share it with a friend. Soon after, another customer asked if Philippe would dip his "man-size" sandwich in a roasting pan of hot meat juices – and a legend was born.

Mathieu sold the restaurant to Harry, Dave and Frank Martin in 1927, and they kept the doors open 24/7 through the Depression and World War II until in 1951, when they were forced to move by something too big to ignore – the new Hollywood-Santa Ana 101 freeway. They've been at their present location ever since and today their in-laws, John and Richard Binder, are in charge, making it a fourth generation family business.

But what was at 1001 N. Alameda Street before Philippe's moved in? The restaurant's website referred to it as a machine shop with a hotel on the second floor, though the latter was probably a rundown boarding house and, given that it was located in the center of the area's "red-light" district, most likely a brothel.

Whatever the truth may be, the racy history is the one that employees mention when talking about the other legend connected with Phillipe's – the "one upstairs." It's said that the ghost of a "lady" – perhaps one who use to ply her trade in the midnight hours – has been seen on the second floor, vanishing when she steps into the next room and leaving behind a strong smell of perfume. An employee named Gloria confirmed that one young staff member named Adrian did see a lady in a red dress several years ago:

"He was very scared (afterward), and completely pale."

Adrian still works at Philippe's, and many staff members have felt something here. One said she felt she was being touched or pushed in the back, and there was a case when the restroom lights were suddenly turned off when someone was alone in the building. These days, Gloria says the other strange presence is that of a former employee:

"There was a lady named Georgina who worked here, and died about six years ago. She always said that when she died she was going to come back to haunt the place, so now we say (when something happens) 'Oh, that's just Georgina.'"

More recently, a regular customer – who has often said she has seen ghosts around the restaurant – said she saw a woman in a purple dress at the table where she had just been sitting. How did she see this woman after leaving the table? The customer was looking in the recently-installed security camera monitor screen, which is located at the 1920s candy counter near the front door.

Other staff could see nothing and thought it was perhaps a reflection from the television screen nearby, but the customer also insisted there was a cold spot at her table:

"She said that she felt a cold draft there, so I went over and put my hand all over the table and around it – but I couldn't feel any draft or vibe."

A search of the *Los Angeles Times* archive only turned up one small story about a sudden and bloody occurrence at this address. The March 9, 1904 edition noted "Lives in Peril" when it reported heavy winds had bought down a number of street signs and injured passersby. One "thing" that measured six by seven fell and landed on top of a Mrs. T. Silberman, knocking her unconscious.

GUSTS TEAR DOWN SIGNS.

Lives in Peril from Heavy Tumbling Structures.

Passer-by Receives Severe Wounds on Scalp.

Whether any ladies from the spirit world are here or not, Philippe's is definitely worth a visit if you want a taste of the old Los Angeles; it's a real old fashioned, sawdust-on-the-floor (six bales per week), jar of pickled eggs (in beet juice), soup-of-the-day kind of place.

Lunch is always a busy time – Philippe's prepares and serves around 300 pounds of pig's feet and prepares 80 gallons of their (very hot) French mustard per week – and you'll see every kind of Angeleno here. Tables are friendly and communal (especially in the section housing the mini Railway Museum) and you're just as likely to end up next to a businessman in a suit as you are a construction worker.

No matter whether their dipped sandwich got its name because Mathieu was French, was nicknamed "Frenchy," the roll was French or the customer was named French, you just have to try one – they serve 17,000 a week. To accompany it I recommend one of their refreshing glasses of beer and, if you visit between October and June, a dessert of their baked apple; it's a customer favorite. Finally, you have to have a cup of their legendary coffee, which costs just 45c per cup. That's a steal for sure, though for 35 years it was an unbelievable 9 cents (yes, you read that right – 9 cents) before rising in price in late 2011 to absolutely no customer outrage; the long lines were still here the next day.

Around the same time Philippe's was immortalized in a short movie called – what else? – *Philippe's Sandwich*. It's a 1950s-era comedy about two young brothers called Flaco and Lino, who, when they realize that their *Mamita* is dying, embark on a journey through Los Angeles in search of a special sandwich for her. It stars Rico Rodriguez as Flaco (you may recognize him as Manny Delgado from ABC comedy "Modern Family").

As for insider tips, remember that it's cash only (there's an ATM here just in case; it's right near the line of old fashioned phone booths) and be sure to pick the middle line – it moves faster (or it seems to, anyway). Upstairs is more sectioned off and a much quieter place to enjoy your sandwich, but then it is the area that's supposed to be haunted...

Daily 6am-10pm
Breakfast: 6-10.30am
www.philippes.com
www.facebook.com/PhilippetheOG
http://twitter.com/PhilippetheOG

Redwood Bar & Grill
316 West 2nd Street
Los Angeles, CA 90012
Tel: 213 680 2600

Tap, Tap, Tap...

The Redwood is the only bar in *Gourmet Ghosts* that has a song written about it (you can download Kim Fowley's "Redwood Bar" from their website). His lyrics say that the Redwood has played host to Jack and Bobby Kennedy and their notorious California-born rival Richard Nixon – though probably not at the same time.

Los Angeles gangster Mickey Cohen has apparently bowled up here too, and it's always been a regular hang out for politicians, lawyers, lobbyists, City Hall employees, journalists, bail bondsmen and the odd celebrity fighting a lawsuit in the Courts nearby.

Secondly, this is the only bar where Jack Sparrow from the *Pirates of the Caribbean* movies could walk in and no one would give him a second glance (the huge anchor by the door is a big clue why, as is the big X on the "treasure map" awning outside). There are recent real movie connections with it too: it was here that Annie (Kristen Wiig) had her first date with cop Rhodes (Chris O'Dowd) in *Bridesmaids* (2011), and Summer (Zooey Deschanel) and Tom (Joseph Gordon-Levitt) sung karaoke here in *(500) Days of Summer* (2009).

Known in past lives as the Redwood Restaurant (with its gaslight-era bar) and as Redwood House, they were originally on 1st Street when they opened in 1942, but they moved here in 1970 when their old building was demolished to make way for the *Los Angeles Times* corporate offices. However, it was just a few years ago that it got this most amazing of makeovers and became a pirate-themed, booty-filled bar/restaurant.

Designer Fred Sutherland flew to a Miami scrap yard in a real life search for treasure, and now the ceiling is painted with maritime flags and all around are barrels, muskets, swords, lanterns, nets, rigging and every kind of maritime kitsch. The contrast with the skyscrapers outside is pretty amazing – a bit like finding an oasis after being adrift in the center of the metropolis.

Bartender Joel Carvalho told me that there were literally many great stories associated with the Redwood. Back in the day reporters from the *Los Angeles Times* would write their stories at the bar, tapping away on their typewriters, and by the door you'll see an old-style red telephone on the wall. The *Times* paid for that direct line for many years, just so that they could get hold of a reporter or photographer the moment they needed one (there's a sticker on the phone with the extension number – 70733).

Carvalho mentioned that when the *Times* was taken over by the Tribune Company the phone was almost cut off – until it was pointed out that there's a phone in the bar next to the Tribune newspaper building in Chicago. The newspaper business has been hit hard in the last few years and whenever I've picked up the receiver there's been no dial tone, but make sure you try it – just in case.

Being a hack's hideout might help explain the fact that despite a long history, few bad stories about the Redwood seem to have made it into print, though Carvalho did talk about a spooky experience he'd had just a couple of weeks before:

"I was in the bathroom and the light in there just... shifted. The light in there is fixed, but my shadow started moving across the wall behind me. My skin started crawling as I watched in the mirror, and I was washing my hands the light dimmed again – it was just strange."

Fellow bartender Dylan Revelo mentioned a couple of strange experiences he's had, the first being in early 2009 when he went down into the storage area. The Redwood is part of a larger building, the California Law Center, and down in the lower lobby/basement is the wonderfully-named Cutey Pie Buffeteria, a small convenience store with a food counter/buffet area that serves the building from 6.30am-4pm weekdays. Aside from candy, soda, chips, fruit and muffins they serve lashings of breakfast – sausage, eggs, hotcakes, burritos – burgers, fries and lunch specials. However, Revelo was there around 2am when they were long closed:

"I came back up the stairs, and out of the corner of my eye I could see through the glass door of the café that there was a man standing at the buffet, like he was in line. I couldn't see his face, but he seemed to be a tall man dressed in a gray suit. For the first time in my life, I got a flood of chills. I had always been a skeptic about that kind of thing, but I never felt like that before: 'I wanna go now.' It was a creepy feeling."

Revelo mentioned it to Vicky, the night building Security Guard:

"She said 'I've had things happen,' and that she had been creeped out too – but she wouldn't talk about it."

A couple of months later, Revelo was sitting at the far left of the bar (near the bathrooms):

"There were only two other people in the bar, and they were in front of me – it was empty otherwise. It was about 7pm, and I was about to start work when I felt a tap on my back – it was a really firm tap, really distinct. I turned round, but there was no one there."

The other two patrons asked who he was looking at, and Revelo said he even looked up at the ceiling to see if it was a drip of water. Then, about a month later, Revelo was working behind the bar late night. He'd already closed the doors, and there were just two guys from that night's band finishing up their beers:

"Suddenly one of the guys gets a weird, bewildered look on his face and turns round, saying 'Something just tapped me on the back.' I said 'Are you kidding?' I hadn't told this guy about what happened to me – I'd never even met him before. I tell you, I work Sunday nights and I close up as fast I can. There's an eerie kind of feeling here at night."

It's quiet in the Redwood during the day and gets really busy at night, but whenever you're here grab yourself one of their white, fairground ride-shaped circular booths and take on a beast of the sea by having some fried calamari. You can also try a Monkey Fist cocktail (Bacardi, Amaretto, pineapple and cranberry juice), a Skinny Pirate (Captain Morgan rum and diet coke on the rocks) or a Moby Dick (Bacardi light, blue Caraçao, pineapple juice, orange juice and a squeeze of lime) and, if you feel like taking a risk, Walk The Plank – a special where if you buy six shots, the seventh one is free!

The menu is far better than you'd get on board a whaler, too: your crew can feast on everything from fish and chips, a chicken pesto panini, landlubbin' mac and cheese or the half pound Angus beef Redwood Burger. A word of warning though: there's a cannon right by the door of the "Galley" (kitchen), so criticizing the cook probably isn't a very good idea.

The days of booze-soaked journalists may have gone and more hipsters than pirates prop up the bar these days, but no matter where you're headed it's worth coming on board the Redwood. After 5pm the parking lots around here drop in price (so you'll have more money) and music fans should take note: there's something here nearly every night (plenty of rock, blues, folk and loud guitars) and even the odd well-known name turns up once in a while.

Sunday – Friday 11am-2am, Saturday 5pm-2am
Happy Hour: Sunday – Friday 4-7pm ($5 draft, $3 Bud/Light, $2 PBR/Tecate, $5 well drinks, appetizers $4-6)
www.theredwoodbar.com
www.facebook.com/theredwoodbar
http://twitter.com/redwoodbar

Spring Arts Tower
Crocker Club and Café Nine
453 South Spring Street
Los Angeles, CA 90013
Tel: 213 239 9099 (Crocker Club) / 213 622 3888 (Café Nine)

The Night Watchman and the Girl in a White Dress

Spring Arts Tower architects John Parkinson and George "Ed" Bergstrom were known for their work across the city – and beyond. Parkinson built most of Spring Street and also the City Hall, the Memorial Coliseum, the Alexandria Hotel and Union Station, whereas Bergstrom designed the Hollywood Bowl and The Pentagon in Arlington, Virginia.

It was reported that the Springs Arts Tower cost more than $1m to build, and it opened its doors in 1915 after being built in record time. Citizens National Bank were the original anchor tenant, occupying the basement and the first three floors, and when Crocker took them over in November 1963 it became Crocker Citizens National Bank – then the 14th largest in America.

Today, the Spring Arts Tower is home to a nightclub, restaurant and bookstore, as well as apartments and offices for artists, architects, advertising agencies, galleries and production companies. It's been used as a location for commercials, pop videos, television shows "24," "Heroes," "Numbers," "NCIS" and "Criminal Minds," and movies including *Rush Hour* (1998), *Meet the Fockers* (2004), *Spider-Man 3* (2007), *Made of Honor* (2008) and *He's Just Not That Into You* (2009). There's actually a movie studio set-up on the 3rd and 4th floor too.

Kevin Taylor, history graduate and former manager of the Spring Arts Tower, has done considerable research on the building, and he said that it has plenty of spooky stories:

"I first came here about seven years ago, and the third floor was like an abandoned old school. It must have been an adult vocational school because there were still desks

*there, old computers, chalkboards and even old gurneys –
they must have taught nursing there too."*

It seems that the night watchman is still making his rounds on
the 3rd floor; there have been reports of a ghostly figure going
around opening and closing doors and the sound of a bunch of
jingling keys:

*"I heard the keys myself, and was spooked because I was
the only one at the time who had a set of keys for the
building. In fact, one of the workers heard the jingling
keys up there just a couple of weeks back."*

In a moment that genuinely gave me a chill, I uncovered an
article in the *Los Angeles Times* archive that revealed there had
indeed been a tragic accident on the 3rd floor – and the victim was
the building watchman. The issue of July 4, 1927 reported that
employees at the Citizens National Bank heard a man groaning
around 10am the previous day, but could not find anyone in
distress.

WORKER DIES IN SHAFT PLUNGE

Building Watchman Found on Elevator Floor

Falls During Night and Bleeds to Death

Torn Clothing Tells Fight to Stanch Wounds

It emerged that sometime during the previous night watchman
Al Brietenbecker had fallen from the 3rd floor down the freight

elevator shaft to the sub-basement, severing a major artery in the fall. Evidence showed that he tried frantically to staunch the flow of blood with torn pieces of his own clothing, but his efforts were unsuccessful and his dead body was found around midday.

The freight elevator is off limits to the public, but luckily Josh Spencer – owner of the Last Bookstore – took me to see it. We passed by the staff dining room (which is one of the old bank vaults and still has the heavy door and wheel handle) and went into the back area – and there was the elevator.

The elevator floor where Al Brietenbecker bled to death

The elevator has a battered and rusted metal door with no call or floor buttons; you pull a lever inside to stop and go between floors.

Al Brietenbecker fell down this elevator shaft from the third floor

As you can see, when you look upwards you can see the deadly cables hanging down the centre of shaft – the same shaft that Brietenbecker fell down nearly 85 years ago.

As for other ghost sightings, Taylor said that they are reported regularly in the basement, as well as the 9th and 10th floor:

> *"The 9th floor – the last one that was renovated when the building was taken over – used to be an urgent care center, and I thought it was very creepy up there. Because it was fixed last it was very dark, was missing lots of light bulbs, and a few years back one of the guards we had just wouldn't go up there. Even the other tenants would dare each other to go up there."*

Moving up to the 10th floor, Taylor said that he has had many reports of a "transparent man" walking around:

> *"It used to be a law office there, and this figure is wearing 1920s attire. I got a report from one of the*

tenants about it very recently. He seems to think that this figure is watching over him and maybe that floor."

On a recent return visit, security guard Ronaldo mentioned the 3rd floor too:

"The sound of high heels are heard all the time, when there's no one there. They're really loud too, as the floors are marble. One new lady tenant even called me up and asked 'Who is that walking up and down the corridor?'"

There's a mirror set up opposite the front desk so security can see who's coming down the stairs at the end of the corridor, but sometimes it isn't a resident or visiting guest:

"There's a little girl in a white dress, carrying a ball in her hand. I've seen her, and so has my brother and another guy."

Around three years ago, Taylor explained that one of tenants took some direct action against the spirits that were present in the building:

"There are lots of artists here, and there was a lot of buzz about the ghosts. He was a musician, and he said 'I can get rid of the ghosts.' He said he had been hired before, and it was apparently some music he played on his guitar. He went off and he did his thing, and true enough, there were no ghost sightings for at about a year and a half – until they started converting the basement vault into the bar."

That conversion was for a bar/lounge that opened in 2009. Two years in the planning, design and development, the Crocker Club features the massive 1960s-era stainless steel bank vault door as part of its chambers and lounges (removing it was never really an option).

courtesy www.crockerclub.com

Almost as soon as he arrived, the co-owner of the Crocker Club reported that he too could hear the distinctive click clack of high heels and smell a strong perfume. According to a February 25, 2009 article in *Metromix*, psychic medium Jack Rourke visited during construction and claimed to have experienced, via extrasensory perception, "a smartly dressed woman in period attire of the late 1940s or 1950s" and referred to her as "Jane."

Inside "The Crocker" it's a haven of retro/nostalgia décor, but since this can be VIP territory (the chambers and lounges all come with private waitresses and service call lights) you might not get to see the whole underground chamber. There's a number of comfy, private booths (the place where customers used to examine the contents of their safe deposit boxes), but the highlight has to be stepping through the huge circular vault door into the Mosler Lounge (named after the company who made the safe).

Then there's the aptly-named Ghost Bar, a sort of private bar-within-a-bar and a nod to the fact that this old building has strange stories to tell. They serve spirits and "ghostini" drinks of all kinds here, and it's appropriate that this used to be a bank, as a night out here is definitely for well-heeled, well-dressed and well-paid!

If you want to take a trip in the building's resident elevators, walk along the marble floor yourself or sneak a look in the mirror by the security desk, then make your way to Café Nine in Suite 900 (on the 9th floor). Its bright turquoise walls, brown sofas and white tables make it seem like an upscale café, and soon after they opened they were already getting more customers than just the building's tenants.

They do healthy breakfasts, sandwiches and salads, but since I had arrived later in the day I went for the easy-to-make turkey Italian wrap. They recommended I try the salmon patty burger though, and a few minutes later it arrived looking like it had come straight out of a magazine. It tasted just as good, and it seems that executive chef Ellen has created something surprisingly sophisticated for an in-building eatery – it really was a nice surprise.

Even if you're not planning a night of cocktails or feeling hungry, the Spring Arts Tower is worth a visit. Bottom corner tenant The Last Bookstore is full of comfy leather chairs, shelves and shelves of used books and is adorned with art works, sculptures and collages (check out the literary "waves" above the door; it's hundreds of books patterned and folded over wires).

They have readings, art events, comedy nights and DJs and a vinyl record store, and bookstore owner Josh has plans to expand to the floor above too – a "labyrinth" of thousands and thousands of books, all priced at $1 each.

Crocker Club: Wednesday – Friday 5pm-2am, Saturday 9pm-2am
Happy Hour: Wednesday all day, Thursday/Friday 5-7.30pm
Café Nine: Monday – Friday 8.30am-5.30pm
www.crockerclub.com
www.facebook.com/thecrockerclub
http://twitter.com/crockerclubDTLA
www.cafeninedtla.com
www.facebook.com/CafeOnThe9thFloor

Alexandria Hotel
The Gorbals and the Down & Out Bar
501 South Spring Street
Los Angeles, CA 90013
Tel: 213 488 3408 (Gorbals), 213 489 7800 (Down & Out)

The Woman in Black, a "Death Luncheon" and the Lost Rooms

In the foyer at the "Alex" is a long list of former residents. Fred Astaire was in room 841, Sarah Bernhardt resided in 1204, Humphrey Bogart hung his hat in 904 and Charlie Chaplin, Gary Cooper, Joan Crawford, Clark Gable, Greta Garbo, Vivien Leigh,

Mae West and many others stayed here at one time or another – imagine borrowing a cup of sugar from one of those neighbors!

Designed by architect John Parkinson – he and his partner George "Ed" Bergstrom designed the Spring Arts Tower opposite, among many others – the Alexandria Hotel opened in 1906 and stood right at the center of Los Angeles and its budding movie industry (it was here in 1919 that Mary Pickford, Charlie Chaplin, D.W. Griffith and Douglas Fairbanks created their United Artists studio and many early movie companies based their offices).

As the list of past residents show, back then it was a famously grand, glamorous venue in which to live, lunch and play – all marble, statues and chandeliers. Opened in 1911, the opulent Palm Court (now a Historic-Cultural Monument only available for private hire) played host to everything from Presidential speeches to dances where silent screen heartthrob Rudolph Valentino (room 1226) regularly sashayed across the floor with a lucky lady partner.

However, when newer hotels like the Biltmore and the Ambassador began to open up further west, the Alexandria quickly slipped downhill, its misfortune following the earlier news that Albert C. Bilicke, the millionaire who funded the Alexandria Hotel, had been one of the passengers killed when the *Lusitania* was sunk by a German torpedo off the Irish coast in 1915.

Then there was the Depression, which forced a four year closure, and the hotel changed hands and was renovated many times over the following years. The Palm Court's majestic skylight was painted black during World War II and the lobby became a temporary home to U.S. Soldiers, and in 1960 the Palm Court was even used as a temporary boxing ring where fans could play $1 to see their heroes Jose Becerra and Raymundo "Battling" Torres train for fights.

In the late 1960s the owners decided to invest $2m on a Victorian-style renovation, and when actresses Nancy Malone and Lisa Mitchell pointed out its illustrious past they were hired to bring back the sparkle by naming rooms after previous residents and hanging pictures of Tinsel Town stars in the lobby. Crime and the local drug trade then became a scourge downtown, but the Alex still never disappeared entirely.

Aside from the many apartments, Company of Angels – the oldest repertory theater in Los Angeles – is based here, and Ilan Hall, winner of the second season of Bravo's "Top Chef" opened his restaurant The Gorbals in the lobby. Right opposite The Gorbals is the wonderfully-named Down & Out Bar (formerly known as Charlie O's).

A glance online reveals that the Alexandria Hotel has inspired many ghost stories, and when I was first researching *Gourmet Ghosts*, Chris Nichols from *Los Angeles Times Magazine* suggested I contact Veronica Gelakoska. She lived in room 353 at the time, and replied by email:

> *"There is a legion of folks who have seen a ghostly little girl here."*

She also said that the ballroom (presumably she meant the Palm Court) is said to be haunted by "many dancers, including a very shy 17-year-old girl," and there have been several reports (including by Nancy Malone) of a woman dressed in a black dress gliding around the corridors, almost as if she was searching for something.

A possible connection to this desperate woman in black might be found in the newspaper archives of the *Los Angeles Times*. On May 28, 1915 the newspaper reported the suicide of Adele Fairchild, a middle-aged woman from San Francisco. She had checked in under a different name and visited a nearby drug store the previous night, but when she was found dying she told the urgently-summoned doctor:

> *"I want to die. I want to die – so much."*

Sordid.

ENDS MISERY
AS DESIRED

Woman Commits Suicide in Hotel Alexandria.

Story of Wrecked Home Out of the North.

Involves Man Well Known in this City.

She got her wish, and was finally free of an apparently unhappy marriage that had been ruined by her affair with her husband's employer, who had also been his longtime friend. Also, the June 6, 1922 edition reported the suicide of Mrs. H. L. Boyden, a middle-aged woman from Lancaster, Ohio. She registered at the hotel a couple of weeks before (without luggage) but had grown "despondent" at her "lack of money and friends" and swallowed a fatal dose of opium tablets. A sad, unsigned poem was found by her body.

"One other bitter drop to drink and
    then—
No more—
One little pause upon the brink, and
    then—
On o'er.
One pang, and I shall end the
    thrall
Where, grief abides, and generous
    deat will show me all
That now he hides.
One moment, al, and then I shall
Discover,
What all the sages of the earth
    have tried to learn.
One plunge and the stream is
    crossed.
So dark, so deep—
And I shall triumph, or be lost in
    endless sleep.
Then onward, whatso'er my
Fate,
I shall not care,
For sin nor sorrow, jors nor hate
Can touch me there."

Years before that in 1910, there were two deaths in two days during the construction of a 12 story annex and a smaller annex over a property next door. Business was booming, and the decision to add more rooms wasn't a difficult one – until September 2, when the *Los Angeles Times* and *Los Angeles Examiner* reported that Louis Jeffries, nephew of boxer James J. Jeffries, was crushed and killed by a falling steel girder at the annex (most likely the larger of the two).

This tragic accident wasn't what made the headlines though. Instead, they were focused on trumpeting the violence that followed when workers brought the body out onto the street.

LABOR-UNION PICKETS STRIKE DOWN BEARERS OF A WORKMAN'S CORPSE.

At the time, Los Angeles was in the grip of a nasty war between the labor Unions and the anti-Union big businesses, and the accident at the hotel quickly generated into a brawl. Several people were injured in the fighting, and the *Los Angeles Herald* reported later that 12 sticks of dynamite had been found on the curb by the hotel.

The very next day there was another similar accident at the site.

DEATH CLOSE.

DROP OF BEAM HURLS WORKER.

MAN FRIGHTFULLY HURT AT THE ALEXANDRIA ANNEX.

Martin Burkwitz had been thrown off a 24,000 pound girder when a cable – possibly the same one as the day before – slipped and he fell from the second floor to the basement, sustaining many broken bones. "Death Close" said the *Los Angeles Times*, and he did indeed become the second victim of the "Fatal Crane Chain," as the *Los Angeles Examiner* called it.

Less than a month later the Los Angeles Times building was bombed and 21 people were killed in what was called "The Crime of the Century," and two Union-linked people were later charged and convicted of the crime.

Nearly two decades later on November 28, 1922 the *Los Angeles Times* headline trumpeted that a "Poison Death Baffles Police" and declared it a "mystery."

POISON DEATH BAFFLES POLICE

Guest at Alexandria Dies From Cyanide

Woman Registered as His Wife is Hunted

Luncheon for Two Ends in Mystifying Tragedy

The *Los Angeles Examiner* went even further:

'GHOST WOMAN' SOUGHT

It was certainly a strange event; a wealthy, young Oregon rancher named Vaden Elwynne Boge had registered himself and his wife at the hotel, saying that she would be coming later with their luggage. He was given a room on the fourth floor, but no one saw a woman or any luggage arrive before he ordered lunch for two from room service. The waiter who delivered the sandwiches, salad, coffee and pie, saw no sign of anyone in the room either, but soon after, houseman James Hirst heard cries coming from the room and then Boge staggered into the hall shouting:

"I believe I have been poisoned. Get a doctor!"

Boge died soon after, and one of the coffee cups was found to contain potassium cyanide while the other was half empty – yet there was still no evidence of any other person. His family thought he might have been engaged, but even after questioning the hotel staff the Police were still in the dark, and a search of the city's docks was ordered to find his luggage.

Dead Man and Fatal Luncheon

Los Angeles Times

The newspapers showed a picture of the lunch tray, complete with its crumpled napkins and coffee cups, but within a couple of days all was revealed about the "death luncheon" – it had been an elaborate suicide plot that the *Los Angeles Evening Herald* suggested had been inspired by a short story called *The Guest* by Lord Dusany (the pen name of Edward Plunkett, the 18th Baron of Dunsany in Ireland).

"Source Of Death Poison Is Found" noted the *Herald*, explaining that Boge himself had bought the cyanide and had apparently been "melancholy and morose" and "blue" for months, possibly due to ill health. There were some sentimental song lyrics in his notebook and the "homicide squad" interviewed 17-year-old Nadine Linginfelter, a distant relative who Boge had been writing to for several months, but she described him as "a brother to me," and no evidence was found of any wife or "love tryst."

"Boge feasted to death alone" was the headline of a small article in the *Los Angeles Examiner* on November 30, and whether it was illness or rejection in love, the real reason behind his "self-destruction" was probably en route in the mail; Nadine's mother said that Boge had written to his mother two days before he drunk the fatal dose.

POLICE SEARCH DEATH MOTIVE

*Man Who Took Deadly Drug
Wrote Mother*

*Letter May Clear Hotel
Poison Mystery*

*Police Find Boge Purchased
Fatal Powder*

Perhaps even more intriguing is the story of a "ghost wing" at the hotel, which has been empty and sealed off for over 70 years. The second, smaller annex of the two constructed in 1910, its story was told by Hal Illingworth in the *Los Angeles Herald-Examiner* on June 24, 1972.

Many years before, William Chick, the owner of a one story business at 218 West 5th Street, had signed an agreement allowing the Alexandria to build over his property as long as he owned the lease on the new annex, which would have several dozen rooms (sources differ on the exact number: 37, 55 or 60). There were no elevators or stairs to the annex, just corridors, but guests including Winston Churchill, Admiral Dewey and actor Harry Lauder probably never even noticed.

The hotel was on the decline though, and soon after movie producer Phil Goldstone bought the Alexandria in 1938 he was so enraged by (either) some party crashers from the annex or one of the tenants protesting against a rate increase that he sealed off the corridors, entombing the rooms forever.

The dust covered windows of the isolated "Ghost Wing" at the Alexandria Hotel

The rooms in this new "ghost wing" had no furnishings at the time, but the old fashioned claw footed bathtubs, 19th century toilets and cast iron radiators soon began gathering dust – and have been ever since. The only possible way in was by ladder from the street, and since construction work on the annex would be expensive and installing an elevator would wipe out several rooms, it was left as it was. Decades passed by, but since the property taxes were still being paid, the authorities were happy to let things stay at a deadlock.

A recent visit to the Alexandria Hotel management bought confirmation of the story (or at least the legend of it), and looking up from the street outside it's easy to see the dust covered windows (see picture). It seemed likely to remain unused and abandoned to history, but in April 2010 a blog about downtown noted that after 75 years of standing empty, the near 28,000 feet of this ghost annex was on the market for $2.6 million. The real estate company website noted that it has a "huge upside" and though it's arguably a bargain price, it's in need of "complete renovation."

The Gorbals restaurant is in the Alex's lobby, and is definitely worth a visit. Named after a neighborhood in Glasgow, Scotland it reflects Hall's background and his choice to serve rather oddball Scottish/Jewish cuisine – and manager Matt Cwern told me that an unexplained guest had already paid them a visit:

> *"Someone took a picture of a group of people, and when we looked at it you could see a strange face in the picture, almost on the shoulder of one of the people. It was white, and you could see the outline of eyes and a nose."*

Although he couldn't get a copy of the picture, he dismissed any notions of it being a light or a reflection:

> *"I thought about that, but the group had their back to the bar, and there are no mirrors or lights in that direction. I was there when they took the photo, and when I looked at it I thought: 'What is that?'"*

I had read reviews about the non-kosher matzo balls wrapped in bacon, and they came on a bed of pinkish horseradish mayonnaise (the color comes from beet juice; apparently a common Jewish favorite). The matzo balls were savory, like polenta, and the long strips of bacon fitted round them perfectly; much better than a "pig in a blanket."

The menu "changes frequently" says Matt, but it's often along the lines of pig's ear, Welsh rarebit (essentially egg on toast), latkes in smoked apple sauce and Persian cucumbers. If you really want to go for it (vegetarians beware!) there is a $50 half-cut, roasted pig head (though it takes about 60-90 minutes to cook, so you have to pre-order).

The dull silver steel-topped bar showcases the bottles of gin, rum, tequila and Scotch (though you can gets beers, wine and cocktails too), and there are benches if you like the communal experience and want to watch the open kitchen, or bar stools that, though they look more like solid wooden crates, are still comfortable.

Just a few steps away is the Down & Out Bar, which is about as close as you can get to a local sports fan's heaven. The "DNO" is a huge place complete with pool tables ($1 each), pinball machines, arcade games, big red booths (and red lights), pictures of 1950s swimsuit girls on the bar and walls, and lots of massive HD televisions showing sports, sports and sports – including UK soccer. Their logo is a soused clown with Xs for eyes, and though it proudly declares itself to be a bar for locals, I found everyone to be very friendly and was instantly comfortable with a 24 oz can of Tecate for $6, though there are drink specials and offers too ($4 Hi Life Tall Boys).

At weekends between 10.30am-3pm Beanie's Pop-Up Brunch (a sort of wet bar/hot plate indoor food stand) in the back corner will serve you up biscuits 'n gravy Benedict, omelets, eggs, pancakes and, from the "Secret Menu," burritos, BLT, Monte Cristo sandwiches – all of them perfect hangover/brunch treats. When I was last there "Beanie" himself was playing pool, and there's often music or a DJ here too.

If sports aren't your thing, then examine the back wall: it has dozens of black and white celebrity mug shots (which they keep right up to date), while behind the bar are huge mug shots of the latest stars to fall from grace.

On your way out, check out the colorful and sometimes bizarre murals on the outside of the windows – they change regularly and are by local artists – and try and get a DNO business card: it says that "If this cardholder is passed out, please return them to the Down & Out."

Other food in the building comes courtesy of Coronado's Mexican Restaurant and Bar, which opened in late 2010 in one of the Alexandria's street level spaces. It's an open, 3,000 square foot restaurant showcasing Latin-American art and – as I can confirm – making delicious burritos. It's owned by Gilbert Coronado and his son Robert, who told me that he was going to "keep making it colorful." They can cook up that big burrito ($6.25), tacos, spicy wings, quesadillas and the like, but the *carne asada* fries alone are worth visiting for.

If you're a late night music fan, then you'll want to check out upstairs in the Alex. Opposite The Gorbals and behind a nondescript door is the Mezzanine, home to the rough n' ready Mezz Bar, whose low, classical design ceiling and creepy cherub faces used to tower over the lobby. Events and hours vary, but you can have a martini or a bourbon in a sort of speakeasy-vibe and catch everything from burlesque to the free monthly comedy club.

Once you're back home, catch the hotel on the silver screen in *Domino* (2005), *Dreamgirls* (2006), *Spider-Man 3* (2007) and *Se7en* (1995), where it was the location of serial killer "John Doe's" apartment.

Gorbals: Monday – Wednesday 6pm-midnight
Thursday – Saturday 6pm-2am
Happy Hour: Monday – Friday 6-8pm ($4 beers, wine 50% off)
Down & Out Bar: Monday – Friday 12pm-2am, Sat/Sun 10am-2am
www.thegorbalsla.com
🛦 The Gorbals
http://twitter.com/thegorbals
www.downandoutbar.com
http://twitter.com/thedownandout

Traxx Restaurant and Bar
Union Station
800 North Alameda Street
Los Angeles, CA 90012
Tel: 213 625 1999

The 1871 Massacre and the
"Tiger Woman" Trunk Murder

Traxx may only have opened a decade or so ago, but it's been a very visible part of the regeneration of downtown LA as both a reminder of the glamorous past and a promise of the future. Not only that, it's located in one of the most beautiful – and famous – places in Los Angeles. Mystery writer Michael Connelly even mentions it in *The Brass Verdict* (2009):

> *"We went over to Traxx Union Station...They gave us a table in a quiet enclosure next to a window that looked out on the train station's huge and wonderful waiting room."*

That waiting room is indeed huge and wonderful, and certainly proves that appearances can be deceptive – from the outside, Union Station doesn't seem that big at all. It looks like a Spanish mission, but inside an English country house/Viking dining hall comes into the mix, the three story high beamed ceilings and the patterned terracotta and marble floors giving it a real sense of grandeur – almost like a cathedral.

With its chandeliers, massive leather chairs and "streamline moderne" Art Deco décor, Union Station is worth coming to see, even if you're not planning on hopping the subway or taking the train across the state or the country. It's a fantastic place for people watching, and the small garden patios on each side of the waiting room are a peaceful, mosaic-covered spot to take your coffee, lunch, newspaper or book. In the early days, passengers disembarked from trains and walked straight through the southern garden on their way out.

Take a seat in one of the big chairs in the waiting room and imagine the station back in the golden age of Hollywood, when nervous young men and women stepped off the train with a suitcase and hopes of being a star. Sadly it usually didn't turn out that way, and they often walked out into the night and were never seen again.

Union Station has made it to the big screen though. It served as a backdrop for *Union Station* (1950) starring William Holden and Nancy Olson, even though the movie was meant to be set in New York, and has made regular appearances ever since in *Blade Runner* (1982), *Predator 2* (1990), *Speed* (1994), *Star Trek: First Contact* (1996), *Pearl Harbor* (2001), *Catch Me If You Can* (2002), *The Island* (2005), *Drag Me To Hell* and *(500) Days of Summer* (both 2009).

There are some celebrities here too. At the top of an escalator at the rear of the station is *A Train* by Bill Bell (1996), one of the many public art projects on the Los Angeles Metro. At first glance it simply looks like 12 flashing vertical nightclub-style lights, but when you get on the elevator the effect is like a movie projector, connecting all the fiber optic patterns and colors together. For just a few moments you see glittering images of a train, a city bus, a Chinese letter and the faces of famous people from history and the movies.

Fresh from designing the Los Angeles City Hall, Union Station was partially designed by father and son team of John and Donald B. Parkinson, though when it opened in May 1939 few people knew that it had virtually been built on top of the site of a bloody and horrifying riot that occurred when Los Angeles was just a small backwater. According to a "Reminiscence" piece in the fledgling *Los Angeles Times* on October 27, 1883, the "Chinese Massacre" took place on October 24, 1871 and saw 500 Anglos and Latinos enter Calle de los Negros (Negro Alley) to attack, robe and murder the Chinese residents of what was then known as "Old" Chinatown.

Recollections of the Chinese Massacre of 1871.

Fearful Scenes Enacted in a Few Hours—A Mob Worse than Wild Beasts—Burial Place of the Victims.

The riot was triggered by the wounding of a Police officer and the subsequent murder of a local saloon owner who came to his aid. Officer Jesus Bilderrain had heard gunfire and found an injured man, Ah Choy, before giving chase into a building and being shot. A bystander named Robert Thompson then opened fire into the building and was himself shot.

It emerged that the dispute was between two Chinese factions arguing over Yut Ho, a woman who had been kidnapped for a forced marriage, but later research suggested that corruption, false evidence and theft also played their part in the racially-fueled violence and lynching that followed. There were 17 confirmed deaths (including some boys), but eight of the ten people found guilty at trial were freed on a technicality, the whole affair seemingly swept under the carpet as an embarrassment to the growing city.

This "Old Chinatown" was later moved to make way for Union Station (Apablasa Street being razed and now buried at least 15 feet underneath it), while Calle de Los Negros became part of Los Angeles Street, which leads straight down to the station.

Rumors of grisly discoveries found during the construction of Union Station are false, though a human burial was found some 70 years later in July 1989, when the Metro Red Line was being built.

The burial was outside cemetery grounds, but identification and a cause of death was impossible to determine: analysis only confirmed that it was an adult around 5ft 3" who had been buried between 1650 and 1950.

However, it is certainly true that several corpses have been found in Union Station. On January 26, 1943 the *Los Angeles Times* and the *Los Angeles Herald-Express* reported the arrest of dining car cook Robert E. Lee Folkes at Union Station.

THE MYSTERY OF LOWER BERTH 13
Murder Strikes on a Running California-Bound Train

MRS. MARTHA VIRGINIA BRINSON JAMES, who was slain in Pullman berth on Southern Pacific's San Francisco-bound West

*Both images by permission of Hearst Communications, Inc.,
Hearst Newspapers Division.*

The "Lower 13" murderer, as he became known, was accused of cutting the throat of new bride Martha Virginia James on the journey between Seattle and California some days before.

Folkes, who had apparently been arrested many times for drunkenness and "molesting white women" was quoted as saying "I didn't do the killing," and evidence was initially hard to find. There was no weapon or motive, though early witnesses on the train had heard James say "I can't stand this any longer," before there was a loud thump.

Cook on Death Train Seized on Arrival Here

Arrested at Union Station for Questioning; Police Check on Stories Told by Two Girls

Folkes later confessed to the crime and was transported back to Oregon under heavy guard to face trial. The key witness was a Marine, Harold Wilson, the occupier of the Upper 13 berth. He had tried to help the dying victim and saw "a dark man" running away down the corridor, but when he gave chase he saw nothing but a trail of blood and an open door.

Just over a year later in early May 1944, the newspapers reported that an antique black trunk sent from Chicago had been opened – just after midnight – by express office clerk Eugene Bildeneau. Inside he made the gruesome discovery of a bound woman encrusted in salt and wrapped in a bloody sheet and various clothes.

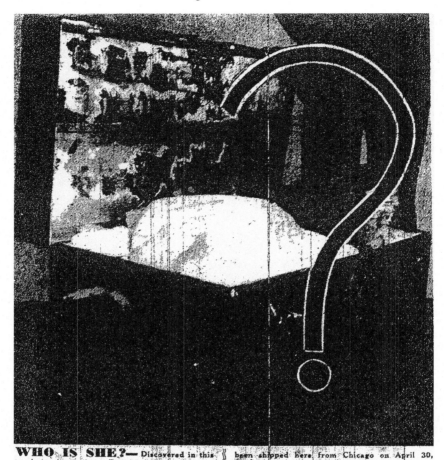

WHO IS SHE?— Discovered in this trunk in the Railway Express offices at Union Station yesterday was the nearly nude body of a ... been shipped here from Chicago on April 30, arriving Thursday. Labels on articles of clothing established the victim's home as being Los An...

By permission of Hearst Communications, Inc., Hearst Newspapers Division.

The trunk had been sent by a man called "John Lopez," who was planning to collect it after taking the bus to Los Angeles. The coroner made an early diagnosis that since there were no visible wounds the victim may have been poisoned, suffocated or died of natural causes, and the newspapers followed the story as the LAPD tried to establish the victim's identity.

Despite suggestions from Chicago authorities that it could be missing person Louise Villegas, she was listed as "Jane Doe 13" while Police began looking for Solyo Villegas, who had hired a cab to take him and a heavy trunk to Dearborn Station.

Villegas and his now-missing wife had recently registered at a hotel as Mr. and Mrs. John Lopez, and when they left the bed was found to have been stripped bare.

Trunk Slaying Admitted by Man Held in Texas

Suspect Confesses He Killed Wife in Chicago in Drunken Argument and Shipped Body Here

A couple of days later the "trunk murder mystery" was solved. Villegas was tracked down in Texas and confessed that he had killed his wife. They had recently bigamously married, and he claimed that she had asked for a divorce so she could marry another man. Despite Villegas' story of a fight, the official cause of death was suffocation and he was extradited to Chicago for trial.

Years before that at predecessor La Grande Station, a sensational double murder saw Winnie Ruth Judd, a 26-year-old medical secretary earn nasty nicknames like "Tiger Woman," "Velvet Tigress" and the "Butcher Blonde."

In October 19, 1931 inspectors looking for illegal deer meat became suspicious when one of her two trunks began leaking blood, so they called her in to collect them. She said she would return with the key, and they noted down her license plate as she was leaving. She never returned of course, and inside one of the trunks, clad only in a negligee, was Agnes Anne LeRoi, 32, while in the other was the dismembered corpse of Hedvig Samuelson, 24, two people that Judd called her "best friends".

The two women had been reported missing from Phoenix for several days – as had Judd – and after tracking the license plate to Santa Monica, Judd's husband agreed to help find her and placed newspaper advertisements begging her to turn herself in. Suffering from an injured hand, Judd did so several days later and told a story of a jealous fight between the three of them over the same man – John J. "Happy Jack" Halloran.

Controversy raged over what happened and Judd initially claimed insanity, though during the unsuccessful trial of Halloran as her accomplice she said that she fired in self defense when Samuelson and LeRoi both tried to attack her – during which she was shot in the hand. The bodies were then shipped to La Grande at 2nd/Santa Fe, with the idea of dumping them in the ocean.

GUARD TRUNK KILLER; FEAR SUICIDE

'Velvet Tigress' Fights to Escape Noose; 'No Doubt of Sanity,' States Jurors

The evidence was damning, and after a sensational trial the *Los Angeles Examiner* reported on February 9, 1932 that she had been convicted of first degree murder:

Ruth Judd, Guilty in First Degree, Doomed to Hang!

She however narrowly avoided execution and was sent to an insane asylum in Phoenix, from which she escaped seven times. A special cell was eventually built for her, and she was finally released in the early 1970s, dying in 1998 aged 93. Later investigation pointed to a second gun and alleged that Halloran was involved, though the truth is unlikely to ever be known. Despite this bloody past and being located in a neighborhood that was once filled with opium dens and women's boarding houses (the code for brothels back then), I just couldn't find any eyewitnesses to any mysterious or spooky events here. "I could tell you many strange stories, but none of them are about ghosts," said Inder, one of the volunteers who staff the information booth (and helps many a lost traveler).

However, if there are any other spirits here, they could well be hiding out. Two places within Union Station are used regularly for weddings, parties, photo shoots and filming; the magnificent hall on your left as you enter (which used to be the ticket office), and then directly across the patio outside – look for the RESTAURANT sign in the glass high above you – is the location of the last "Harvey House" station restaurant/lounge.

An Art Deco fantasy of crazy, zig zag floor tiles and a u-shaped counter and balcony, it was one of a chain of eateries that were popular in the days before buffet cars, and was designed by visionary architect Mary Jane Colter. Her work was inspired by Hopi, Zuni, Navajo and Mexican motifs and she seemed to have a great connection to Native American beliefs – maybe even the supernatural. She suggested the name of one of her most famous commissions – the isolated Phantom Ranch at the bottom of the Grand Canyon – and perhaps the closed-off remains of her work at Union Station are a safe supernatural sanctuary (at least for now).

Over 1,500,000 passengers pass through Union Station every year, and many of them drop in to owner/chef Tara Thomas's Traxx Restaurant for a bite. Taking its cue from the splendor of the station around it, the lunch and dinner menu at Traxx is high-end, expensive dining (Waldorf salad, hangar steak, jumbo lump crab cakes, a Reuben with corned beef and Russian dressing on rye), so it's not quite the place for a quick snack before you catch your train.

As for me, I always prefer to go across the waiting room to the Traxx Bar for one of their famous Traxx Martinis (two parts Hendricks Gin, a hint of dry Vermouth and a float of Dubonnet

Rouge). You can order food in the bar (it comes from the restaurant) and my recommendation is the Traxx Burger "cooked to your liking."

There's a definite *film noir* feel in the bar, and when you go in at night you can only see silhouettes: are they drinkers drowning their sorrows, reveling in an affair, celebrating a reunion, or just killing time? The outdoor tables are roped off like a private club, and since the restaurant and bar both have luxurious, brown leather seats too, they fit right in with Union Station – it's as if they have been here since day one.

Also, if you're a First Class passenger on the West Coast Starliner, you get breakfast fruit and orange juice and even a drink as early as 9am (Bloody Mary's are very popular at that time of day the bartender assured me). Union Station itself is open 24 hours a day – like Los Angeles, it never stops.

Lunch: Monday – Friday 11.30am-2.30pm
Dinner: Monday – Saturday 5-9.30pm
Traxx Bar also open Sunday 1.30-8pm (sometimes later)
www.traxxrestaurant.com
❑ Traxx Restaurant
http://twitter.com/TraxxRestaurant

Chapter 4
Mid-Wilshire

El Coyote
7312 Beverly Boulevard
Los Angeles, CA 90036
Tel: 323 939 2255

Sharon Tate's Last Meal and The Back Room...

If there's one place that everyone in L.A. seems to know, it's El Coyote. A Los Angeles institution, it was opened by Blanche and George March on March 5, 1931 at 1st Street and La Brea and moved a little further up the street to Beverly Boulevard some 20 years later.

John Wayne was often seen at the bar, Princess Grace and Prince Rainier of Monaco once walked in unannounced, and a young Drew Barrymore spent many evenings with her famous family here. One time Penélope Cruz and then-boyfriend Josh Hartnett were chased by paparazzi after arriving and finding that all the more private booths were taken, while other people who have slid into a booth here include Kevin Spacey, George Lopez, Kathleen Turner, Jim Carrey and Quentin Tarantino.

El Coyote has sailed quietly through the decades, though August 8, 1969, is definitely a notorious date in their history: that was the night when a heavily pregnant Sharon Tate and her friends Jay Sebring, Wojciech Frykowski and Abigail Folger ate here.

It was probably their last meal, as in the early hours the next day they – and another unrelated person – were brutally killed by members of Charles Manson's "Family" in arguably the most infamous murder in Hollywood history.

'RITUALISTIC SLAYINGS'
Sharon Tate, Four Others Murdered

Arnoldo, a manager who has worked here for decades (he's currently in his 30th year) admitted that it was the most frightening story about El Coyote – except for this one:

> *"There was a beautiful waitress from Alaska who worked here about four years. She said that she could feel different energies – a kind of "sixth sense" – and wouldn't go into the back room when the lights were out, ever. She couldn't say what it was (in there) but she got shaky and real scared."*

A colorful, noisy restaurant/bar that's deceptively large (eight rooms and a patio), there's definitely the chance for some star spotting here, though you must come early to avoid a long wait for dinner. Mid afternoon it's much quieter, and you can settle into one of the booths and relax with chips, salsa and one of their famous house margaritas or a Coyote Cosmo (vodka, triple sec, cranberry juice, DeKuyper and peach schnapps).

I've been coming here since I first arrived in Los Angeles, and the corn tamales are one of my regular choices. The chicken taco salad in its crispy shell is surprisingly filling for something so healthy, and the burritos come highly recommended – they could sink a battleship. There's also the "Enchilada Howard," which was named in honor of their very first customer. El Coyote serves around 1000 meals every day, and with the decorative chili pepper fairy lights and mirror/shell mosaics that Blanche made herself on the walls, it's definitely a legend in its own lifetime. See if you can find the "Mexican man" (complete with sombrero) in his glass case.

Sunday – Thursday 11.30am-10pm, Friday/Saturday 11.30am-11pm
www.elcoyotecafe.com
El Coyote Cafe
http://twitter.com/elcoyotecafe

Original Farmers Market
6333 West 3rd Street
Los Angeles, CA 90036
Tel: 323 866 9211 / 866 993 9211 (toll free)

Arthur and Earl – long gone but still here…

For several generations of Angelenos, the direction to "Meet me at 3rd and Fairfax" has meant a trip to one of the city's most famous and lively outdoor landmarks, the Farmers Market. They celebrated their 75th Anniversary in 2009, and now several million visitors a year come eat, drink and shop in a place that originally started out as a simple dairy farm.

The owner of those 250 or so acres back then was Arthur F. Gilmore, and his life changed overnight when he accidentally struck oil in 1905 (an event that allegedly inspired "The Beverly Hillbillies" television show; the CBS studios are right next door). Gilmore gave up farming almost immediately, and over the following decades "Gilmore Island" became not only the source of Gilmore Oil, but home to the Farmers Market and sports events of all kind.

Gilmore had a passion for speed, and in 1934 the Gilmore Stadium opened its doors to showcase midget car racing (the cars all running on Gilmore Gas, naturally). Fans could also watch rodeos, wrestling or boxing, and the stadium was also home to The Bulldogs, the very first football team in Los Angeles. Baseball got a look in too, and nearby Gilmore Field (built in 1939) was home of the aptly-named Hollywood Stars, a minor league baseball team part-owned by celebrities including Bing Crosby, Barbara Stanwyck and Cecil B. DeMille.

They knocked it out of the park from 1939-1957, but even with star-studded crowds and Jayne Mansfield as "Miss Hollywood Star" in 1955 they were displaced in town when the Brooklyn Dodgers arrived. The stadium, field and even the later drive-in movie theater disappeared over time too (the field is now the CBS parking lot), but they're not entirely forgotten: you can see memorabilia at numerous displays around the market and there's a vintage "gas station" with an automobile waiting to be filled up with Gilmore's very best.

The story of the Farmers Market itself began when entrepreneurs Roger Dahlhjelm and Fred Beck came up with an idea that they thought could help fight a way out of the Depression. Earl B. Gilmore – AF's son – was in charge by this time, and in July 1934 a number of farmers paid 50 cents and drove onto an empty patch of his land to sell fresh flowers, fruit, vegetables and more. Customers soon came from miles around, and a sharp-thinking woman named Blanche Magee began selling sandwiches out of her picnic hamper to the hungry farmers – and then to their customers.

She opened the first restaurant here, Magee's Kitchen, and Magee's Nuts soon after. Both are still open for business, and Magee's Nuts grinds about 100,000 pounds of fresh peanut butter every year (movie legend Lauren Bacall has hers shipped to New York). It's been run by Phyllis, the daughter-in-law of Blanche, for several decades now, and on one notable day in 1964 a group of four British lads named The Beatles paid a visit and sent a thank you letter for the "fab" peanut butter when they got back to Liverpool (it's on display in a frame).

The Farmers Market is certainly one of the most popular places in Los Angeles, and it seems that the Gilmore dynasty is still keeping an eye on the hot spot that they created. When asked about the supernatural side of the Farmers Market, David Hamlin of WHPR instantly mentioned a former employee who worked in the Gilmore Adobe, the former Gilmore family home that was built in 1852 and became the company office:

> *"For a number of years the late KC Marelich worked there. She was in that structure every day and the nature of her work kept her there many evenings as well. I knew (and admired) KC and I knew her to be a completely sensible and rational woman with a solid grasp of reality and a good head on her shoulders. She was absolutely convinced that there was a presence in the adobe – a spirit or ghost – and she was quite certain that it was either Arthur or Earl Gilmore."*

In all likelihood Earl was born, lived and died in the Adobe, and Hamlin thought that the continuing presence of Gilmore (father and son?) has been one of the reasons that the Market has remained so constant and so successful. Marelich died several years ago, but Hamlin noted:

> *"She shared her story with me personally, and I can attest to the fact that she well and truly believed it."*

Sadly the Gilmore Adobe is not open to the public, but there is another unusual story about a mischievous – and thirsty – Arthur Gilmore. In December 2008 Security Director Virginia Champeau was leading a meeting with five other staff members in one of the Farmers Market office rooms (they're on the upper deck), and had been to The Coffee Corner below to get her favorite drink, black coffee with a dash of cream:

> *"But it was too hot and I burnt my tongue, so I put the cup down on a filing cabinet in the room, right by one of the staff who was leaning on it, and then turned back to the meeting. When I turned back a little while later there was nothing there but a ring of coffee on the cabinet – the cup was gone! That room's door only opens in, so no one could have come in and taken it without all of us seeing them, and we were all so confused that we went to the kitchen to look for the cup – it was in the trash."*

I asked whether the person leaning on the cabinet had perhaps let temptation get the better of him, but she said no:

> *"He wasn't near the cup, and besides that we could all see him. He never left the room either."*

She mentioned it to Shariff, then the Market Manager, who had been working at the Farmers Market for around 30 years:

> *"He looked at me and said: 'You know that's how Arthur Gilmore liked his coffee – with just a little cream?' So my advice for anyone here in the future is: put some sugar in it!"*

Though this coffee-snatching happened in the office and Marelich only ever felt a presence in the Adobe, it's not at all hard to imagine that Gilmore – and his son – often take a stroll around the rest of the Farmers Market, just to see that all is well.

As for recommending a place to eat here, that's a difficult question: there are so many choices. For many Angelenos (including me) the Farmers Market is a second home, an outdoor office (Walt Disney worked on some of his Disneyland designs here) and a popular place to meet up. You'll often find me at EB's Bar (which was named in honor of Earl), and if you're hungry you really can't go wrong anywhere, no matter what time of day it is.

Patsy D'Amore's argues that it was the first place in L.A. to sell the new-fangled "pizza pie" and there's popcorn, ice cream and donuts too (Bob's Doughnuts bakes around 1,000 a day – go for the raised glaze). You can also try something from nearly 20 different ethnic or cultural cuisines including New Orleans gumbo, Brazilian barbeque and Indonesian/Malay/Indian curry. Fish fans can sample the shrimp at Tusquellas Fish & Oyster Bar or there's French, Mexican, Texas BBQ, Chinese food – the list goes on and on.

If you twist my arm, I'll admit that some of my favorites include the Gumbo Pot (try the Gumbo Ya Ya, sweet potato chips and chocolate beignets), the ever-busy Pampas Grill (sirloin, lamb, Brazilian sausage, chicken and beef), or Du-Par's, the old-style US restaurant/bakery with their "Beat The Clock" meal between 4-6pm – the time you arrive is the price you pay.

One insider's tip I do have is to take your food upstairs to the Dining Deck. Not only is it quiet but there's often a cool breeze blowing through the windows, which offer some great views of the Hollywood Hills. The occasional movie and television star can be seen wandering around the Farmers Market too, and Greta Garbo was one of the earliest fans – it's changed quite a lot from the days when all the diners had four legs and udders!

Louis DeRosa's grandfather opened Marconda's Meats in 1941, and like most of the 100 stalls here it's a family business – something that he feels makes the Farmers Market unique, and something a visitor should not miss:

"It's different than any other place in the state. It's like a step back to different times, and as modern and high tech as life is, the flair is still for old time service."

Open daily, stall hours vary
www.farmersmarketla.com
www.facebook.com/farmersmarketla
http://twitter.com/Farmersmarketla

HMS Bounty
Gaylord Apartments
3357 Wilshire Boulevard
Los Angeles, CA 90010
Tel: 213 385 7275

"He heard a huge thump on the roof..."

The "Food & Grog" sign and the porthole swing doors might make you think the HMS Bounty is perhaps the very definition of a themed bar/restaurant, but as the old mechanized cash register suggests, there's a difference: it's been around for 90 years.

Opened as "The Gay Room" in 1921, it's on the street level of The Gaylord apartments that were built by eccentric millionaire Henry Gaylord Wilshire (the man who also gave his name to the famous 16 mile Boulevard that runs from downtown to the beaches of Santa Monica).

An influential figure in the history of Los Angeles, Wilshire was an outspoken Socialist who won and lost several fortunes before dying destitute in 1927.

The bar was called the "Dining Room" in the 1950s and after acquiring the nautical decorations – many paintings and scale models of the ship involved in the 1789 mutiny – it officially became the HMS Bounty in 1962.

Busy at lunch and always crowded at cocktail hour, it was a favorite for celebrities and musical legends like Duke Ellington and Sarah Vaughn, who sometimes played here after gigs at the

Cocoanut Grove in the Ambassador Hotel opposite, a place where black performers weren't allowed to eat or drink.

Today, Mexican-born Juan Castaneda (known to everyone as "Ramon") explains that he keeps the HMS Bounty "ship shape and Bristol fashion" (an English naval term that means he runs it the way his mentor and former owner Gordon "Gordie" Fields would like it), and an article on the wall notes that Ramon started here as a teenager and has worked every job until he now has a controlling stake in the bar.

As for any unusual stories, he mentioned the rumor of a tunnel connecting "the Bounty" to the Ambassador Hotel, the location of Robert F. Kennedy's 1968 assassination, but admitted that though the Ambassador itself was said to be haunted, no ghosts have ever taken the tunnel across to visit.

In The Gaylord, Senior Resident Manager Esther Fenton said that strange happenings were so common here that they were often mentioned just in passing, and that it's only new residents who say anything:

"Lots of people here have seen and felt things, but they always seem to be unthreatening, even playful. Sometimes I can be in an apartment and get a chill, but it seems things happen all over the buildings – especially the 8th, 9th and 14th floor – and even in my apartment on the 1st floor."

Fenton herself has a regular unexplained experience:

"Often when I turn off the television at night and go to bed, it turns itself back on. Sometimes I wake up in the night and it's been switched back on again – and I am certain I didn't leave it on. I never feel threatened; it's more something mischievous I think. One night I even shouted out 'leave the damn thing off!' and it didn't turn back on again."

She also mentioned that she spoke to a woman resident on the 8th floor who had a story to tell. Leaving the apartment with her son one morning, the boy asked: "Who's that lady by the elevator?" but when she looked down the corridor, there was no one there. She also said that some residents have claimed to see a child in one of the corridors and that they feel they're "not alone" when they're in the basement or in the building late at night.

In the lobby, displays of menus, old keys, signing-in books, magazines and monogrammed bars of soap confirm its place in local history, and black and white pictures show that it was a favorite residence for many silent movie actors and actresses (Ronald Reagan had an apartment there at one time).

Unfortunately, some guests chose to permanently end their stay by "taking a header off the roof":

"Around 20, 25 years ago the new owner – still the owner now – was outside on the patio and he heard a huge thump on the roof of the HMS Bounty. He knew what it was straight away. We have an alarm system on the roof now, so no one can get up there."

The *Los Angeles Times* archives doesn't contain any reports of suicides at HMS Bounty or The Gaylord, though there was a deadly fire here on February 27, 1951 that undoubtedly shook one of Hollywood's legends:

Louis B. Mayer Brother Dies as Bedroom Burns

The headline didn't even mention the name of the victim, Rudolph W. Mayer, brother of the MGM legend, who had died from a heart attack after a blaze began in his bedroom. The apparent cause was a discarded cigarette.

Ironically, on a recent visit the friendly Desk Clerk told me that Wilshire himself was "fire mad" and had rooms constructed so that even if two gallons of gas was set alight with a match, it wouldn't be dangerous. He added that about five years ago the sprinklers were activated when a toaster caused a fire, and they gushed so fiercely that the room was soon a foot deep in water. That water eventually cascaded down the stairs, causing more damage than the fire itself, and the attending firefighters said that this was probably one of the safest buildings in Los Angeles.

A number of older residents have also passed away while they were living here: noted businessman Fred L. Baker (1927), ex-Dallas Federal Bank official William Barnes Newsome (1929), pastor's wife Minnie Aked (1934), Estelle Loeb, widow of the former French Consul (1935), and noted songwriter and vaudeville star Gus Edwards (1945). Edwards discovered Eddie Cantor and other talents of the era, and was played by Bing Crosby in the 1939 movie of his life called *The Star Maker*.

Lastly, even though The Gaylord is a residents-only building, bar customers must go through a door with a huge wooden "Sailor's Rest" carving on it to visit the bathroom. Men will need to take a trip down to the basement in the elevator, but the ladies' is in the lobby, and there have been stories of a cheeky ghost pinching women on the behind when they're in the smallest room – and even a face leering at them in the mirror!

Whether or not there are any strange spirits in the building, it's certainly worth visiting the HMS Bounty for a very friendly welcome and a semi-surreal nautical experience. The low ceilings make you feel like you're stepping into a ship's galley, there are more portholes on the wall and nearly every booth has a plaque above it celebrating past and present regulars and proving that this is more than a novelty bar.

The seagoing theme continues on the "Bill of Fare," which is surprisingly extensive (it is very surf n' turf, but there's also burgers, lamb, steaks, salmon, beef, chicken, pork, shrimp and salads). You can also have soup from "the kettle" and select from Mr. Christian's Board (including the "Bounty Combination," a half sandwich with dinner salad or soup) or the dignified-sounding London Club or the Monte Cristo from Captain Bligh's Board.

The Koreatown locale probably inspired the cartoon for the daily "Wise Man" drink special (a beer and a shot of whisky), and though the menu warns that "prices subject to change while eating," it's a great place for a drink or something more hale and hearty. As for insider tips, it's worth knowing that the "Wise Man" special actually applies all day, and that there's a special $3.95 menu from 12.30-5.30 on Sundays too.

Monday – Saturday 11am-2am, Sunday 12pm-midnight
Happy Hour: 5.30-9.30pm (beer and a shot $5.50)
www.thehmsbounty.com
HMS-Bounty
www.thegaylordapartments.com

Mandrake Bar
2692 South La Cienega Boulevard
Los Angeles, CA 90034
Tel: 310 837 3297

A Ghostly Photograph and a Deadly Robbery

As some might recognize immediately, the name of this bar has a connection to things devilish and dangerous. A plant within the nightshade family, the mandrake is not only poisonous and contains hallucinogens, the roots often make it look like a human figure, which was why neo-pagan religions often used it in magic rituals.

From the Book of Genesis onward, mandrake has been described as potion to seduce a woman, and it's appeared in comics, manga, video games and even the movie *Pan's Labyrinth*. Fans of JK Rowling will know all about the mandrake too; when you pull one out of the ground it screams so loud that unless you're wearing earmuffs, it kills you!

Co-owner Flora Wiegmann-Heitzler chose the name after a friend suggested it to them, and had no idea about its origin:

"We liked the word first, then figured out what it all meant."

Flora, her husband Drew and third co-owner Justin Beal rebuilt the bar after buying it in 2005, and then threw open the doors to the public in June 2006:

"It's pretty much always been a gay bar, and we know that because when we were building we found a plastic box above the bar. It had been deliberately put there, and it was a time capsule. Inside it had business cards from every bar that had been here before, some handwritten notes and other things. We saw the past names of the bar: Manhandler (there was a big hand round the "H" on the logo), JJ's Irish Pub, Maverick's, Wonderbar and others."

Back in October 1981 when the bar was called Manhandler, Warren Kaslo of Schuyler Falls, New York was killed in a hold up here, and the *Los Angeles Times* article of June 17, 1982 noted the unusual ending to the story. Having plugged away for eight months, Wilshire Division detectives Fred Miller and Sherman Oaks finally got their man, Allen "Babe" Geller, when they – bizarrely – arrested him in a hospital. Geller had gone there to get treatment for gallstones and thought that Det. Oaks was a doctor – until he took out handcuffs.

By the early 1990s, this location was the home of JJ's Irish Pub ("Where Irish Guys Are Smiling"), and the owner was a man named Seamus. His boyfriend – Flora didn't know his name – worked as the cook, and had a sudden and tragic end:

> *"One night he left the kitchen and stepped out for just a moment – and had a heart attack. Died right there. Seamus came in just once, soon after we opened, to wish us luck. He looked older than he maybe was – he was in a wheelchair – but he never mentioned it."*

Having grown up in what she felt was a haunted house (the previous owner had hung himself in the basement), Flora felt she was sensitive to "that stuff" and quickly felt something when she was first working at the Mandrake:

> *"I was here alone, tiling the ladies bathroom, and something felt weird – like I wasn't alone and that there was someone outside. At night here I never feel like I'm by myself – it's like there's still someone in here."*

Amazingly, there is photographic evidence that might prove something otherworldly is still in the bar:

> *"When we were building the place out – dry walling etcetera – my business partner Justin was taking pictures all the time so we could see how things looked. Then he took a picture where there was a strange light in the corner."*

© *Justin Beal*

On the left side of the picture there's a large, human-sized apparition or shape, and though the apparition has never been seen since, Flora dismisses any idea that the picture is a hoax:

> *"The picture is totally real. We were standing at the bar later, and when Justin looked at the picture and saw that, he kind of freaked out. We had no idea what it could be, until an old timer at the bar mentioned that the apparition was in exactly the same place where the cook – Seamus's boyfriend – had died."*

The decor is rather minimalist, a mix of glittery silver (there's a giant disco ball and a shiny bar) and pine paneling that's reminiscent of a sauna. New artworks were recently installed here as well, and the crowd is always hip and lively. There's no serious food at the Mandrake now, just a limited selection of snacks like cured meats, cheeses, fresh baguette, nuts and olives, but there's a plethora of beers and cocktails to choose from, and the Happy Hour can be a tough choice: choosing between a shot of whiskey and a Pabst Blue Ribbon or a Tecate and a shot of Tequila.

As for entertainment, there's something on here almost every night (it could be an art launch, storyteller, DJ, singer, band or a movie night) and if you can't visit, you could always click on their website "archive" section and see the ghostly photograph and a couple of business cards from the past bars. As they say here:

"Yes of course, always Mandrake!"

Sunday/Monday 6pm-midnight
Tuesday – Thursday 5pm-midnight
Friday/Saturday 5pm-1am
Happy Hour: Daily 5-7pm ($5 PBR and a shot of whisky or Tecate and a shot of tequila, $2 off house cocktails)
21+ only
www.mandrakebar.com
www.facebook.com/mandrakebar.com
http://twitter.com/mandrakebar

Sweet Lady Jane (formerly Ma Maison)
8360 Melrose Avenue
Los Angeles, CA 90069
Tel: 323 653 7145

Orson Welles' Favorite...

In a town where looking fabulous is the golden rule, it's hard to imagine that a bakery selling devilishly gorgeous and sinfully tasty cakes, breads, buns, cookies and other sugary delights is as endlessly popular as Sweet Lady Jane's.

Owner Jane Lockhart opened the doors in May 1988, though she hadn't initially set out to be a baker – she found the desserts that she bought were "too sweet" and starting making her own on the kitchen table at home.

Years before it was Sweet Lady Jane's, this address was the location of Orson Welles' favorite restaurant, Ma Maison. The *Los Angeles Times* of October 21, 1982 ran a piece mentioning Welles, whom then-owner Patrick Terrial noted:

"My family has been taking care of him for three generations."

Ma Maison also hosted Michael Caine, Woody Allen and Frank Sinatra, and first employed Wolfgang Puck (the celebrity chef who caters the Oscars every year). But they also employed John Sweeney, who murdered actress Dominique Dunne in 1982.

Today, locals and movie stars alike still come here for a treat – including the ghost of *Citizen Kane* legend Orson Welles, who famously loved food so much that he still holds the record for the most hot dogs eaten in on sitting (18!) at Pink's hot dog stand at Melrose/La Brea. Lockhart explained that in those days Welles ate here every day at his regular table – which today would be in the back corner – and has allegedly been seen here since his death:

"Customers come in regularly and ask about Welles, but as for the smell of his favorite brandy or cigars, well…"

Their Old Fashioned Chocolate Cake is my major temptation (you think you'll never even finish a slice, but somehow you do), and though it's very small inside (there's barely room for a handful of tables) it's always very busy. Also, judging by the fancy cars parked outside with their flashers on, they do a thriving take-out business too, and you can read newspaper clippings about some of their famous customers on the wall.

Welles died of a heart attack aged 70 in 1985, and Lockhart admitted that while she has never seen him checking out the desserts, his cigar would certainly be out of the question:

"California restaurants are all non-smoking now, and I don't think customers would appreciate the smell mixing with the cakes and pastries. The staff and I just see it as more of an urban legend – a good story."

Monday – Wednesday 7.30am-10.30pm, Thursday – Saturday 7.30am-11.30pm, Sunday 9am-9pm
www.sweetladyjane.com
www.facebook.com/sweetladyjanebakery

Couldn't Get A Table
–Mid-Wilshire

Despite my best efforts to find an eyewitness or something in the archives, these places just didn't have enough to make it into the chapter – but still had a great ghost story.

Antonio's
Tel: 323 658 9060

Lucky For Some...

Antonio's has a reputation as a place where there's something magic in the air. Or maybe lots of black cats have been seen here. Either way, it seems to be the restaurant where a long list of celebrities like Tom Hanks, Julia Roberts, Jennifer Aniston, Jennifer Lopez all hung out – just before they hit the big time. On the walls and the website are dozens of pictures of stars including Dennis Hopper, John Wayne, Warren Beatty, Sidney Poitier, Marlon Brando, Rod Stewart, Mick Jagger, Johnny Depp, Robert Pattinson, Pierce Brosnan, Benicio Del Toro and Pamela Anderson – they've all enjoyed a night out here.

Over 50 years ago, owner Antonio Gutierrez arrived from Monterrey, Mexico and began waiting tables at a restaurant. One day he saw an empty lot on a nearly-deserted stretch of road and, after he bargained the owner down from to $5,000 to $3,800, set about building his own restaurant. As for unusual stories, the sprightly and outgoing Gutierrez did mention something in an interview with local newspaper *The Larchmont Chronicle*:

"The ghosts shut the lights on and off and ring the bell to pick up food. Once when I was in the kitchen they were pulling at my shirt."

He won't be drawn on who he thinks this ghost could be, though he says that Frank Sinatra spent many nights here in his regular spot, and so did eccentric billionaire Howard Hughes – he was here so often that he even had a phone installed at his table, and though it's now in a private room, Antonio will happily give you a peek if you ask.

He also noted that when the restaurant was being constructed, builders discovered several caskets in the ground – a possible sign that this site dates back to the time when the area was under Mexican rule. There was no evidence of these caskets or anything else in the archives, though there is definitely a good spirit here: their very own brand of tequila, complete with a movie star-handsome picture of a young Antonio on the label.

The menu includes his mom's original recipes, which ensures that the restaurant is always busy. It's serious, traditional Mexican fare – any of their tamales are a knockout, and you can't go wrong with any of the Monterrey specials – while their Thursday daily special *albondigón rebozado* (cabbage leaf stuffed with beef chorizo and herbs) is surprisingly innovative. Also, no matter what you choose you must save room for the fried banana dessert.

Lunch: Tuesday – Friday 11am-4pm
Dinner: Tuesday – Friday 5pm-11pm, Saturday 12pm-11pm, Sunday 12pm-10pm
www.antoniosonmelrose.com

El Carmen
Tel: 323 852 1552

Is "Mama" still here?

When El Carmen originally opened at La Brea and 3rd Street in 1929, it was right at the edge of town. Even the famous red trolley cars didn't go out that far, so pioneering owner Encarnación Gomez was the queen of all she surveyed – though few people knew that a restaurant had been the last thing on her mind.

Just two years before she was preparing to return to Mexico to take her place as First Lady when her husband General Arnulfo Gomez "*El Hombre Sin Vicios*" ("The Man Without Vices") became one of the many victims of Mexico's dangerous political world.

Even *Time* magazine reported on his capture, court-martial and execution in Mexico City (November 21, 1927) and while his death was met with a great outpouring of emotion (and a small village in the Mexican state of Durango was named after him), it left Encarnación almost penniless.

Determined, she pawned her jewelry, gathered together some family recipes and did something that – at the time – was unthinkable for a widow: she went into business for herself. Despite opening the same month as the 1929 Stock Market crash, it wasn't long before directors Cecil B. DeMille and D.W. Griffith were sitting at the counter, and throughout the Depression and World War II the friendly welcome from "Mama" kept people coming in.

By 1947 it was a regular haunt for artist Diego Riviera, young singer Mario Lanza and actor John Wayne, while her granddaughter Montserrat Fontes recalled target practice with .22 pistols in the back alley!

When Encarnación moved further west to the current location in 1951, her hungry guests followed. For 40 years she sat at the cash register in this *taqueria* (Spanish for taco shop), and though another business had rented some of the space by the time her grandson Paulino Fortes sold the restaurant in 1997, it was a fixture of the now-hip and fashionable 3rd Street.

The new owners transformed El Carmen into a tequila bar with a *lucha libre* (Spanish wrestling) theme – cult Mexican movie posters and colorful masks – and today it's a snug place with red lighting, sparkly lamps, a mounted bull's head and a sensual décor that's ideal for fun or a romantic night out.

Things may have changed, but it seems that Encarnación still likes to visit her old bar and see how things are going; bartender Paige Gentry had had a very recent experience:

> *"Last Sunday I was in the bar alone, listening to the jukebox and getting ready for opening. Suddenly the jukebox switched off. This is something that never happens – it runs off a separate amp and power source that's never turned off – yet when I went in back to check it, it was turned off."*

She also had a very sweet experience soon after she started working here:

"We have a jar of candy in the office, but my bag and hoodie were on the opposite side of the room. When I picked my bag and hoodie up later to leave, there were Reese's Pieces inside."

This may of course just been a friendly co-worker, and though there have been many reports among the staff of strange shadows, there's nothing unusual in the newspaper archives.

Encarnación is doubtless happy her joint is still jumping though, and one piece of advice still applies from her reign: if you want a table, make sure you arrive early. The tasty tacos and huge portions of guacamole are a must, but the reasons many Angelenos love it here is the choice of liquid libations; El Carmen has around 450 tequilas to choose from!

Though it's one of my favorite places to take people from out of town, a night here can quickly get expensive with a list like that, so another option is to come for the Happy Hour when chips and salsa are free, guacamole is $2, margaritas $4, cans of Tecate $3 and two tacos and rice and beans $5. Keep an eye on that clock though!

Monday – Friday 5pm-2am, Saturday/Sunday 7pm-2am
Happy Hour: Monday – Friday 5-7pm
f Tito LaBrea
www.elcarmenla.com
www.facebook.com/ElCarmenOn3rd

Chapter 5

Westside & Beaches

Culver Hotel
9400 Culver Boulevard
Culver City, CA 90232
Tel: 310 558 9400

Munchkins, Tunnels and Harry's Game

courtesy Culver Hotel

The Culver Hotel has a strong connection with arguably the most popular movie of all time, *The Wizard of Oz*.

During the making of the movie around 120 of the little people who played "Munchkins" stayed here, and the stories of their exploits – some myths, some true – have become legendary. Over the years this group of tiny actors has been accused of everything from drunken shenanigans to all-out orgies, and even though other movies including *Last Action Hero* (1993), *Stuart Little 2* (2002) and even some early Laurel & Hardy movies filmed here, the "Munchkins" are still blamed for most of the unusual and mysterious things that have happened.

Either way, the movie business certainly played its part in the story of Culver City, which was founded in 1917. When movie production exploded in the 1930s and 1940s, the Culver Studios was a major player, and the city's founding father Harry Culver thought this area was the perfect location between the sun, sea and sand of Santa Monica and the glitz and glamour of Hollywood.

Enjoying the special half day holiday, 8000 guests attended the 1924 opening of what was then called the Hotel Hunt, and Culver soon began persuading actors, celebrities and producers to come and stay in his luxury accommodation.

Cast members from *Gone with the Wind* and of course *The Wizard of Oz* (both 1939) were soon gracing the hallways, though it's hard to imagine today's movie stars staying in a hotel with only one bathroom per floor. Nonetheless, Clark Gable, Greta Garbo, Joan Crawford, Buster Keaton, Ronald Reagan and others all had part-time residences within these walls.

According to their legend the hotel was once owned by Charlie Chaplin, who then lost it to John Wayne in a game of poker. "The Duke" was said to have been propositioned by the Black Panthers for ownership, but he refused and later donated it to the YMCA (the Hotel paid tribute with the John Wayne Presidential Suite). All in all, the Culver Hotel has been a local landmark from day one, and following one of many restorations it was placed on the National Register of Historic Places in 1997 (keep your eyes out for the plaques).

Appropriately enough, the most prominent ghost here is the spirit of Harry Culver, whose own story is worthy of a movie – especially the romantic way he met his wife. One day while standing on a train platform he saw a vision in a yellow dress and a straw hat. The woman was young beauty Lillian Roberts and Culver, a number of years her senior, convinced a friend to invite her to a party where he would be in disguise as their chauffeur. His friend and his wife sat in the back leaving Miss Roberts the only remaining seat – next to the "chauffeur."

He had offices on the second floor for over a decade, and even though he died in 1946 it's said that staff members occasionally see his ghost wandering the corridors and keeping an eye on what's going on. Milena Aalunni, who runs Private Events, Catering and Filming here, admitted that some guests have had unusual experiences:

> *"There have been some reports about pictures that move and won't stay straight, and faucets turning themselves off and on. Also, sometimes in the Conference Room – Harry Culver's old office – the windows have moved and banged shut, even though there's no wind outside."*

Whether Harry's here or not, many people find the Culver Hotel an unexpected surprise when they pop in for a cocktail or something to eat. Aside from the fabulous Art Deco look, the Lobby Lounge/Bar can get really busy (especially during the Happy Hour) and there's live music – usually jazz – every night and at weekend lunch time. Give one of these cocktails a whirl: the Marilyn Monroe (prosecco, Campari and elderflower), the Culver Lemonade (Sagatiba Pura rum, fresh mint, lime, sugar and pomegranate juice) or a Dirty Harry classic martini with Absolut vodka and olives.

To eat, I find it hard not to have the Atlantic Salmon (with creamed spinach and cous cous), or there's the indulgent Black Truffle Mac & Cheese with black truffle shavings and parmesan (and I also add bacon for $2 more).

Lobby Lounge: Daily 11am-11pm, Afternoon Tea 3-5pm
Lobby Bar: Daily 3pm-close
Brunch: Daily 7am-4pm
Happy Hour: Daily 4-7pm ($3 beer, $4 house wine, $6 cocktails, $5/6 starters)
www.culverhotel.com
www.facebook.com/theculverhotel
http://twitter.com/culver_hotel

Basement Tavern at The Victorian
2640 Main Street
Santa Monica, CA 90405
Tel: 310 396 2469

Delia is still in the building....

The Victorian is a vintage building with an unusual story. Not only was it moved from its previous location (1003 Ocean Avenue, near the Fairmont Miramar hotel) to where it is now, it's been rumored that someone came along for the ride.

Around 120 years ago this Queen Anne-style Victorian house was the residence of one of the early families of Santa Monica, optometrist Dr. George Kyte and his wife Mary. Even though George died just a few years after Mary in 1940, their distinctive-looking home was still known as "the Kyte House," and after spending many years as a hostel it was included as part of a plan to bring a "Heritage Square" to the city instead of being razed to make way for condominiums.

In 1973 it and another similar house on the lot – the "Roy Jones House" – was moved lock, stock and barrel along the sea front and past the Santa Monica Pier to Main Street. That second building became the California Heritage Museum, a museum that explores the development of Southern California from the Civil War to the early 20th Century, while the Kyte House was due to be converted into a luxury restaurant.

Strangely, moving the houses was the easiest part of the process: legal, business and community wrangles held up the Heritage Square for years (the *Los Angeles Times* even reported in May 1976 that the project was "dead"), but by 1978 the Kyte House had opened its doors as The Chronicle Restaurant. Years later it was renamed The Victorian, and now it plays host to weddings, corporate events and private parties.

In early 2010 a small bar opened in the basement, and was named after its almost secret location – you actually have to go round the back of The Victorian and past the dumpsters in the alley, but then you can't miss it: there's a red door with a big, blue eye painted on it.

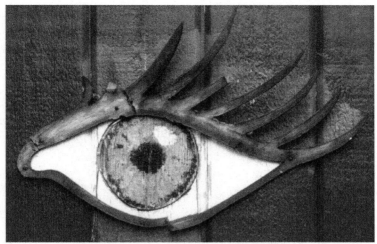

courtesy Basement Tavern

When the building was still on Ocean Avenue it was owned for a time by a woman named Delia, yet after the move to Main Street it was rumored that no one knew what had happened to her. Ashia – the manager of The Victorian – told me that around the time The Basement opened, two of Delia's nieces (one who lived in Italy, the other in San Diego) visited and walked round the house recalling some happy memories – even though it was when the building was literally somewhere else.

Ashia also said that in the early days, when there was just her and another employee in The Victorian, a "few things" had happened: lights turning on and off, flickering shadows, "things moving," and "the feeling that someone was there." She mentioned the idea that Delia might still be here to the nieces, and they "both replied that 'we would not doubt that whatsoever.'"

The manager of The Basement, TJ Williams, agreed that "Delia" might still be in residence, and that he's "definitely experienced a few things." More than that, he says that "everyone on staff" has heard strange noises in the building, especially in the very early hours of the morning after the bar has shuttered for the night. The Victorian is long closed by then, but Basement employees have often heard something overhead on the first floor:

"I've heard it three or four times: running footsteps, the sound of opening drawers and opening doors. It wasn't

clanking pipes or house noises, and we've gone upstairs with a flashlight and looked around, but all the doors are locked and no one is there. One night it happened a couple of times and we were all thinking 'let's get out of here.'"

This phenomenon happened most recently in late summer 2010 and early 2011, and TJ mentioned that they created the "Delia Elixir," a special cocktail of bourbon, agave, raspberries and lemon, in honor of her. There was however no evidence in any of the Los Angeles newspaper archives of anyone named Delia, so perhaps her "disappearance" got mixed up with the death of Mary Kyte, who died back in 1937 (and as was tradition in those days, lay in state in the house before being taken to the cemetery).

Delia or no Delia, The Basement is very glamorous inside, with big, glittering chandeliers and high-backed leather chairs that give it a speakeasy feel. If you come here at night, be prepared to wait in line – this was a popular spot as soon as it opened – though you might have more luck during Happy Hour, when a "Delia" is $5 (it's normally $8).

The Happy Hour also sees 50% off the food menu (except for the charcuterie and cheese plates) and the Pizza and Basement Burger with tomatoes, arugula and bleu cheese are recommended, though do watch out for the jalapeños on the burger – they give it a kick! If you have any more room, try the truffle parmesan fries ($8) and stay for the live music, which happens almost every night.

Monday – Sunday 5pm-2am
Happy Hour: Daily 5-8pm, all night Sunday
www.facebook.com/BasementTavern
http://twitter.com/basement_tavern

Georgian Hotel
1415 Ocean Avenue
Santa Monica, CA 90401
Tel: 310 395 9945

The 8th Floor

Just a stone's throw from the beach – a swimmer or surfer could probably see its distinctive turquoise coloring – the Georgian Hotel was one of the first "skyscrapers" in the area when it was built back in 1933, and it was the dedicated vision of Rosamund "Rose" Borde. She had already opened another hotel called the Windermere some twenty years before, but for the Georgian she hired an architect to bring her ideas of Romanesque Revival and Art Deco to life, and over the following decades her personality and business savvy led to the Windermere being nicknamed "The Lady" in her honor.

Santa Monica was quite secluded in those days, and celebrities like Clark Gable and Carol Lombard quickly made it their favorite hideout. Its basement restaurant was perfect for a discrete rendezvous, and the hotel also had a beauty parlor, barber shop and playground (though the fact that the restaurant was one of the last holdouts against Prohibition definitely helped too). The hotel continued to grow in the 1940s and 1950s thanks to the growing aircraft industry in the area, and in the 1960s the hotel reinvented itself with then-unthinkable luxuries like an en suite bathroom in every room.

There was tragedy for the Borde family though. Nearly a century ago Rose's sister-in-law Celine, 28, left the Windermere Hotel "with neither hat nor money" and disappeared, reported the *Los Angeles Times* of December 19, 1909.

DIRE FEARS.

GOES FOR WALK, RETURNS NOT.

YOUNG WOMAN'S FATE IS PUZZLE AT SANTA MONICA.

She had arrived several months before after suffering a nervous breakdown, but had been in "good health and spirits" and was packed and ready to go home to her teaching job in San Luis Obispo when she went out for her "usual afternoon walk." She was spotted "gazing into the water" on Santa Monica Pier – and was never seen again.

BODY IDENTIFIED.

Remains of Miss Celine Borde Are Brought to. Santa Monica from Up the Beach.

Her body was "cast up by the sea" around 30 miles away on January 5, 1910 and was so badly decomposed – it was missing its hands and face – that it was only identified by a silver butterfly piece of jewelry, and, though suicide seemed the likely cause of death, the Coroner ruled otherwise, as the *Los Angeles Herald* reported:

TEACHER'S DEATH SAID TO HAVE BEEN ACCIDENT

Evidence Presented to Coroner's Jury Indicates That Miss Celine Borde Fell from Pier

Also, the view from the Georgian Hotel was the last thing that several people ever saw. The *Los Angeles Times* reported on August 27, 1949 that "Beverly Hills Psychiatrist" Dr. Boris Sergei Ury, 42, either jumped or fell the 70 feet from the window of his sixth floor room.

Beverly Hills Psychiatrist in Death Plunge

The *Los Angeles Examiner* featured a picture of Ury's blanket-covered body on the street, and it was noted that he had been in ill health and was having marital problems.

8-Story Fall Kills Indian Girl; Companion Held

On November 21, 1955 it was reported that Dolores Birdtail, a 21-year-old "Indian girl" from Montana had "plunged to her death" from James G. Warlick's room. Dolores and her sister Ophelia had met Warlick and Paul Maxey a few hours before, but the *Los Angeles Herald-Express* reported that Warlick had "scratches on his chest and neck and chest" from when she "resisted" him. He was held on suspicion of murder, but days later he told the Coroner's jury that he was walking toward the elevator when he heard "a muffled cry or sob or yell." Maxey confirmed this, and Ophelia testified that Dolores had said she wanted to leave:

> *"But Dolores told me that 'if any of these guys start bothering me, I'm going to jump out of the window.' I didn't believe her. I told her I was going. She said she was staying. That was the last I saw of her."*

The coroner ruled that it was either an accident or suicide, and Warlick was released. Just a few years later on May 28, 1958 another short piece noted that Joan Harris, a mother of two who had been living nearby after the recent separation from her husband, had fallen to her death from the roof here.

Inside the recently-renovated hotel, you may get the chance to hear – and maybe even see – Rose herself. It's said that loud sighs and gasps are heard in the Veranda Restaurant when it's been empty; footsteps too. There have even been reports of someone saying "Good Morning" to staff.

However, as the hotel itself, their PR gave a clear – but confirming – reply to my email:

"The Georgian does not like to participate in any coverage about the hotel being haunted. The staff that may have had encounters are tired of talking about it, and the hotel doesn't want to present itself to the public as a place that's haunted. Sorry."

Whether or not you have any luck on your visit, follow in the footsteps of movie stars – and infamous figures like actor "Fatty" Arbuckle and gangster Bugsy Siegal – by having a drink on The Veranda and watching the waves. You can have breakfast (house favorite is the French Toast Soufflé) and lunch out here too, though dinner is only served in the Lobby inside.

There's a Mediterranean-inspired tapas menu, and a bar opens here from 3.30pm – you should try their special Art Deco martini called "The Georgini." It's a mix of Absolut vodka and Hpnotiq Liqueur (which is Georgian Hotel blue and is a mixture of fruit juices, vodka and a touch of cognac) and is shaken with ice and served with a lemon twist.

Breakfast: Monday – Friday 6.30-10.30am, Saturday/Sunday 6.30-11.30am
Lunch: 11.30am-2.30pm
Dinner: Sunday – Thursday 3.30-9pm, Friday/Saturday 3.30-9.30pm
www.georgianhotel.com
www.facebook.com/Georgianhotelsm
http://twitter.com/georgianhotelsm

The Arsenal
12012 West Pico Boulevard
Los Angeles 90064
Tel: 310 575 5511

Mysterious Lucien and Paddy the Dead Drinker

The Arsenal has been a fixture on the Westside for over 130 years – an unbelievable amount of time in this city – and it has the checkered history to match. Of course, when it was first built in 1874 by Count Cortez del Cota this area was known as New Spain (the days of "California" were a long way off) and drinks and food were not on the menu; this building was a store for weapons.

The first documented Santa Ana winds (known by the more sinister name of "Devil Winds") flattened the building, and it was left to rot for over 20 years before Guillermina Garcia and her son Diego raised it from the rubble and opened the doors again – but now as a saloon. Gold seekers and farmers would come to drink their "special" firewater and listen to native Mexican songs and music, but then that was all swept away in the 1916 Great Flood (along with much of the surrounding area).

L'Arsenal Hot emerged out of this disaster in 1929, and since this was the age of the speakeasy, people flocked from miles around to relax from the day's work and catch the occasional risqué show. Sadly, one of the patrons failed to put out their cigarette properly one night, and in 1949 a raging fire consumed everything. "L'Arsenal" was again rebuilt, and the story of the designer was as interesting as the building he re-imagined.

Born in 1889 and allegedly linked to French nobility, Lucien Le Carre was a radical artist, poet, WWII soldier and movie designer. Often down on his luck, he was introduced to L'Arsenal by none other than Bertolt Brecht and Aldous Huxley, and soon become a regular fixture drinking at the bar – so much so that the then-owners let him live upstairs. Amazingly saved from the 1949 fire by the owner's dog, a grateful Le Carre embarked on what was to be the last project of his career. His design included the weapons on the wall, but just a few years after the successful reopening he disappeared and was never heard from again.

Sounds like it could be a movie, doesn't it? Like it's almost too good to be true?

There's a longer version on the Arsenal's website – and a picture supposedly of Le Carre in a swimming pool – but since I couldn't find anything in the newspaper archives to confirm any of these facts (even about the fire, or Le Carre and his alleged father, who somehow seems to have been born in the 17th century), it's probably best to take it all with a big pinch of salt.

Nearly 55 years after Le Carre's "work" got its public debut, The Arsenal came under new management again and a complete restoration and renovation was promised. Patrons who loved the weapon-lined walls, separate bar and intimate atmosphere feared the worst, but the new management – wisely – kept the old feel while taking it up a notch at the same time.

Another remodel took place in summer 2011, and to celebrate the reopening and the new menu, filet mignon, burgers, champagne and cocktails were all at 1950s prices for a week.

courtesy www.arsenalbar.com

One time when I visited The Arsenal I got talking to some of the older guys drinking at the bar. They said that there was a ghost here, and that they called him "Paddy." Apparently he was a fellow "old timer" and had actually died there one night while sitting in the room with the weapons on the wall.

It seemed that all the staff felt a little uneasy being there late at night – so many strange things had happened and been attributed to "Paddy":

"Everyone says they've had to do a double-take with some of the shadows – that they've seen something."

Other strange happenings include one of the kitchen staff finding all the oven burners on full flame – something that couldn't have gone unnoticed (or without causing a problem):

"Also, there were two bartenders here late – after closing – and they heard banging noises from one of the bathrooms. They both went to look, but there was nothing there. As soon as they left the bathroom, the banging started up again."

Today, The Arsenal is split into three sections: an outdoor covered patio and indoor bar with a distinct modern-style club lounge feel, though the stately section with its red booths is still present and correct (it's an "atmosphere ideal for seduction or break-ups," one of the old menus used to suggest). Sadly, most of the weapons are now gone – too many were getting stolen by patrons and souvenir hunters – and the juke box has increased its output to include everything from the Sex Pistols to Dylan to The Beatles to Sinatra.

There's plenty of live music here too: DJs most nights, and – best of all – Tuesday night, when from 9pm a magician goes from table to table doing sleight of hand and up-close magic (definitely the best time to visit).

Try the Old Fashioned cocktail (Kentucky bourbon, soda, bitters, sugar, maraschino cherry and a splash of orange juice) or, if you have a sweet tooth, the root beer float (Kahlua, Galliano and cream topped off with Coke) and the delicious beignet-battered Oreos. In between those the sliders are a popular choice, and there are six kinds of fries including mac n' cheese. Their pizzas are great too, though if you want to stick with the overall theme then try The Arsenal of Flavor, a burger with gouda cheese and the trimmings.

Even though Le Carre "disappeared" in 1953, "Paddy" might still be hanging around, so it seems true to say that the spirit of the "old" Arsenal still remains.

Monday – Friday 5pm-2am, Saturday/Sunday 6pm-2am
Happy Hour: Monday – Friday 5-7pm, Saturday/Sunday 6-8pm
(Beers $3-4, cocktails/house wine $4, various appetizers $5-6)
www.arsenalbar.com
www.facebook.com/thearsenalbar
http://twitter.com/thearsenalbar

Paradise Cove Beach Café
28128 Pacific Coast Highway
Malibu, CA 90265
Tel: 310 457 2503

The Ghost of Millie

Around 50 years ago Joe Morris bought about 70 acres of Paradise Cove, and his son and current owner Bob recalled many happy times that the family shared in a "kickback beach community" that was full of fishermen. The whole family was heartbroken when "Papa Joe" later sold up, but Bob stayed in the restaurant business (he owned Gladstone's at one time, as well as many others), but when he and his wife Kerry had their son Timothy in the mid-1990s he felt it was time to come back home.

courtesy www.paradisecovemalibu.com

A location for movies like *Beach Blanket Bingo* (1965), *Indecent Proposal* (1993), *Lethal Weapon 4* (1998), *Monster-in-Law* (2005) and television shows including "Gidget," "Baywatch," "Alias," "The Rockford Files," "Sea Hunt" and "Malibu Run," there's no question that this beach bar and restaurant has one of the best ocean views, to say nothing of one of the most glamorous addresses in that hideaway of movie stars, moguls and millionaires – Malibu.

But aside from gazing at the Atlantic, checking out the historical photographs, walking along their private beach or strolling out on the pier, there may be something else to look out for when you arrive. Originally there was a recreation center with a coffee shop, bar and hot dog stand here, and from the 1970s until Morris arrived it was a restaurant known as The Sandcastle.

Chuck Weiser began working at The Sandcastle in 1980, and one night he had an encounter with the former owner of the coffee shop – a woman who had died a short time before:

"I was working there one night – the place was closed and empty – and I took a break to have a cup of coffee when I saw someone down the aisle that used to lead towards what used to be the patio in front."

On his own in the building, Weiser recalled reaching for his pistol:

"Just to make sure it was there. I always had a gun there, just in case, and I thought to myself 'Goodness gracious, someone's come in.' But it wasn't."

Traveling – "almost floating" – towards the beach was a "white form, with no features or face, and there was "no noise, nothing," other than something he "instantly recognized":

"I watched and saw that it wasn't a human being! When I saw the way that it was walking – it was very unusual and distinct – I realized that it was the former owner of the coffee shop. She has what we call a "farmer's walk." She was large for a woman, which this apparition was, and it was tall – like she was – too. Then suddenly, it evaporated all of a sudden and I thought to myself: 'Christ's sake; that was Millie!'"

Weiser was certain it was Millie because of where he saw her:

"All day, all summer, she would walk between the coffee shop she rented and the hot dog stand on the patio."

Other enquiries unearthed the story of a waitress who is still keeping an eye on her tables. Bob Morris chuckled about his unpaid supernatural staff member and then suggested speaking to the (very real) General Manager, Pablo de Torre, who was certain of one thing:

"Yes, things happen here late at night when we close up. One time a couple of us were standing in the kitchen and a huge pile of plates was pushed onto the floor from a shelf near us. Another time some dishwashers heard a noise and when they turned round they saw ramekins (small side pots) being thrown out through the kitchen door along the floor – and there was no one in there."

De Torre noted that this supernatural waitress was another veteran of The Sandcastle, the restaurant that preceded the Paradise Cove (which opened in 1998):

"I haven't seen her myself, but I used to live in a place in Mexico where there were spirits and I believe in it. It's not frightening – I think she's just having fun with us."

If you come here for breakfast, make sure you order the Malibu Country Breakfast (three eggs with country sausage, ham or apple-smoked bacon – I prefer the bacon) or the Portobello mushroom crab Benedict – their own invention – is great too. Fish are a big deal here too (as you can tell from the tanks) and the calamari appetizer is their dinner best seller, though you can get almost anything that lives in the sea – including a Gigantic Iced Seafood Tower. Costing the market value price, it's great for a group and contains lobster, shrimp, salmon, mussels, scallops, calamari – you get the idea.

There are also Pablo's own special tacos, chicken, ribs, sandwiches, burgers (the BBQ onion burger is a popular favorite) and, if you're feeling adventurous, order the Sandwich "In" Soup, and find out why this soup needs to be eaten with a fork and spoon. Also needing some heavy lifting is their Mile High Chocolate Cake, and if you have The Works – which comes with chocolate, vanilla and strawberry ice cream as well – you'll certainly need a stroll on the beach afterward to work it all off.

Some insider tips: there's music on Tuesday, Wednesday and Thursday nights, and you should arrive early if you want to rent a good hut, beach chair or umbrella (they're around $50 each). Cabanas can be rented too, but are at least $350 and must be reserved in advance. Also, though there are surf boards on the wall and that cocktail-friendly "kickback" atmosphere is still present, this is Malibu. Even the hippest of surfer dudes are banned from bringing their boards, and dog lovers must leave their best friends in the car. Finally, save yourself a walk and get your parking ticket validated before you leave.

Daily 8am-10pm, Holidays 7am-closing
Breakfast: 8-11.30am
Lunch/Dinner: 11am-closing
www.paradisecovemalibu.com
www.facebook.com/paradisecovebeachcafe
http://twitter.com/ParadiseCove

The Queen Mary
1126 Queen's Highway
Long Beach, CA 90802
Tel: 877 342 0738

A Supernatural Vortex and The Grey Ghost

The *Queen Mary* may have long since retired to a life of luxury in Long Beach, but the many ghostly stories hidden behind her 2,000 portholes have scared fans of the supernatural for decades (and she was even temporarily called *The Grey Ghost* around 60 years ago). Movie fans will immediately recognize her as the fictional "SS Poseidon" from *The Poseidon Adventure* (1972) and its 1979 sequel, but not many people know that Paul Gallico's original 1969 book was inspired by a near-disastrous event that actually happened to the *Queen Mary*.

In December 1942 she was carrying just over 16,000 American soldiers from New York to England when she ran into a gale and was hit by a rogue wave some 28 meters (92 feet) high. Dr. Norval Carter was part of the 110th Station Hospital on board, and he wrote that at one point she "...damned near capsized. One moment the top deck was at its usual height and then, swoom! Down, over, and forward she would pitch." It was later calculated that the ship tilted around 52 degrees and would have capsized had she rolled over to 55 degrees. At that time the ship was around 700 miles off the coast of Scotland, and any rescue would have been unlikely.

The *Poseidon* adventures are not the only time the *Queen Mary* has graced the big screen; check out *Batman Forever* (1995), *Escape from L.A.* (1996), *Being John Malkovich* (1999) and *Pearl*

Harbor (2001), while on television she has been in "Murder, She Wrote," "The X-Files," "Arrested Development" and "Cold Case." The *Queen Mary* was also the location for the 30th birthday party of actor Vincent Chase (Adrian Grenier) in the third season of "Entourage," and teen pop sensations The Jonas Brothers shot their video for the single "SOS" here.

Built in Clydebank, Scotland and originally known as "Hull Number 534," the *Queen Mary* is a relic of the Golden Age of transatlantic travel. She sailed the North Atlantic Ocean from 1936 onward and was specifically designed to be the first of a two-ship weekly express service on the busy route from Southampton to New York via Cherbourg, France.

She continued this run after World War II until she was retired from service in 1967, and she's been a museum and hotel ever since, with 2011 seeing the 75th anniversary of her maiden voyage.

The *Queen Mary* has overcome many problems in her time too. Construction was temporarily halted because of the Depression in 1931, and her very name itself was controversial. As was customary with all Cunard Line's ships, they planned a name ending in "ia" and were thinking of *Victoria*, so they approached King George V and asked if they could name the liner after Britain's "greatest Queen." He happily replied that his wife, Queen Mary, would be delighted!

Unwilling to offend the King, the ship was subsequently christened the *Queen Mary*, though rumors persisted that this wasn't the first choice. Then-chairman of Cunard, Sir Percy Bates, told *Washington Post* editor Felix Morley that he would only reveal the truth "On condition you won't print it during my lifetime," though there were also suggestions that the name was simply a compromise between recently-merged Cunard and the White Star Line, the latter traditionally used names ending in "ic" – like their *Titanic*.

Interestingly, comparisons between the *Queen Mary* and the *Titanic* show that the *Queen Mary* beat the legendary vessel in almost every area: it was longer, heavier, and had more portholes and decks than the doomed ship. It also needed many millions more rivets to build it and had a greater overall and cruising speed at its command.

Though now docked permanently in Long Beach, the *Queen Mary* has had an unsteady journey there as well.

There was initial debate about whether she should be a hotel, a theme park or just preserved as an ocean liner, then there were temporary closures, talk of bankruptcy and a number of owners (including Disney). Even the funnels had to be replaced with aluminum replicas during early construction.

There's been plenty of renovation, restoration and improvements over the years as well. The funnel was repainted its original "Cunard Red" color and the lifeboats repaired, while today's guests will find iPod docking stations and flat screen televisions in the 300-plus rooms and eight suites. Those electronic gadgets would be puzzling to past passengers like Bob Hope, Clark Gable and Winston Churchill (who has a restaurant named after him here), and though around 1,500,000 visitors now come onboard every year, many people who have stepped on deck never left again.

Reports of ghosts first started after the *Queen Mary* came to rest in California, but since then she's been the subject of paranormal investigations by radio, magazines and television shows like "Ghost Hunters," "The Othersiders" and UK show "Most Haunted". *Queen Mary* historian Will Kayne feels that the ship isn't necessarily haunted; it's more that so many people have been on board over the last 75 years or so:

> *"People get very emotional when they come here, and I think it's because lots of energy has passed through the hull of the ship. In World War II it was a prisoner ship and a troop carrier, and many people died on board."*

There could be more to it though, as Kayne recalled some of the reactions of the psychics and paranormal investigators who have come onto the ship:

> *"Behind the aft (rear facing) wall of the first class swimming pool there used to be a row of dressing boxes (rooms), and they have all claimed that there is a vortex – a spiraling area of energy – there that's a link to the spirit world, like a sort of gate."*

There is some startling and unusual photographic evidence that might support the idea of a vortex, though it was taken elsewhere on the ship. In the center of the picture you can clearly see an unusual shape – a large, white angular spiral (or vortex) – moving from one corner to another, while in the background there is a steel door.

© Karen & Jason Miller

This specific watertight door was in fact the scene of a fatal accident in the 1960s, though out of respect for the victim's family I was asked not to describe it in detail. Whether it qualifies as a gate or link it's impossible to know, but when Jeff Milller sent a copy of the picture by email he apologized for the quality; he said it's been looked at so many times over the years it's now covered in fingerprints.

As you can see from the time clock in the right bottom corner, the date was 9th November 1999 and Jeff was attending the annual Halloween event with his mother Karen, brother Jason and friend Cheryl Jones, who also emailed me about an unusual sighting later:

"We all were walking around exploring the Queen Mary late that night when we stumbled across an old service elevator. We all got into the elevator and it was a bit tight in there. One of us pressed the up button a few times to take us back up to the deck, but the elevator went down instead. After a few moments it stopped and two people got on (I believe two women) dressed entirely in white kitchen uniforms. The elevator then continued down without the down button being pressed. The elevator stopped again after a few moments and the two people in white uniforms got off. They completely ignored our presence in the elevator – and it was a tight fit, with six people packed in there. In fact, they spoke to each other as if the four of us weren't even there."

A puzzled Jones wondered if the women were perhaps *Queen Mary* staff members, and if so, "Were they current, alive staff members?" Jeff admitted that the group had certainly been partying, but that Cheryl was "pretty with it," and whether the women were perhaps in period costume for an event or not, Kayne noted that people with a "special connection" to the spirit worlds are not the only ones to have noticed things here:

"Some guests have felt things by the swimming pool – chills, their hair standing on end – and then there's the steel hull resting in the water. Steel and water are both big conductors of energy, and the Queen Mary is kind of in the right place at the right time."

It's certainly been a place for (fictional) murder – the victim at the beginning of movie *Someone To Watch Over Me* (1987) is found in the pool area – but Kayne mentioned that the Security Guards who patrol the lobby often hear splashing from the empty first class swimming pool, and there are regular reports of a little girl heard crying in the nursery.

All the visiting psychics and investigators feel that she died in the swimming pool, but the complete story is a mystery. There are no notes in any of the ship's log books about such an incident, and (perhaps because of the vortex nearby) opinions are divided about whether she was even a passenger on board. There have been reports of women dressed in vintage 1930s bathing suits here too, and the discovery of wet footprints on the tiles – despite the pool being drained years ago.

There have been other sightings of ghostly children as well. In May 1991 a Property Services manager was aboard one of the ship's aft elevators when she heard the sounds of children playing and then a child calling "mommy, mommy" through the elevator control panel. But the panel only operated from inside the elevator, and passengers weren't allowed on the lower decks in any case. Then, when she checked her own radio, it was turned off.

On another early morning in January 2000, a Property Services crew member was vacuuming in the Exhibit Hall when it suddenly began to get very cold. Feeling that he wasn't alone, the man turned around to see a girl standing there sucking her thumb and staring at him.

She stretched her arms toward him as if she wanted to be picked up, but then he saw her eyes begin to glow and realized that she wasn't standing – she was floating! The spirit of this little girl was seen at least three times that month.

There's also the tragic undated story of baby Leigh Smith. Despite the efforts of the ship's surgeons she died a few hours after birth, and an infant's cry has been heard during the night opposite the room that used to be the third class children's playroom.

The ghosts of several very glamorous lady passengers have been seen here too. The Queen's Salon, the ship's former first class lounge, has been the location for sightings of a beautiful woman dressed in a white evening gown and dancing by herself, while another Woman in White (surrounded by a purple aura) was seen on "B" Deck in June 1992 by two housekeepers.

Then in March 1994, one of the ship's telephone operators and the Front Desk clerk saw a graceful woman in a flowing, powder blue dress walking across the lobby – and then disappearing into this air. Perhaps these three ghosts are one and the same; a passenger who, for whatever reason, never went home and continues to parade around the ship to this day?

Officially, there were 49 deaths associated with the *Queen Mary*. The first one took place in 1934 while the ship was under construction, and though there are no figures available about how many perished on board during World War II, there is a terrifying story from the time she had been painted camouflage gray for the war effort. Adolf Hitler had offered a $250,000 reward and the Iron Cross to any U-boat captain who could sink *Grey Ghost* (as she was then), and on one mission she collided with her escort, British cruiser *HMS Curacao*.

Under orders not to stop for any reason, the *Grey Ghost* had to race away as hundreds of men struggled to survive in the water. Over 330 soldiers perished, and the accident wasn't reported until the war was over. Some 40 years later a television crew left a microphone running overnight in the exact spot onboard the *Queen Mary* where the two ships collided, and when the tape was played back the next day, the desperate sounds of pounding and even screams seemed to be heard.

The numerous ghosts on the *Queen Mary* are well documented online, but since these nearly all these events and ghosts seem to be related to a time before she arrived in Long Beach, there was no archival evidence of any of them in the *Los Angeles Times*. In fact, the only stories uncovered in the archives both told of a tragic prank and a terrible accident.

The *Los Angeles Times* and *Los Angeles Herald-Examiner* of March 18, 1974 reported that Wayne Paul Hussey, 19, was on his way back from a rock concert with two friends. "Slightly intoxicated," he stripped to his shorts and jumped 85 feet from the sundeck, hitting the water flat on his stomach and immediately disappearing under the water.

> **A shipboard "streaking" prank had fatal consequences for a young man in Long Beach Harbor. Police said Wayne Paul Hussey, 19, removed his clothes just at closing time on board the Queen Mary and jumped into the water from the upper deck. Friends notified police when he did not surface nearby, and divers recovered his body after a seven-hour search of the water near the ship.**

A spokesman for the *Queen Mary* said that several people had jumped from the liner before – once for a $250 bet – but until then there had been no fatalities or even injuries. Ironically, the very day before the *Los Angeles Herald-Examiner* had run a picture-heavy article on student pranks – including streaking.

THOSE FABULOUS FADS

Streaking is a modern college fad—but in previous years, students ate goldfish, records, jammed into VW bugs or phone booths and one fellow managed to stuff four billiard balls into his mouth. Not to be outdone, 50 British students crowded onto one bed.

Also, on December 6, 2011 the *Los Angeles Times* reported that a local woman – also suffering from the effects of too much alcohol – accidentally fell over the railing of the ship down to the water below. One of the ship's employees, two Long Beach police officers and the woman's boyfriend jumped in to save her, but she died later in hospital.

A popular place for events, parties and weddings, the *Queen Mary* is certainly unique and romantic – the ship itself is an impressive sight as you drive toward it – and there's plenty to do onboard. You can go shopping, try your hand at the classic cruising sport of shuffleboard, take a Pilates or yoga class or even have a massage in the onboard spa. There are regular live performances too – jazz and blues to piano shows and dinner theater – and around a dozen tours that will help you find out more about this historic vessel.

For supernatural entertainment, "Ghosts & Legends" is an interactive special effects show filled with animations of the ship's haunted past, while "Haunted Encounters" is a guided tour of the ship's most haunted areas and reveals the *Queen Mary*'s most famous ghosts. Newest attraction "Paranormal Spirit Box" sees Paranormal Investigator Erica Frost using a P-SB7 device to make contact with the ghosts on board, while the most genteel choice is "Dining with the Spirits," which takes place on Sunday evenings and includes a chat with your paranormal guide during dinner at Sir Winston's Restaurant, and then a supernatural tour.

I was first in line when "Haunted Encounters" began, and I still have the Paranormal Passport that I was "issued" when I stepped on board. The tour started with a movie, and then a group of us were guided round the ship as our flamboyant guide – the late paranormal investigator Peter James – told us all about the unexplained events and ship's ghosts. It's all great fun, but at times you do feel – especially in the depths of boiler room or looking up the endless corridors – that this isn't a quiet, undisturbed place. When you're down in the very bowels of the ship in the near dark, make no mistake: it's scary!

It was a relief to get back on deck, and although there are restaurants, cafés, a deli, a breakfast bakery and even a champagne bar for Sunday Brunch, I ended up getting a much-needed drink in the Art Deco Observation Bar and walking out onto upper deck to look at the lights of Long Beach. There are many other kinds of tours too, but interest and excitement in the *Queen Mary* and her ghosts naturally reaches its peak around Halloween, when the annual horror event emerges from the depths – and the shadows – to scare all mortals who dare enter their mazes.

All in all, the *Queen Mary* is guaranteed to make your hair stand on end – especially if you arrive with your tongue in your cheek and ready to scream – though the last word goes to Erika Testo, the Marketing Manager of the *Queen Mary*, who admitted that while she hadn't personally seen any paranormal activity:

"Some of the reports are too close in detail to be coincidence. There are a lot of places on the ship where it feels odd like you are not alone, so I do believe that there is something that cannot be explained here."

Daily 10am-6pm; restaurants, stores, tours and event hours vary
www.queenmary.com
www.facebook.com/thequeen.mary
http://twitter.com/TheQueenMary

Couldn't Get A Table –
Westside & Beaches

Despite my best efforts to find an eyewitness or something in the archives, these places just didn't have enough to make it into the chapter – but still had a great ghost story.

Patrick's Roadhouse
Santa Monica
Tel: 310 459 4544

Still Bill's...

You can't miss Patrick's Roadhouse. Not only is it painted green and covered in shamrocks, it's right by the Pacific Coast Highway – so the ocean view alone is worth the trip.

In the late 19th century, the world's longest pier was built near here as part of a plan to compete with the port at San Pedro. The plan failed, and soon the pier and the railroad line were closed, the passenger depot and buildings abandoned like a ghost town by-the-sea. Years later they were resurrected as a stop on the "Red Car" Los Angeles mass transit system, but that idea was soon crushed by the automobile, so one of the rooms became a roadside joint called "Roy's".

It was here, their legend goes, that Bill Fischler and his children stopped in for lunch and had a very bad hamburger. The disgruntled owner challenged Fischler to buy the place and make his own hamburgers, so Fischler did just that and named it after his five-year-old son Patrick.

Recently divorced, the boisterous and outgoing Fischler was aged in his 50s and saw this as a second bite at the cherry, so he expanded Patrick's by buying up the Entrada Motel next door and then decorating it all with his unique sense of décor – they call it "yard sale meets relic meets antique oddity – at the movies."

The self-styled "poor man's Getty Museum" has been here since 1974, and has had a sense of humor and a good time ever since.

Breakfast is the best time to visit (and star spot) and the current owner and host is Silvio Moreira, who worked for Fischler and took over when he died. That was back in 1997, though it's not hard to believe the stories that he's still here, keeping an eye on the restaurant that became a celebrity favorite. He seems to be happy, only apparently dropping some pots and pans in the kitchen every now and then, though many years ago a chef quit his job because he was supposedly getting stared at by Fischler's ghost.

Moreira refurbished the restaurant when he took over, and just as he was about to hire someone to repaint the outside mural, the original artist – a man in his 70s named "Silvani" – arrived out of nowhere. He'd apparently been living in a camper, and repainted the mural in just a few days.

As for solid proof that Patrick's Roadhouse is haunted – by Fischler or anyone else – Moreira told the *Palisadian-Post* on September 24, 2009:

> *"I wouldn't call it haunted, but (Fischler's) definitely still guarding it, making sure it's protected."*

There have also been reports of the ghost of a woman dressed in black at the back of the restaurant. She has been heard crying, and some believe that she suffered a broken heart when she fell in love with one of her "customers" at the old hotel next door, which may have also operated a brothel.

The Roadhouse is a quirky place, and since it's near celebrity hideaway Malibu, it gets plenty of famous visitors. Actor and former California Governor Arnold Schwarzenegger has a regular table (just like Johnny Carson used to), and other stars including Lucille Ball, Ted Danson, Sean Penn, Julia Roberts, Tom Cruise, Sylvester Stallone, Cindy Crawford and Nicole Kidman have eaten here over the years.

Also often seen here is Patrick Fischler himself, now all grown up and a successful character actor. You'd recognize him from "Lost," "Mad Men," 2010's *Dinner For Schmucks* (he was the guy with the vulture), and the recent 1947 era Los Angeles video game "L.A. Noire," in which he digitally played mobster Mickey Cohen.

Being a diner, the food is "Traditional American," which means big, filling breakfasts, burgers and fries, hot coffee and so on, though some of their egg dishes – Silvio's and Eggs Florentinovich – are a tribute to the current and former owner, while eggs and Canadian bacon on a muffin is a real tongue twister: it's called Eggs McKarageorgevitch!

Also, courtesy of a recipe from Schwarzenegger's mother is the dish Bauernfruehstueck (Farmer's Breakfast), a huge multi-egg omelet stuffed with bell peppers, red peppers, sausage, mushroom, ham, potato, tomatoes, bacon and whatever else tasty is around. No need to *sprechen sie deutsch* to order it though: it's known as "The Governator Special."

A couple of tips: it's surprisingly small inside so there's nearly always a wait for a table, and be ready to circle around – parking is very limited around here.

Monday 8am-4pm, Tuesday – Friday 8am-9pm
Saturday 8am-10pm, Sunday 7am-8pm
www.patricksroadhouse.info
www.facebook.com/PatricksRoadhouse
http://twitter.com/patsroadhouse

Chapter 6
Off The Menu

Privé Salon (formerly the Original Spanish Kitchen)

Four Oaks Restaurant

Janes House

Paulist Productions (formerly The Sidewalk Café)

The Ghost Restaurant and Pearl's Curse

Today it's a hair salon with a spa upstairs, but for around 40 years it was a famous local mystery – a "ghost" restaurant called the Original Spanish Kitchen. Under cobwebbed chandeliers, cutlery, crockery and salt and pepper shakers remained on the tables gathering dust like a gourmet *Marie Celeste*, frozen in time for decade after decade with no explanation.

As far back as the 1970s the-then business next door put a sign in their widow offering $1 for information about their "mysterious neighbor," so it's not surprising that it got a reputation as being haunted. If you looked through the grubby windows it was as if time had stood still, and sometimes a ghostly figure was seen moving around inside.

Bob, the manager at the nearby El Coyote, said that "a few years back" he and friend "who had nothing better to do" went down to have a look. One of them knocked on the door and a "pale, old woman" cracked the door a little and told them to "go away or she'd call the cops."

The sad story of the Original Spanish Kitchen has been covered by the *Los Angeles Times* several times over the last 30 years, and it all began when John "Johnny" Domenic Caretto was a co-partner in a branch that opened downtown in 1926 (it's long gone now). A few years later in 1932, Johnny and his dancer wife Pearl realized their dream and opened their own Original Spanish Kitchen here on Beverly Boulevard.

It was an immediate success, and celebrities and stars of the day such as Bob Hope, Van Johnson, Buster Keaton, Howard Keel, Linda Darnell and John and Lionel Barrymore became regulars. Movie icon Mary Pickford had her own special booth in a corner by the door, and as well as always giving autographs to fans she often gave Johnny recipes, which he'd then add to the menu.

Pearl and Johnny lived happily on the second floor, but then Johnny got bad news: he'd been diagnosed with Parkinson's disease. In 1961 the symptoms became too much, and he checked into a Hollywood rest home. Expecting he would soon return, Pearl put up a "Closed For Vacation" sign and began to take care of him. Sadly, Johnny died a few years later, and Pearl never felt that she could quite fill his shoes as a gregarious and popular host. She remained living here and paid her property taxes, but was rarely seen from that day on.

Unsurprisingly, there were other rumors: Johnny had been murdered, the couple had killed each other in a jealous argument, or there had been a shoot-out. None of these were true, though the story of the Original Spanish Kitchen was the inspiration for an episode of the *Lou Grant* television show in which the 30-year-old murder of the owner of "Baby Duarte's Cantina" was solved by the team of the "LA Tribune" newspaper.

Enquiries came in about whether the building was for sale – it was worth around $1m – but the reclusive Pearl wasn't interested, and the neighbors were happy to respect her wishes, helping out from time to time with repairs or delivering groceries and medicine. After the building was vandalized in 1980 Pearl moved elsewhere, though she instructed her daughter from a previous marriage, Patricia Arnold, never to talk about the restaurant: she just wanted to be left alone.

Even though both the Carettos are now long gone (and hopefully reunited), memories of the Original Spanish Kitchen still remain. After extensive renovation, in 2001 the new owners left the letters "Spa" on the ancient sign outside and covered over the rest with a sign saying Cafe.

The Privé Salon downstairs is where the actual restaurant was, and co-owner Simone Dufourg revealed that though her father-in-law (and famous resident stylist) Laurent D was "not a believer," the stories were well-known and, after he felt an "intensely cool breeze" when he first looked around, he insisted on a "clearing." During this "clearing" the Arizona psychic apparently said that there were "angry spirits here," and, moments later, a mattress "came flying down from the landing." Doors kept unlocking themselves too, and even though it seemed that someone or something didn't want them there, the clearing was complete in around half an hour.

She added that there haven't been any reports of anything strange since, though the *Los Angeles Times* of March 1, 2009 reported that employee Lane Lenhart has noticed lights suddenly going on and off, while upstairs at the Ona spa (where Johnny and Pearl had lived) manager Eugenia Shakhnoff told me about a similar strange electrical anomaly:

"Soon after we had opened there was a group of us talking about the old stories (of the Original Spanish Kitchen) and suddenly all the phone lines lit up. There was no ringing and no one on any of the lines, but for about five minutes they were all flashing. You know what they say; when you talk about something you attract it?"

One of the spa guests who overheard our conversation said she had heard some of the stories too and, after we had all frightened the wide-eyed Receptionist, Shakhnoff mentioned that some of Pearl's relatives had once come to visit:

"They were either cousins or nieces from New Jersey, and they had come to see the place. I think they even said something like the real story was not quite as it was."

Shakhnoff reasons that "ghosts might still need their hair done," though it does seem that Pearl is unhappy about other people cooking up delicious dishes on her turf – several restaurant/café's have come and gone since she left. Le Petit Saint-Tropez was the third restaurant to close here in March 2011, and oddly it was the first one too – it had originally opened in 2007. The Eden Roc Café opened for just a few months in between, but now it's an empty space again and any prospective new tenant must be wondering whether it's worth trying to banish Pearl's curse.

To be fair, it seemed to be more of a private restaurant that catered to the clients and staff more than locals or visitors. You could walk straight into the café from the salon or from an entrance in the parking lot, and it was so set back from the street that many people might not have even known it was there. It's a shame, because for those in the know it was a bit of a hidden treasure. It was quiet and peaceful inside, with a Buddha statue, stream feature and cabanas that made you feel like you were overlooking the

Mediterranean Sea. You could even browse through the art books picked by French owner/designer Yves Castaldi.

The last word goes to Pearl. When she was tracked down by *Los Angeles Times* reporter Michael Szymasnski in 1989, she was reluctant to talk about the restaurant and clearly still heartbroken at the premature end to her own love story:

> *"Isn't it sad how so many people never find their one true love?"*

Four Oaks Restaurant
Bel Air (West Hollywood & Beverly Hills)
Closed/Off The Market

Hidden Discoveries

Over 100 years the Four Oaks developed from a simple coach stop to a well-regarded restaurant, but since 2005 it has been up for sale. In 2010 they even reduced the price to just under $3m, but now it is off the market for what could be a number of reasons. This is a popular and romantic spot though – Steve McQueen and Vincent Price were regulars – so why have there been no takers? Could it have anything to do with the fact that it's slap bang at the center of several haunted stories?

Named after an ancient oak tree that split into four branches (the tree has long since gone; it was razed to make way for – what else? – a parking lot) the story of the Four Oaks began in 1880, when Beverly Glen's main road was a just river bed. A small inn and café was built by this memorable oak tree to cater for cowboys and cattlemen, but then came the bounty of the gold rush. Prohibition was good news for this out-of-the-way place too, and bootleg liquor followed by a trip upstairs to see one of the "ladies" was a popular night out for men from miles around.

Its walls could certainly tell some stories, and during a remodeling in the 1960s owner Jack Allen came across some fascinating artifacts of the Four Oaks' wild past: old whisky and wine bottles, a fully operational hidden still and some secret stairs going to the nearby house of someone who clearly liked his wine, women and song. They also found some old lipsticks and rouge pots, and might have unearthed something else too; a busboy who slept at the restaurant soon after woke up to see a large, illuminated figure in the darkness – it was the last time he ever stepped foot inside the building.

Today the Four Oaks is still empty, it's future unknown.

Janes House
Hollywood
Events Only

The Sisters

Although it's somewhat hidden at the back of a mini-mall, this turreted, ramshackle wood-shingled Victorian/Dutch Colonial building is over 100 years old, and was once the private "Misses Janes School of Hollywood."

Back then this gravel street was known as Prospect Avenue, and in 1903 the house was bought by Herman Nelson and Ruth Janes, one of Hollywood's founding families. They moved in in 1905 and by 1911 Mary and her daughters Carrie Belle, Mary Grace and Mabel were teaching the children of "discriminating parents of Hollywood" from kindergarten through 8th Grade at a monthly tuition fee of $5. PTA meetings really must have been something when the proud pops included Charlie Chaplin, Douglas Fairbanks or Cecil B. DeMille!

The school closed after World War II and the Janes' brother Donald set up a gas pump in the front yard as Janes Auto Service, then when Carrie Belle's husband died in 1964 they rented out some space to a florist and other vendors. Things seemed to be on a decline, and there were legal wrangles with city Building Inspectors about fireproofing: the *Los Angeles Times* reported that Mary Grace said the house was "sturdy as ever," and that "My sister and I did more for Hollywood than any of these people they're always talking about, that Hollywood Bowl crowd."

Two years after Grace died in 1973, Guy Miller, inventor of the Vocabumat (a learning aid/table mat with foreign phrases and translations on it) moved in as a kind of caregiver and janitor, but when Mabel and Donald both passed away in 1978, it was virtually the end. The house itself was saved forever when it was awarded Landmark Status in 1980, and an ailing Carrie Belle was the last one of the family to leave in 1982, dying in a nursing home in Studio City in January the following year aged 94.

The new owners retained the overall style in what they developed as the Janes Square Landmark Shopping Center (there's a Janes Square sign wrought in the iron gate as a tribute to the tireless teachers), and the Visitors Information Center for Hollywood took up residence in Janes House soon after. After that it was the short-lived Memphis restaurant, and then Janes House bar and lounge, which lasted barely as long.

I attended an event here and looked around; inside it's all dark wood, chandeliers, ancient windows, grand chairs and tight staircases, the light shining out of the windows making it look like a haunted house. Plans are again underway to make Janes a fashionable bar/club, and with two bars already in place – as well as some very risqué old photographs in the bathrooms – it could at last be time for this old house to be right back in the center of things.

As for any strange tales, the only thing I found online was that doors and windows were reported to open by themselves, and other things would move around by themselves too. There's no newspaper or archive evidence at all however, and since it's now only occasionally used for private events and parties, it could be that the Janes sisters have got their home back again – interviewed in her nursing home by the *Times*, Carrie said:

"I wouldn't think of staying here. I want to stay at my own kind of place. I'm going to go home."

There are a couple of restaurants in the Shopping Center, so you could check out Janes House at the back and choose either New Orleans party fare at Five OFour or Mexican food at Te'Kila, which offers an eight pound "El Gigante" burrito if you're really, really hungry. There are Happy Hours at both places; daiquiris and margaritas for all!

Paulist Productions Building (formerly The Sidewalk Café)
Pacific Palisades

The "Hot Toddy" Murder Conspiracy?

Today it's an office building and is off limits to the public, but 75 years ago the ground floor of this Pacific Coast Highway location was a successful roadhouse café owned by Thelma Todd, the beautiful actress known as "Hot Toddy" and "The Ice Cream Blonde." She starred alongside Laurel & Hardy, Buster Keaton and, perhaps most famously, with the Marx Brothers in *Horse Feathers* (1932) and *Monkey Business* (1952), though today her mysterious death is still unsolved and was an early example of a "conspiracy theory".

Body of Thelma Todd Found in Death Riddle

Todd was found dead in her car on December 16, 1935 and her death filled the first five pages of the next day's *Los Angeles Times* and *Los Angeles Examiner*, and for days afterward too. She was parked a short distance away from the café in the garage of her on/off boyfriend, director Roland West, and was found by her maid. The LAPD initially ruled the death an accidental suicide, but things didn't add up, and many felt that there was more to it than that.

A suicide seemed unlikely to her friends, and some thought that the jealous West might have locked her out because he was angry at her late night partying. Perhaps Todd had turned on the car to keep warm, fallen asleep and accidentally killed herself by carbon monoxide poisoning? Or maybe she simply fell asleep and West didn't even know she was there?

The name of infamous New York gangster Lucky Luciano came up too, and a 1991 television movie "White Hot: The Mysterious Murder of Thelma Todd" saw Loni Anderson playing Todd and former Bond villain Robert Davi (*Licence to Kill*) playing Luciano. Had Luciano wanted to begin illegal gambling at the café and Todd refused? Or did he want her for himself?

Either way, there's little evidence that Luciano ever even visited Los Angeles.

Another theory said that she was murdered by her ex-husband, Pat DiCicco, a playboy who had a history of violence against women. Though there were no signs of a struggle, Todd's corpse was found to have a bloody broken nose and a tooth in her mouth, and her blood/alcohol level was extremely high.

Finally, some recalled a report in the *Los Angeles Examiner* about Todd receiving threatening letters earlier in the year. She had dismissed other similar letters as pranks, but two mailed from San Francisco and one from New York demanded she pay $10,000 or "our San Francisco boys will lay you out. This is no joke."

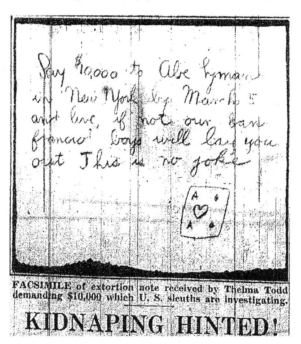

FACSIMILE of extortion note received by Thelma Todd demanding $10,000 which U. S. sleuths are investigating.

KIDNAPING HINTED!

By permission of Hearst Communications, Inc., Hearst Newspapers Division.

Todd was frightened enough to hire private security, though the Department of Justice dismissed the threats as a joke. There were even accusations that it was all a publicity stunt, but then in late August the *Los Angeles Times* reported that Harry Schimanksi from Long Island had been arrested for sending the letters.

Since Todd's body was cremated, the only thing left of her was her movies and, later on, her star on the Hollywood Walk of Fame. West allegedly confessed his guilt on his deathbed in 1952, but the case remained classified as an accidental suicide, and reports of Todd's ghost or smells of gas fumes (at her former home and in West's garage) are inconclusive too.

Bibliography/Sources

Newspapers/Magazines

Chapter 1 – Hollywood

"Suicides Yesterday Epidemic" – *Los Angeles Times*, pA18, June 20, 1929

"Picture Actor Leaps To Death" – *Los Angeles Times*, pA3, December 9, 1932

"Film Player Tries Suicide" – *Los Angeles Times*, p7, February 4, 1940

"Youth Scalded On Meal Job" – *Los Angeles Times*, pA2, November 1, 1932

"Will Live Like Real Mandarins" – *Los Angeles Times*, pV1, April 7, 1912

"Borrowed From The Far East" – *Los Angeles Times*, pV1, January 11, 1914

"Six Frisky Baby Black Swans Guarded From Candid Cameras" – *Los Angeles Times*, pA15, February 27, 1938

"Fayette Moore, Film Producer, Ends Life" – *Los Angeles Times*, p2, May 22, 1955

"Elderly Actor Beaten to Death" – *Los Angeles Times*, pD11, March 12, 1979

"Police Check Possible Link in Actor Slayings" – *Los Angeles Times*, pB21, March 13, 1979

"Death Near Young Woman" – *Los Angeles Times*, pII10, January 7, 1910

Chapter 1 – Hollywood (continued)

Opening of All Star Café and Speakeasy – *Hollywood Independent*, February 28, 2001

Kaufman, Amy. "Stars' prints set in cement, not stone" – *Los Angeles Times*, pA14 December 29, 2011

Kingsley, Grace. "The Four Hundred Club" – *Los Angeles Times*, p17, November 1, 1925

Lindgren, Kris. "Nurse Arrested in Slaying of Actor, 84" – *Los Angeles Times,* p29, May 26, 1979

Mikulan, Steven. "Hollywood, Straight Up" – *LA Weekly*, May 4, 2000

Ram, Jason. "A Heavenly Haunt: My Experience at the Yamashiro Restaurant"

Chapter 2 – West Hollywood & Beverly Hills

"Suspect in Pool Slaying Seized at Home" – *Los Angeles Times*, pB14, September 15, 1973

"Sunset Strip Triangle! Swank Hotel Man Slain" – *Los Angeles Herald-Examiner,* Vol. XCII, p1, January 29/30, 1963

"For The Record" – *Los Angeles Times*, pA4, April 24, 2009

"Ketchup 'Massacre' Has the Beanery Bouncing" – *Los Angeles Times*, pD4, February 20, 1969

Andrews, Colman. "In Any Storm" – *Saveur Magazine*, Issue 56, Jan/Feb 2002

Graham, Sheilah. "A Gadabout's Notebook" – *Los Angeles Times*, p8, December 2, 1936

Knoedelseder Jr., William K. "The Tragic Death of a Comic" – *Los Angeles Times,* pF1, June 5, 1979

Murphy, Jean Douglas. "Yod in His Heaven -- in Los Feliz Area" – *Los Angeles Times*, pE1 December 8, 1972

Pool, Bob. "Ghosts are on tap all year long in West Hollywood" – *Los Angeles Times,* pA39, A42, October 30, 2011

West, Richard. "Barbara Hutton, Reclusive Woolworth Heiress, Dies" – *Los Angeles Times*, pA1, May 12, 1979

𝒞𝒽𝒶𝓅𝓉𝑒𝓇 3 – 𝒟𝑜𝓌𝓃𝓉𝑜𝓌𝓃

"Police Seek Mysterious 'Thin Man,' New Figure in Black Dahlia Case" – *Los Angeles Times*, p2, January 24, 1947

"Mary Pickford Sued by Pair for $8,083,750" – *Los Angeles Times*, pB1, January 25, 1957

"Mary Pickford Tells of Balking on Liquor Deal" – *Los Angeles Times*, pB1, May 26, 1961

"Heart Victim Dies As Autos Collide Head-On" – *Los Angeles Times*, p10, August 11, 1953

"Death Plunge" – *Los Angeles Herald-Express*, August 11, 1953

"Seven Stories He Leaps: Cannot Die" – *Los Angeles Times*, pII1, August 21, 1918

"Two Fearful Falls: Two Men Killed" – *Los Angeles Times*, pA6, September 10, 1903

"Fell To His Death" – *Los Angeles Record*, p1, September 9, 1903

"Market Opening" – *Los Angeles Times*, pV1, October 21, 1917

"Up Again, Down Again" – *Los Angeles Times*, p11, November 21, 1901

"Sailor Killed as He Walk Angels Flight" – *Los Angeles Times*, pA, September 1, 1943

"Display Ad No 9 No Title" – *Los Angeles Times*, pI3, September 18, 1919

"Cline Poisoning Inquiry Widens" – *Los Angeles Times*, pA9, November 9, 1933

"Oviatt Denies He Financed Radical Unit" – *Los Angeles Times*, p16, April 13, 1965

"Obituary 1 – No Title" – *Los Angeles Times*, pD4, March 28, 1974

"Gusts Tear Down Signs" – *Los Angeles Times*, pA8, March 9, 1904

"Philippe's Founder Recalls Busy Days…" – *Los Angeles Times*, p27, August 27, 1951

"Worker Dies In Shaft Plunge" – *Los Angeles Times*, pA8, July 4, 1947

"Ends Misery As Desired" – *Los Angeles Times*, pII3, May 28, 1915

Chapter 3 - Downtown (continued)

"Believe Woman Ended Her Own Life" – *Los Angeles Times*, pII1, July 6, 1922

"Labor-Union Pickets Strike Down Bearers Of A Workman's Corpse" – *Los Angeles Times*, pII1, September 2, 1910

"Drop Of Beam Hurls Worker" – *Los Angeles Times*, pI7, September 3, 1910

"Fatal Crane Chain Claims 2nd Victim" – *Los Angeles Examiner*, September 3, 1910

"Poison Death Baffles Police" – *Los Angeles Times*, pII1, November 28, 1922

"New Theory In Hotel Suicide" – *Los Angeles Evening Herald*, November 29, 1922

"Source Of Death Poison Is Found" – *Los Angeles Evening Herald*, p1, November 28, 1922

"Boge Feasted To Death Alone, Police Believe" – *Los Angeles Examiner*, November 30, 1922

"Police Search Death Motive" – *Los Angeles Times*, pII1, November 29, 1928

"A Reminiscence" – *Los Angeles Times*, pO 4, October 27, 1883

"Ensign's Bride Slain in Berth on Coast Train" – *Los Angeles Examiner*, Vol. XL No. 44, p1 January 24, 1942

"Quiz Suspect in L.A. on Murder in 'Birth 13'" – *Los Angeles Herald-Express*, Vol. LXXII p1, January 26, 1943

"Cook on Death Train Seized on Arrival Here" – *Los Angeles Times*, pA, January 26, 1943

"Trunk Slaying Admitted by Man Held in Texas" – *Los Angeles Times*, p1, May 10, 1944

"Love Nest Murder Suspect Arrested Aboard Steamer" – *Los Angeles Times*, pA7, June 5, 1929

"Confesses Weird Slaying" – *Los Angeles Evening Herald & Express*, pA-3, April 6, 1950

"Cryptic Messages Scribbled Across Dead Divorcee's Body" – *Los Angeles Times*, p2, April 6, 1950

Chapter 3 – Downtown (continued)

"Red-Haired Divorcee's Death Told By Waiter" – *Los Angeles Times*, pA3, April 7, 1950

"Man, 73, Drowns in Hotel Bathtub" – *Los Angeles Examiner*, September 13, 1951

"Husband Joins Crowd, Learns Wife is Suicide" – *Los Angeles Times*, pA1, January 3, 1956

"School Principal Killed In Plunge from 11th Floor" – *Los Angeles Times*, p2, April 22, 1946

Fuss, Marilyn. "Now 91, An Artist Recalls When Walls Were His Canvas" – *Los Angeles Times*, pC7, October 12, 1976

Gray, Olive. "Genius Honors Local Builder" – *Los Angeles Times*, pB9, December 24, 1927

Illingworth, Hal. "A Ghostly Past" – *Los Angeles Herald-Examiner*, p13, June 24, 1972

Malnic, Eric. "Man Convicted in 2 Dismemberment Murders Sentenced" – *Los Angeles Times*, January 5, 1982

Marek, Arthur L. "Guard Trunk Killer; Fear Suicide" – *Los Angeles Herald-Express*, February 9, 1932

Rochlen, A.M. "Ruth Judd, Guilty in First Degree, Doomed To Hang!" – *Los Angeles Examiner*, Vol. XXIX No. 60, February 9, 1932

Smith, Jack. "1st St. Losing the Redwood – Forum and Watering Hole" – *Los Angeles Times,* pC1, January 23, 1970

Stafford, Guy C. "Mrs. Judd Found Guilty Of First-Degree Murder" – *Los Angeles Times,* p1, February 9, 1932

Theisen, Will. "Seeing Spirits At Crocker Club" – *Metromix*, February 25, 2009

Timmons, Joseph. "Ghost Woman Sought in Hotel Poisoning" – *Los Angeles Examiner*, p1, November 28, 1922

Weinstock, Matt. "Some Strange Turns Taken By The Twist" – *Los Angeles Times*, pB6 April 25, 1962

West, Richard. "Witness Gives Grisly Details of Couple's Slaying, Dismemberment" – *Los Angeles Times*, p OC-A6, July 17, 1981

"Victim Shipped Here by Man in Chicago" – *Los Angeles Examiner*, Vol. XLI, No. 147, May 6, 1944

Chapter 4 – Mid-Wilshire

"Louis B. Meyer Brother Dies as Bedroom Burns" – *Los Angeles Times*, p4, February 28, 1951

"Mexico: More Deaths" – *Time,* November 21, 1927

Deutsch, Linda. "When the Stars Eat Out" – Associated Press / *Los Angeles Times*, pN40 October 21, 1982

Doyle, Alicia. "Spirits About At Melrose Eatery" – *Larchmont Chronicle*, May 5, 2006

Fontes, Montserrat. "Memoir: My Grandmother's Third Street" – *Westways*, September 1988

Graham, Nancy. "'Doctor' Has Bad News For Patient" – *Los Angeles Times*, pWS1 June 17, 1982

Torgerson, Dial. "Ritualistic Slayings" – *Los Angeles Times*, p1, August 10, 1969

Chapter 5 – Westside & Beaches

"Dr. George I. Kyte's Funeral Will Be Conducted Today" – *Los Angeles Times*, p12 August 24, 1940

"Obituary 3 – No Title" – *Los Angeles Times*, pA18, July 28, 1937

"Goes For A Walk, Returns Not" – *Los Angeles Times*, pI10, December 19, 1909

"Body Identified" – *Los Angeles Times*, pII8, January 10, 1910

"Teachers Death Said To Have Been Accident" – *Los Angeles Herald*, January 8, 1910

"Freak Mishap Kills Man, 75" – *Los Angeles Times*, pA1, August 27, 1949

"8-Story Fall Kills Indian Girl" – *Los Angeles Times*, p2, November 21, 1955

"Man Grilled as Indian Girl Plunges to Death" – *Los Angeles Herald-Express*, November 21, 1955

"Girl's 8-Story Plunge 'Accident or Suicide'" – *Los Angeles Examiner*, November 26, 1955

"Mother of Two Falls to Death" – *Los Angeles Times*, p2, May 28, 1958

Chapter 5 - Westside & Beaches (continued)

"The Southland: Streaker Jumps Off Ship, Drowns" – *Los Angeles Times*, pOC2, May 18, 1974

"Those Fabulous Fads" – *Los Angeles Herald-Examiner*, pA-3, March 17, 1974

"Fatal Dive Probed" – *Los Angeles Herald-Examiner*, March 18, 1974

"Woman in fatal fall at Queen Mary had been drinking, police say" – *Los Angeles Times*, December 6, 2011

Aushenker, Michael. "Patrick's Roadhouse on PCH is GHOULA's Latest Haunt" – *Palisadian-Post*, September 24, 2009

Siegel, Barry. "Santa Monica's Classic Land Battle" – *Los Angeles Times*, pG1, May 13, 1976

Chapter 6 - Off The Menu

"Body of Thelma Todd Found in Death Riddle" – *Los Angeles Times*, p1, December 17, 1935

"Actress Gets Death Threat" – *Los Angeles Examiner*, March 6, 1935

"Mystery Guest New Clue In Thelma Todd Tragedy" – *Los Angeles Examiner*, Vol. XXXIII – No. 6, p1, March 6, 1935

Harvey, Steve. "Original Spanish Kitchen mystique lives on" – *Los Angeles Times*, pB2 March 1, 2009

Larsen, David. "Ready For Diners, Never Opens" – *Los Angeles Times*, pD1, June 29, 1979

Morian, Dan. "Owner Dies; Home's Future Uncertain" – *Los Angeles Times*, pWS1 January 20, 1983

Szymanski, Michael. "Frozen in Time – Mystery, Romance Flow From Legendary Kitchen Abandoned 28 Years Ago" – *Los Angeles Times*, p1-1, December 28, 1989

Torgerson, Dial. "Building Inspector Persistent" – *Los Angeles Times*, pF1, June 25, 1967

Books

Baldwin, David. *Royal Prayer: A Surprising History* – Continuum International Publishing Group: New York, 2009

Bishop, G/Osterle, J/Marinacci, M/Moran, M. *Weird California* – Sterling Publishing Company: New York, 1996

Carter, Walter Ford/Golway, Terry. *No Greater Sacrifice, No Greater Love: A Son's Journey to Normandy* – Smithsonian Books: Washington DC, 2004

Connelly, Michael. *The Brass Verdict* – Little, Brown & Company: New York, 2008

Greenwood, Roberta S. *Downtown By The Station: Los Angeles Chinatown 1880-1993* – Institute of Archaeology UCLA: Los Angeles, 1996

Hauck, Dennis William. *Haunted Places: The National Directory* – Penguin Books: New York, 1996

Henstell, Bruce. *Los Angeles: An Illustrated History* – Knopf: New York, 1980

Holzer, Hans. *Haunted Hollywood: Ghostly Encounters* – Bobbs-Merrill Company Inc: New York, 1974

Jacobson, Laurie and Wanamaker, Marc. *Hollywood Haunted* – Angel City Press: Santa Monica, 1994

Marie, Carol. *Milt Larsen's Magic Castle Tour* – Brookledge Corporation: Los Angeles, 1998

Ogden, Tom. *Haunted Hollywood: Tinseltown Terrors, Filmdom Phantoms, and Movieland Mayhem* – Globe Pequot Press: Guilford, 2009

Sarlot, Raymond R. and Basten, Fred E. *Life at the Hollywood Marmont* – Roundtable Publishing: 1987

Various/ed. Andre Balazs. *Hollywood Handbook* – Universe Publishing: New York, 1996

Websites

www.1947project.com

www.allstartheatrecafe.com

www.bell.k12.ca.us/origfamily/pages/arthurgilmore.htm

f Bizarre-Los-Angeles

http://blogdowntown.com/2010/04/5244-a-ghost-building-for-75-years-alexandria

www.britannica.com/blogs/2009/02/haunted-hollywood-3-grauman%E2%80%99s-chinese-theater-10-oscar-related-ghost-stories-in-honor-of-the-academy-awards/

www.chinesetheatres.com/webcam.html

http://cinematreasures.org/theaters/496

http://creepyla.com/blog

www.donray.com/spanishkitchen.htm

http://eliasofsonora.net/encarnacion.html

http://ghosts-hauntings.suite101.com/article.cfm/haunted_vogue_theater_hollywood#ixzz0Pn87XfOQ

www.ghosttheory.com/2008/04/07/los-angeles-city-of-roaming-angels

http://ghoula.blogspot.com

www.hauntedhoneymoon.com

www.hauntedplayground.com/photos.htm

www.la.com/ci_12509820?source=rss

www.lapl.org

www.LATimeMachines.com

www.latourist.com/index.php?page=haunted-hollywood-story

www.loopnet.com/Listing/16635502/2181-N-Beverly-Glen-Blvd-Los-Angeles-CA/

www.loopnet.com/Listing/16621566/216-W-5th-St-Los-Angeles-CA/

www.michaelconnelly.com/video/photo-gallery/

www.onbunkerhill.org
www.pacificelectriclofts.com
www.paulistproductions.org/building1.html
www.prairieghosts.com
http://search.proquest.com.ezproxy.lapl.org/index?selectids=latimes
www.seeing-stars.com/Landmarks/JanesHouse.shtml
www.spirits66.com
http://theshadowlands.net/places/california2.htm
www.unsolvedmysteries.com
www.wikipedia.org
www.willkern.com/roosevelt.html

And the websites of each location in the book.

About The Author

Originally from London, James T. Bartlett has been living in Los Angeles since 2004 and has been a freelance journalist since 1999. He has been published in over 90 magazines and newspapers including the *Los Angeles Times*, *Angeleno*, *Los Angeles Magazine*, *LA Weekly*, *Westways*, *Hemispheres*, *Delta Sky*, *Voyager*, *Thirsty? Los Angeles*, *Variety*, *Fortean Times* and *The Historian*. He is also a contributor to BBC Radio and RTE Radio 1 in Ireland, and blogs for BBCAmerica.com. You can contact him at jbartlett2000@gmail.com